JASON T. HARMONY
IN
THE RED TAIL HAWK

By T. J. Hand

RANCH
HAND

Publishing

DEDICATION

I dedicate this book to my lovely wife Judy, whose father, Edgar, is a novelist in his own right. Although, to some, writing a novel might seem like a lot of time consuming hard work, it's actually the easy part compared to editing the book, which Judy has done. Judy has worked with me through every step of the way on this novel. Through every chapter and each individual page correcting my atrocious spelling. She's listened patiently as I've read each phase of this story to her for her reaction, for her suggestions and also her input. She's helped me research numerous items in the story line that I had no first-hand knowledge about. They say as people grow older together they start to become as one. That is certainly the case in our lives. Judy is and has always been the air beneath my wings.

CHAPTER ONE

As I knelt by the shallow stream in the morning sun looking for flakes of gold in my pan, I noticed a stray horse not more than 40 yards away from me drinking from the cool water. Suddenly, from out of nowhere, a Jeep came racing up the creek bed and came to a skidding stop not far from the horse and me. There sat a beautiful woman. Her bosoms seemed to be swollen, they were stuffed so tight in her low cut tank top shirt. Her cut-off jeans were so short and tight they seemed to show every part of her lovely body.

"Hey, Stud!" she shouted as she stood up in the jeep.

I dropped my gold pan, jumped up and said, "That's what my girlfriends call me but my real name is Jason."

She turned around and said, "I'm not talking to you, stupid. I'm calling my horse."

She started to step down from her Jeep when her right foot slipped on a mossy rock and into the shallow creek she went. She sat there in the cool water trying to get to her feet. The harder she tried to push herself up, the more she kept slipping back into the water. When she realized she wasn't getting any place fast, she let out a lady like cry for help.

After her second cry for help, she looked me straight in the face and yelled, "Well, aren't you going to help me?"

As I surveyed her situation, which was more laughable than serious, I said, "Oh, were you talking to me? I thought you were talking to your horse."

This was the first vacation I'd been on for over five years. Working as a mechanic and a part time gumshoe kept me very busy. I worked at Mr. Bill Henderson's Auto Shop as a mechanic. The man had a thriving business with a five-stall garage and three mechanics. I'd been working there for the last five years from 8:00 am to 4:30 pm, Monday through Friday. Life was beginning to seem like an endless work order of cars and trucks, every day going to the same white stucco building with the big yellow sign that read Henderson's Auto Shop. The only break I got was on weekends. Weekends were my favorite part of life, the most creative part. That was when I got to play Detective Jason T. Harmony. I worked closely with the Meade Brothers, Ted and Landen, who owned and operated Meade Investigations, and who were two very curious looking fellows.

Ted was only 30 years old but he had snow-white hair. It had been that way since he was born. It was some type of genetic imbalance. With his six-foot frame and his muscular build, not many people ever commented about his odd hair color. Although he looked like a bouncer for a motorcycle gang, he was one of the nicest guys you'd ever want to meet. I once saw him release a fly that was trapped in a spider web and about to be devoured by the resident spider. He was also a champion for the underdog.

His brother Landen was more direct and to the point. Although he was the older of the two by a whopping three years, he was also the smaller of the two. At five feet six inches, he weighted a mere one hundred and forty pounds. He had a handle bar moustache and a big firebreak down the middle of his head where nothing would grow except for a sunburn. I guess you could call him the brains of the operation when it came to the two of them.

The Meade Brothers were the only private investigators in our growing community of Jefferson City, Nevada. Although they were freelance investigators, they did quite a lot of work for Bill Montgomery, the legal beagle in our community, and they would occasionally assist Arby Fillmore, our County Sheriff. It always gave me a shot of adrenalin to work with these brothers. There was never a dull moment when we worked together.

Three days ago we'd just wrapped up a case that had puzzled our community for some time. It started off quite simple but took an odd twist the deeper we got into it. When it started out I was working at the shop on a curious work order. This particular vehicle had been in our shop just three months ago. At that time I had done a complete brake job on the vehicle. Now it was back and the complaint on the work order said that the brakes were making a grinding sound when stopping. The reading on the odometer showed it had only gone a little over 2000 miles. I jacked it up and took off the tires to check out the brakes. I couldn't believe what I saw. The front brakes were worn down, metal to metal, almost no brake material left what so ever and the back brake lining was so thin you could almost see through it. The vehicle belonged to Mrs. Willcon, an elderly woman who lived down the street not far from our repair shop. Her husband, who was quite a few years younger than her, had supposedly gone off to a meeting a few months ago and never returned. It was later found out that his suitcase and some of his clothes were missing so it was assumed that he had run off and left her. Most of the people around town figured he'd run off with a younger woman because he had been known to run around with a few. But no one knew for sure.

When I took off the brake pads and shoes, I checked the brake calipers and rear actuators for malfunctions. I could find nothing out of order. If this was a bigger heavier vehicle with a lot more mileage I could perhaps understand this type of brake wear but this was a smaller midsize pick-up truck with power brakes and a little old lady driving it. Nothing added up. I walked over to the Boss and showed him the brake lining to see what he wanted to do.

"Must be a bad batch of brake linings," he said. "I can call the parts store and have the brake lining replaced for free but we'll have to charge her for labor."

That sounded like a fair solution to me. It had nothing to do with our workmanship. When you own a repair shop, you're in the business to make money, not do free brake jobs. I went back to the truck and continued on the brake job and waited for the parts store to bring out the new brake linings so I could wrap up the job.

When the brake job was finished I took it out for a test drive to check the brakes. Just to make sure everything was working as it should and most of all to make sure it stopped. Most mechanics say they stand behind their brake jobs. That would be the safe place to be if you weren't sure of your workmanship. I always made the claim that I stood in front of my brake work because I was sure of my work.

As I was pulling into the parking area in front of our garage after completing the test-drive on the truck, I saw two boys about nine or ten being chased by an overly large Red Tail Hawk. They were running and screaming for help as the hawk kept diving at them. I started honking my horn in an effort to scare the hawk away but it wasn't having much effect. The horn in this particular truck sounded like a toy horn on a kiddy car.

"Dink! Dink! Dink! Dink!"

Finally the two boys ducked for cover in one of the stalls of our shop. The hawk, sensing it wasn't a good idea to follow, discontinued its chase and flew straight up in the air. When it had gotten about a hundred feet in the air, it started circling. It made three large circles and then took off flying north at a high rate of speed. This was definitely the first time I'd ever seen anything like this before. I parked the truck in our lot and hurried inside to make sure the boys were all right. By this time a group of people began to gather outside our building. They'd witnessed the strange happening and were curious about it.

As I ran into the shop I yelled out to Mr. Henderson, "Call Sheriff Arby and tell him to get down here ASAP! We've got a situation that needs his attention!"

The two boys were beet red and were trying to catch their breath from all the running they had done. They were little Jimmy Fowler and Billy Barnes, a couple of mischievous kids that lived in the cul-de-sac down the street from the apartment complex where I lived on Oak Park Drive. When I came up to the boys, I could see blood on the back of Jimmy's shirt.

"Are you boys alright?" I asked.

"I'm OK," said Billy, "but that bird hit Jimmy's back with his claws and almost knocked him down!"

"I'm OK," said Jimmy, "but my back hurts a little."

"Take your shirt off and let's have a look," I said.

When he took his shirt off I could see two scrape marks on his back. Both were about three inches long and not very deep into the skin. There was dried blood around the scrape marks but no signs of bleeding right now. I knew that birds of any type don't carry rabies but claw marks that pierce the skin can cause a serious infection. I called out to Mr. Henderson to call 911 and get the paramedics here to take care of Jimmy's cuts.

"What in the world happened?" I asked. "Why was that hawk flying after you? Did you do something to make it angry?"

"No, Mr. Harmony," Billy answered. "We didn't do anything to upset the bird. We were just hiking out in back of town on the B.L.M. land. When we came to Wild Cat Ridge we started climbing up the side of the mountain trying to get up to the top. We got about half way to the top when out of nowhere this huge hawk appeared and began swooping down toward us."

"You were probably by its nest," I said, "threatening its offspring."

"No!" Jimmy replied loudly wiping his nose on his shirtsleeve that he held in his hand. "We were on the side of the ridge. There was no place for a nest."

"Anyway, as the bird kept getting closer," said Billy rubbing the back of his hand across his eyes wiping away some tears, "we worked our way down the ridge to the ground. When we hit the ground we began to run as fast as we could!"

"But the bird kept following us!" said Jimmy excitedly. "It swooped down and hit my back. It almost pushed me down!"

As the boys kept talking I thought to myself about how much damage a Red Tail Hawk could actually do to a person if it was trying to harm them. Judging by the marks on Jimmy's back, the bird wasn't in its killing mode. Just then I heard a loud voice outside the shop.

"Everybody break it up here! Move on! Move on! Get on back to your own business! I'll take care of everything here." It was Sheriff Arby talking to the crowd outside. I could always tell Sheriff Arby's voice. It was so deep and forceful sounding. It matched the tall heavyset frame of his body.

As the crowd dispersed he walked in the shop, looked over at the two boys and me and said, "Jason T. Harmony!"

I said, "At your service, Sheriff."

"What in the world is going on?" he asked.

After I explained what I knew about the hawk incident, he turned and started talking with the boys. About that time, the paramedics came driving around the corner with their siren blaring. I ran outside the door to the sidewalk and waved them down. Then I pointed to the inside of the shop. They turned into the parking lot and slowly proceeded to drive into the shop. When they stopped they quickly got out of the van they were driving. As they stepped out I instantly recognized the driver. It was Mary Jenkins, a girl I had gone through High School with. She grabbed the medical bags, said a quick hello to me, and then hurried over to examine the boys. Her partner was new in town. I'd seen him around a few times but I'd never met him.

He walked over to the boys and said, "Hi. My name is Jim. I'm here to help you. Where do you hurt?"

After looking at the boys, Mary and Jim decided it wasn't life threatening. They put some antibiotic ointment on the claw marks and bandaged the area. As they worked, I talked with Sheriff Arby.

"Jason," he said, "what do you think about this hawk attack? Do you think it's a fluke? We've never had anything like this happen around here!"

"Well, I'll tell you, Sheriff, I kinda think the boys must have inadvertently gotten around the hawk's nesting area" I said. "That's the only reason I can think of that would cause a hawk to attack a human."

"Birds! Birds!" he said. "That's all I need here. I've got people speeding through town like it was a freeway. I've got homes being broken into and shop lifting at the new supermarket down the street. Juvenile delinquents running wild throughout the area, a report of a missing person and now I've got to add birds to the list of crimes going on around here?"

"Sheriff," I said. "Why don't I get a hold of the Meade Brothers? We can drive on over to the B.L.M. land and take a look around this weekend. Maybe we can shed some light on this bird attack."

"That sounds like the best idea I've heard all day," he said. "Be sure and let me know what you find." As he began to walk back to his squad car, he turned and said, "You know, Jason, I sure wish I had a dollar for every cockamamie thing that happens in this town. I'd be a rich man." Then he began to laugh. While he was getting into his squad car a vehicle went racing by. The Sheriff turned to look at me and a big smile broke out on his face. He turned on his flashing lights and siren and drove after the vehicle in hot pursuit.

The paramedics were finishing up and preparing to leave when Mr. Henderson shouted out, "I'm paying you boys to work on cars, not stand around and watch paramedics. Now, get back to work!"

The rest of the day went by rather slowly. It seemed that the clock wasn't moving at all. When it came time to clean up the shop and put our tools away, I took out my cell phone and called Landen Meade. While the phone rang in my ear I locked my toolbox and got ready to call it a day.

On the third ring Landen answered with his usual, "This is Landen. What's up?"

"Hey, Landen. This is Jason," I said. "How's it going?"

"Hellooooo, Jason. It's going quite well actually. What's on your mind?" he asked.

I proceeded to tell him about the hawk attack and how I'd talked with Sheriff Arby about taking a run out to the B.L.M. land and looking around.

"Did he mention anything about paying us for this little endeavor?" he asked.

"I just assumed," I said, "that he would pay your usual hourly rate."

"Jason," he said, "you never assume somebody is going to pay you. People are always extremely happy to receive your help at first, in this type of business. But when the work's all done and the cases are all wrapped up, people don't care anymore about your services. They're less likely to want to pay you. When you are contacted about a job in this business you always establish a price that you will be paid for your services. I realize that this business is not your livelihood. You have your mechanical abilities to fall back on. But this is the way that Ted and I make our living."

As I listened to the endless jabbering on about the financial aspects of this undertaking I finally interrupted him and said, "So I take it you don't want to investigate this thing for the Sheriff?"

"No! No!" he said. "I didn't say that. I just want to make sure we'll be paid for it. I'll give Arby a call," he continued, "and work it all out."

"Sounds good to me," I said. "Do you want to meet in front of the Wal-Mart store Saturday morning?"

"Yes, that would be good," he said. "Let's say about six in the morning."

As we said our goodbyes I stuck my phone in my pocket and headed out the door on my way home.

CHAPTER TWO

Saturday morning, with a thermos full of hot coffee, a mug in my hands and a cooler of water and soft drinks that were already loaded into the back, I got in my car and drove down to the Wal-Mart parking lot. I pulled into the parking lot and noticed that the Meade Brothers were nowhere to be found. I parked my car, turned off the engine and then sat quietly drinking my coffee while thinking about the day to come. It was only 5:45 a.m. so I had a little time to kill. I always tried to be early for my appointments. It was something that my Father had instilled in me years ago with a silly little jingle. He used to say, "When you're late, you make people wait. Be an early bird and you'll get a good word". I always wondered, when I was little, what a good word was. Was it something they handed out to people who showed up early? Was it a prize of some type? I didn't realize until I was in my teens that it meant a good reputation for being a dependable person.

It was a few minutes after six when the Meade brothers came driving into the parking lot. It wasn't hard to recognize their van. It had a yellow flashing light on the top. On both sides it had a picture of a Sherlock Holmes looking fellow holding a magnifying glass. Above the picture in bold letters it said **MEADE INVESTIGATIONS**. Below the picture in smaller letters it read Find A Need, Call A Meade. As they came driving up they turned on their yellow flashing light and honked their horn. I got out of my car and walked over to their van.

When Ted opened his window I shouted out, "I thought Sheriff Arby told you that he'd let you put that flashing light on your truck if you only used it for emergencies?"

"This is an emergency," Ted said smiling. "Landen hasn't had his morning coffee yet and he just can't operate until he does."

"I've got a thermos full of coffee," I said, "if he's got a cup."

Landen produced a cup that I filled up with coffee. As he sipped his coffee I said, "I've brought along some equipment I thought we might need. I've got a 50 foot length of rope, a pipe wrench, a lead bar, a gun and a candle stick."

"Well, it looks like we're all ready to play a game of *Clue*. Did you bring along Colonel Mustard, too?" Ted asked, laughing.

"No, but I brought along Professor Plum," I said, smiling. "Actually I was just testing to see if Landen was in his operating mode yet. But I did bring along a cooler with some soft drinks and some bottled water."

"Good thinking," said Landen. "We'll need something cool to drink when that sun gets high overhead."

I loaded the cooler into the van then I said to Ted, "We'll need to stop at Willy's Pit Stop to pick up some ice for the cooler."

"OK," said Ted. "Just remind me to stop when we get close to the place."

Willy's Pit Stop was a gas station/convenience store on the outskirts of town. It was an older place, built back in the 50's. Slick Willy himself was in his early seventies. He was as skinny as a rail, about six feet tall with short gray hair and always chewing on a toothpick. He and his wife, Loretta, had owned and operated the place for as long as I can remember. Loretta was a shy woman and she usually stayed in the back room, stocking supplies, doing bookwork and watching TV. Willy got his nickname because of some of the tricky and shady deals he pulled. The more gullible the person was, the shadier the deals were. For instance, in his younger years he once sold a guy a new tire for a good deal of money. The only problem was the tire had a tiny pinhole in it, which caused it to leak about ten pounds of air each week. After about seven days, the guy came in and complained about his new tire being low on air. Slick Willy went out to air up the tire and then charged the guy a dollar. The next week the guy comes back with the tire low on air again. Slick Willy goes out and airs the tire up and charges the guy another dollar. The third week the guy comes back with the tire low again. By this time he's fit to be tied.

The guy marches in to Slick Willy's office and says, "Look, I bought this tire from you and it keeps losing air. I want you to fix this tire right now!"

Slick Willy says, "I'm sorry, sir, but we just sell 'um. We don't fix 'um."

"Look," the guy says, "I have a warranty on that tire and I want it fixed."

"Let me see that warranty," says Slick Willy. As he looks at it he says, "This here warranty guarantees that tire against road hazards, tread wear and warpage. It says nothing here 'bout losing air."

The guy takes a deep breath and says, "Fine. Give me my warranty back and I'll go out and air the tire up myself."

"I can't let you do that," says Willy.

"And why not?" the guy asks.

"Insurance purposes," Willy says.

"Insurance purposes?" the guy shouts.

"That's right," says Willy. "My insurance only allows authorized people to use that there air hose."

"Well," says the guy who by now was getting very irritated, "if you think I'm going to come in here every week and pay you a dollar to air my brand new tire up then you must be insane!"

"Now, calm down a minute," says Willy. "I'm sure we can work something out here. Let's see here." He thinks for a minute and then says, "I know what I can do. For $10.00 I can give you the Official Course on Air Gauge Operation and Authorization."

The guy says, "Why in the world would I want to give you $10.00 just so I can air up my own tire?"

"Well, sir," says Willy, "that will allow you to air up any tire, any time you want for free."

"For free!?" shouts the guy. "What do you call the $10.00? That's not free!"

"Well, sir," says Willy, "that's what we in the business call an initial start up fee."

Back in those days Slick Willy had the only place around for miles where you could buy gas and oil and also air up your tires. So the guy says, "I'll give you $5.00."

Willy says, "$5.00 plus tax."

The guy sighs and says, "OK. You got yourself a deal."

Willy takes the money and leads the guy out to the air hose. Then he watches while the guy airs up his own tire. When the guy is through, Willy says, "By the authority vested in me I hereby grant you the official usage of this here air hose."

With that, Willy walks back into his office and the guy gets into his car and drives off.

After putting the cooler in the back of the Meade van, I locked up my car and got in the back. We then proceeded on our way.

"Is everyone buckled up?" asked Ted as we were driving out of the parking lot. Landen and I both nodded yes. Then Ted says, "We're off to the B.L.M. land."

The area that we were heading for was owned by the Federal Government. It was acquired years ago and was under the control of the Bureau of Land Management, a department of the Federal Government, hence the initials B.L.M. It was a huge section of land out back of the town that went on for miles and it was occupied by every wild life creature you could think of. But what most people enjoyed about this area were the wild mustangs. They were really a beautiful sight. If you were lucky enough to catch a glimpse of them galloping as free as the wind along this untamed countryside, it was something you'd always treasure.

"OK," said Landen, "we're going to concentrate our investigation on the Wild Cat Ridge area. The boys were climbing the ridge when the bird first swooped down at them. I've brought a shotgun along just in case. I know it's against the law to shoot a Red Tail Hawk but I checked with Fish and Game and they assured me you can legally shoot any animal, reptile or bird if they are threatening your life."

After driving for a short while we neared Willy's Pit Stop. I reminded Ted to pull into the place so we could pick up some ice for the cooler. Ted and I jumped out of the van and walked over to the ice chest just outside the front door of the building. Landen stayed in the van drinking his coffee. When we opened the lid we saw that it was completely empty.

"Well that's just great," said Ted. "What are we going to do now?"

"Let's go inside," I said. "Maybe Willy's got some ice in there."

We walked inside and saw Slick Willy leaning on the counter reading a newspaper with a toothpick sticking out of his mouth. As he looked up from the paper a smile crossed his face.

"Good morning, gentlemen. How may I help you today?" he asked as he stood up straight and moved the toothpick to the other side of his mouth.

"We wanted a bag of ice," said Ted, "but there's none in the cooler outside."

"Well, sir," said Willy, "I apologize for that but some feller come in here yesterday afternoon and said he was going to buy eight bags of ice from the cooler. At $2.00 a bag, that's $16.00 plus tax. Now that cooler only holds ten bags of ice so I says to the guy, *"Hey partner, it looks like you could save yourself some money if you buy all the bags in the ice chest. I'll let you have every bag in the cooler for $25.00 tax included."* He couldn't resist the deal I gave him and he bought all the bags right there on the spot."

"What in the world would somebody want with that many bags of ice?" Ted asked.

"Well," says Willy fingering his toothpick, "I figure he must have been havin' one of them there wild parties or something."

"So you don't have any ice left?" I asked.

"Now, I didn't say that!" Slick Willy says. "I do have a few bags left in the back ice box. But I figure, in this warm weather, and the fact that the ice truck don't come by to restock my cooler till this afternoon, that now I'm forced to charge a little more per bag. Supply and demand, ya know."

"Just how much is it going to cost us for one bag of ice?" I asked.

"I figure about $4.00 a bag should do it," said Willy.

"We'll give you $3.00," said Ted.

Willy thought for a minute and then he said, "$3.00 plus tax and you got yourself a deal."

Ted looked at me and said, "This guy's good."

I nodded my head and said, "Better give him the money before he tacks some type of surcharge on it."

We both broke out laughing as we walked out the door with the bag of ice. When we got to the van we sprinkled the ice in the cooler over the bottled water and soft drinks.

"What took you guys so long?" Landen asked after we got back into the van.

"We got robbed," said Ted.

"Really?" said Landen sitting up straight in his seat. "Should I call the Sheriff?"

"I don't think it would do much good," I said. "He'd probably rob him, too."

Ted and I started laughing again. Landen said, "What's so funny? You just said you got robbed."

"Yeah," said Ted, "and by an old man named Slick Willy."

"Oh," said Landen relaxing back down in his seat, "that old coot."

We pulled back on the main road and went for a little over a mile before we came to the turn off for the B.L.M. land. It was a dirt road about twenty feet wide and full of potholes and ruts.

The dust and dirt flew in all directions as we traveled down the road. The land was dry and rocky, mostly considered desert land and not much good for anything. The road ended abruptly after about a half mile so we parked the van in a small turn around area and got out. We could see Wild Cat Ridge from where we stood.

"Make sure you bring some water with you," Landen said. "This hot dry desert air will dry your insides out in no time."

I opened up the cooler and grabbed a couple of bottles of water for myself. Ted and Landen did the same. The good thing about bottled water is that you can stuff them in the side pockets of your pants and keep your hands free for other things.

"Everybody have their cell phones on?" asked Ted.

"Mine's on," I said, "and the digital camera on it is ready for snapping pictures."

"I've got mine on," said Landen, "and I've also brought along the new digital camera we bought last week for Meade Investigations. I figure if we don't have to shoot this hawk maybe I can zoom in on it with the camera and get a good close up picture of it so we can tell a little more about it."

"Good thinking," Ted said. "I'll grab the shot gun and some shells just in case." He grabbed four shells and stuck them in his right shirt pocket.

Landen walked over and closed up the van. "Let's boogie," he said and we took off for Wild Cat Ridge.

As we walked along we could see the morning sun starting to rise. If everything went well, we hoped to be back at the van by no later than 12:30 p.m. Once the sun was straight overhead in this vast desert area it got unbearably hot. There was nothing to shade yourself with out here. You were lucky if you could find a rock formation that could cast a shadow large enough to cool your body off in the hot afternoon sun.

While we continued walking I said, "I sure don't know what little Jimmy and Billy were doing hiking out here by themselves in the first place. They might have ended up dead from heat exhaustion. This is miles from town."

"That could have been a distinct possibility," said Landen.

"They probably should have been spanked when they got home," I said.

"I don't know about spanking little Jimmy," said Ted, "but I sure wouldn't mind spanking his mama. She is one hot babe."

"Yeah," I said. "I saw her down at the 7-11 the other day in this tight little dress. Boy she was..."

"Gentlemen!" Landen said. "And I use the word loosely, please keep your minds out of the gutter."

Silence fell upon us for a few moments as we walked along. Ted and I looked at each other but we decided it was best to keep our mouths shut. We'd gone about a half of a mile when we spotted something lying on the ground up ahead of us. As we got closer we could see that it was a canteen. I bent over and picked it up.

"It's half full of water," I said.

"It probably was dropped by the boys when they were running," said Landen. "We might as well bring it along with us. You can never have too much water out here."

The closer we got to the ridge, Landen began snapping pictures with the telescopic lens on the new digital camera. He took pictures of the top of the ridge, the sides, the bottom and the area in between. About ten minutes later we reached the bottom of Wild Cat Ridge. The ridge was roughly 150 feet in elevation and stood out from the desert floor like a monument placed there by the Gods. Its rocky surface made it easy but dangerous to climb. Although the large rocks seemed to be quite stationary they could slide out from under your feet without notice and you would go tumbling down the side of the ridge.

While we stood at the bottom, we gazed skyward looking for the big hawk that had attacked the boys. There was nothing but blue skies above. No hawk to be seen anywhere.

"What's on the other side of this ridge?" I asked.

"I'm really not quite sure," said Landen. "I believe it's just more flat rocky type of land. Why do you ask?"

"Well, I've never been over that way. I was just kind of curious," I said.

"There's actually a way to get to that section of land off of Highway 88," Ted said. "It's a very steep grade that the truck drivers all hate because it's hard climbing up the grade. They usually end up going as slow as 5 mph as they near the top, and coming down it they have to use their brakes a lot so it's hard on their trucks either way they go."

"Yeah, I remember it now," said Landen. "They call it No Pay Grade because they burn more diesel fuel and have more wear and tear on their trucks than it's worth."

The whole time we talked, Landen was casually snapping pictures of the area.

"The boys said they climbed about halfway to the top of the ridge," I said.

"I'm surprised they didn't fall and kill themselves," Ted said.

"Young boys seem to have an indestructible self defense system built into them," said Landen. "They can do a lot of things older people could never get away with. Their bodies are more flexible and wiry. The older a person gets, the stiffer their bodies get," he continued, "and the slower their reflexes get."

Looking up at the ridge I could see no sign of a hawk's nest or offspring of any type. "I think I'll climb up the ridge just a bit and take a look around," I said.

"OK," said Landen, "but don't come crying to us if you fall on your butt."

"If I slip," I said chuckling, "I'll aim for one of you to break my fall."

While I began to work my way up the ridge, I tested each foothold to make sure it wasn't going to slide out from under me. When I got about a third of the way up, I turned and looked down. That was a mistake. I hadn't really realized this before, but I wasn't too comfortable with heights. I decided that it would be better not to look straight down so I gazed out into the distance.

While inching my way up, I spied a shiny object. It was very small, about the size of a green pea lying about three-quarters of the way up the ridge. It gave off a greenish metallic glow in the sunshine. If I turned my head, sometimes it would disappear. It was only visible when it was reflecting in the direct sunlight. About halfway up I started feeling a little odd. I felt like I was enriched with something but I just didn't know what it was. I reached for my cell phone to try and get a picture of this shiny object above me on the ridge. As I reached my hand into my pocket searching for the phone, I glanced down momentarily and saw Ted and Landen standing far below on the ground. They looked so small. Then I realized exactly how high up I was, just hanging onto the side and standing on rocks that could slide out from under my feet without notice. My queasiness over heights had suddenly disappeared. I was at peace with the world. I pulled the phone out of my pocket and held it up over my head and aimed it in the general direction of the shiny speck. It was impossible to look into the screen and focus it from the angle I was at, just holding onto the rocks with my right hand. This only left my other hand free for using the camera.

"What are you doing up there?" yelled Landen. "Are you OK?"

"Yeah, I'm fine," I said. "I'm trying to take a picture of something up here."

"What is it?" he asked.

"I'm not sure," I said. "It's something shiny up toward the top of the ridge."

As I snapped the camera on the phone, blindly, trying to capture a photo of the shiny speck, I saw a shadow cross over the side of the ridge.

"It's the hawk!" yelled Landen. "Right above you!"

Glancing down, I saw Ted with the shotgun in his hands raising it in the air. I looked up just in time to see the huge hawk diving straight down toward me.

"Shoot it!" yelled Landen.

Ted held the rifle in his hands aiming up toward the big bird.

"Shoot it!" Landen yelled again. "Kill the damn thing!"

Suddenly I felt a thrust against my back with enough force to knock the cell phone out of my hand and send it tumbling down the side of the ridge. I scrambled to cover my head with my free arm to guard against any further attacks when the rocks gave way and I started to slide down the ridge. Grabbing wildly with my hands to latch onto any object I could to stop my decent down the side of the mountain, I heard a shot ring out below.

"You missed it!" yelled Landen.

"I wasn't trying to hit it!" answered Ted loudly. "I just wanted to scare it away!"

"You need to kill it!" screamed Landen. "Before it attacks again!"

While the two of them argued about the hawk, I was continuing to slide down the side of the ridge, all the while picking up momentum the further down I slid. Suddenly I heard another load blast go off.

"You missed it again!" Landen yelled.

"I'm not trying to hit it!" yelled Ted. "I told you I'm just trying to scare it away!"

As I slid down the ridge frantically grabbing for whatever hold I could find, I remembered something I had learned in the Boy Scouts as a young boy when we use to go on hiking and camping trips. When climbing up the sides of hills or walking down on slippery surfaces, always turn your feet sideways. This not only makes your body a lot more stable but it gives your feet a much wider surface rather than just the tip of your foot to negotiate the rocks, mud and slippery areas. I instantly turned my feet sideways and hoped for the best. Part way down the ridge I was able to catch a solid rock sticking out of the side of the hill with my hands. As I grabbed it, quickly my feet wedged up against the side of the ridge stopping my decent. At last I was stationary again. My heart was beating so fast it was hard to catch my breath. As I held onto the side of the rocky surface, I looked around for the hawk. I knew if it were to swoop down on me again there was no way I could protect myself from an attack. I gazed around but could see no sign of the bird.

Just then Ted shouted, "Jason! Are you OK?"

"I think so!" I yelled back. "My chest is a little sore from sliding down the side of the ridge but I don't think it's anything serious."

"I'm glad to hear you're OK!" yelled Landen. "I'm sure it had nothing to do with the expert marksmanship my brother just performed!"

"Very funny!" said Ted. "The bird flew away didn't it?"

"Well, yes," said Landen. "The bird is gone."

"Then I accomplished what I was trying to do," said Ted. "I told you I was trying to scare the bird away."

Landen said, "Oh, the bird left alright, but it probably left from sheer boredom. I'm sure it had nothing to do with your shooting ability."

As I listened to them bicker back and forth I started to work my way down the side of the ridge. I had only fallen about 25 feet but it seemed like a mile when it was happening. I glanced around for my cell phone that had fallen out of my hand but it wasn't anywhere to be found. I figured something a small as a cell phone and gray in color, as mine was, would probably be pretty hard to locate on this rock hill.

With all the excitement the time had passed quickly. It was now past 12:00 noon and starting to get downright hot. The hotter the sun baked the area the hotter the rocks got on the ridge. By 2:00 in the afternoon it would be almost impossible to climb around on the mountainside without burning your hands. The rocks were already starting to warm my hands as I neared the bottom.

I stepped off the last few rocks and my feet touched the ground. I pulled one of the bottles of water out of my right side pocket to take a nice long drink. By now it was warm and not very satisfying. I slipped off my shirt to check my injuries. There were numerous scrape marks on my chest and the sides of my arms. Mostly small abrasions but nothing was bleeding. Landen and Ted examined my back where the hawk had struck. There were two bright red marks from where the hawk's feet had touched but the skin was not punctured.

"You're probably going to have some pretty good size bruises there tomorrow," Landen said. "But for now I think you'll be just fine."

As I slipped back on my shirt I glanced around the area hoping to find my cell phone. I thought to myself about how mild this attack really was. If that hawk had wanted to, it could have ripped my back open with its talons. Instead it thrust against my back with its talons fully open. None of this made any sense.

"Jason," said Ted, "I think I see your phone over there by that pile of loose rocks."

We walked over and sure enough, there it laid, a little scratched up but still intact. I picked it up and scrolled through the pictures I had snapped while I was on the ridge.

"Did you get any good shots?" asked Ted.

"It's really hard to tell," I said, looking through the pictures. "I need to take them home and download them onto my computer. How did you do with your camera, Landen?"

"Well, while Ted was shooting and missing the bird," he said, "I was shooting and hitting. I got quite a few shots. We'll have to take them back, blow them up larger and study them."

We walked back to the van and it seemed to get warmer with each step we took. By the time we reached the van I had finished my second bottle of water and couldn't wait to get into the cooler and grab a really cold bottle of water. I opened the lid and both Landen and Ted grabbed something cool to drink.

As we leaned back against the shady side of the van enjoying our cool drinks, Ted said, "You know, even though we had to pay $3.00 plus tax for the bag of ice I think it was money well spent."

Landen and I both agreed as we slowly sipped our drinks. When we had finished with the cool drinks, we loaded up our equipment and got into the van, then headed for home.

CHAPTER THREE

When we pulled back into the Wal-Mart parking lot I was dead tired and sore all over.

"Let's all go home and relax," said Landen. "We can continue later. I think we all need a break now."

"That's the best idea I've heard all day," Ted replied.

"Yeah, I think I'll go home and take a nice warm bath," I said.

I unloaded the cooler and my thermos from the van and put them back into my car. Then I got in, waved bye and headed back to my apartment. When I got home, I unloaded the thermos and cooler from my car and drained the water from the cooler, caused by the melted ice, in the grassy area of the complex. When I got to the porch I noticed the weekly newspaper lying by the door. I opened the door and put the ice chest and thermos just inside the door and went back out and picked up the paper then went back inside.

I made myself a sandwich and walked over to the phone to check my answering machine for messages. There weren't any new messages. No news is good news, I thought to myself. I grabbed the newspaper and sat down at the table. I glanced through the paper as I ate my sandwich. On page two they had a small story about the hawk attack that was just a couple of paragraphs. When I finished my sandwich I lay down on the couch to rest and continued looking through the paper. I guess I was so tired from the day's activities that I must have fallen asleep, because when I opened my eyes and looked at the clock it was already quarter to seven. I got up, walked into the bathroom and started the water running in the bathtub. I went into the bedroom and grabbed a change of clothes and lay them out on the bed. I went back into the bathroom, took off my dirty clothes and got into the tub. The heat of the water felt good on my sore body.

After soaking in the tub for quite a while I got out, dried myself and went to the bedroom and got dressed. After putting on the clean clothes, I went back to the bathroom and spruced up my hair and gave myself a shave. I slipped on my good shoes, picked up my keys and walked out the front door.

Saturday nights in Jefferson City, Nevada would be pretty boring to a person from a big city. There usually wasn't much going on. About the hottest place in town was Sadie's Bar and Grill. They usually had a local country band playing dance music. If you liked to dance and have a few beers it was the place to go, although it could get pretty rowdy sometimes, depending on the mood of the crowd and how much alcohol they had consumed. The more respectable people in town would probably be found playing Saturday night bingo at the local Moose Lodge. It gave them the chance to get out of the house and have a little fun and maybe win some money in the process.

If you had the gambling bug, you could always go to Wally's Diner and Club House. Wally had a room off to the side of the main dining room that had twenty or so slot and poker machines where people could try their luck. For myself, I had other plans for the evening. I figured it was my civic duty to go by little Jimmy's house and check on her, I mean his condition. When I got to the house I heard some music playing in the background. I knocked on the door and after a few seconds it swung open. There stood Jimmy's mama.

I said, "Hi. I came by to check on Jimmy. Is he healing up from the hawk attack?"

"Oh Jimmy's doing just fine," she said, but he's not here. He's staying at Billy's house tonight."

"Gosh," I said, "I'm sorry I missed him."

"Your name's Jason isn't it?" she said.

"Yes, ma'am," I said. "Jason T. Harmony."

"What's the 'T' stand for?" she asked.

"Trustworthy," I answered with a smile on my face.

Then she started to giggle and said, "My name is Connie. Connie Fowler. Would you like to come in and talk for a while?"

"Sure," I replied. "If your husband doesn't mind."

"Oh, I'm not married," she said. "Not anymore."

When I walked in I noticed the tight jeans and the cowboy boots she was wearing. "Were you planning on going someplace?" I asked.

"No," she said. "Why do you ask?"

"I just thought that with your jeans and boots on you might be going out to do a little dancing," I said.

"You know," she replied, "I used to go out dancing all the time but I haven't done it in quite awhile now. Can I get you something to drink? A glass of wine, a beer or soft drink"

"Thanks," I said. "I'll take a small beer if you have one."

"All I have is Budweiser. Is that alright?" she asked.

"That's fine," I said, "I like Budweiser."

She went to get my drink and I thought to myself, *How lucky can I get? Here I am, not only standing in this lovely woman's house, but she's getting me my favorite brand of beer. She must think I'm pretty hot.* She handed me a beer and her long silky black hair accidentally brushed against my hand. *I'm in love.* I thought to myself.

"So, Jason," she said, "you work at Henderson's Auto Repair?"

"Yep. I've worked there for quite a while now," I said.

Connie motioned towards her couch and said, "Would you like to sit down?"

"Sure," I said.

We walked over and sat down on the couch and then Connie asked, "Do you like it?"

"Like it?" I asked looking into her lovely blue eyes.

"Yes," Connie said. "Do you like working for Mr. Henderson?"

"Yeah," I said. "It's alright I guess. It gets a little hectic at times but it pays good and Mr. Henderson is a decent man to work for."

As I took a sip of my beer, Connie smiled and said, "I like to drink beer too."

"Why don't you have one with me?" I said.

"I can't. I get too giddy and start acting silly," Connie replied. "I will take a sip of yours, though, if you don't mind."

"Heck, no. Go right ahead," I said.

I handed her the beer and she took a sip, and then said, "I've been looking for a part time job around town but nobody seems to be hiring right now."

"What kind of work do you do?" I asked.

"Oh, I do a lot of things," she said. "I'm really good on computers, at typing and organizing files. I've done clerical work. I've been a cashier and I've even worked at the casinos as a black jack dealer."

"That's certainly a wide variety of skills," I said. "I'm sure you'll find something."

As we talked and laughed she had the radio playing softly in the background. Suddenly a lively song came on called *Boot Scoot Boogie* and she said, "I love that song. It makes me want to dance."

"Well, let's dance then," I said. When we got up she turned the radio up a little louder and we started to dance back and forth, kicking up our heels and do-si-doin' to the *Boot Scoot Boogie*. Although I'm not that good of a dancer, I was doing pretty dog gone good, even if I do say so myself. When we were done and Connie had turned the radio down, we collapsed on the couch laughing.

"I haven't done that in a long time," she said. Then she tenderly grabbed my hand and said, "Thank you for dancing with me."

"No. I want to thank you. A beautiful woman like you could dance with any man she wanted too." As I gazed into her eyes she came closer to me and as our lips were about to touch, suddenly there was a loud knocking on the front door.

"I better get that," she said. Then she slowly turned her head and reluctantly got up and walked to the door.

When she opened the door I heard a voice say, "Hi. I'm Ted. Ted Meade from Meade Investigations. We're investigating the hawk attack on your son, Jimmy. I just came by to see how little Jimmy is doing. Do you mind if I come in?"

"No, not at all. My name is Connie Fowler," she said. "It is very nice of you to check on Jimmy but he isn't here right now. He's spending the night at his friend Billy's house."

She opened the door wider and in walked Ted. His white hair looked like it had just been styled. He was wearing tight black pants and a tight black t-shirt that showed all the fully developed muscles in his upper body. In his right hand he was holding the canteen I'd found on the trail to Wildcat Ridge.

"I brought this for Jimmy since I was coming to check on him," he said, giving the canteen to Connie. "I found it up at the Ridge and figured it was probably his or Billy's."

I thought to myself, you lying dog. I found that canteen, not you.

She set it down on her end table she said, "Yes, its Jimmy's. He's been looking all over the place for it. I'm so glad you found it. Thank you so much."

While he stood there soaking in all her gratitude he turned his head and caught a glimpse of me sitting on the couch. "Oh, hi there, Jason" he said. "I didn't think I'd find you here."

"Yeah, I sure bet you didn't," I said with a smile on my face.

"Oh, do you two know each other?" Connie asked.

"Yeah. We've met," I replied.

"Can I get you something to drink?" she asked Ted. "A soft drink or a beer?"

"Yes, ma'am," he answered. "I'll take a beer if it's no trouble."

"Oh, it's no trouble at all," she said brightly.

When she went to her refrigerator to get Ted a beer I looked at Ted and said, "I think I hear Landen calling you."

Connie heard me from the kitchen and asked, "What did you say?"

I thought real quick and said, "I said, I think I have some sand in my shoe," loud enough for her to hear this time.

"Oh, I just hate that," she said. "It makes my foot feel so uncomfortable." Connie brought Ted's beer in and she handed it to him, then she set back down on the couch next to me. Ted came over and set down on the couch on the other side of her. Connie said, "It sure is nice that both of you are so concerned about Jimmy. It makes me feel good knowing that he is so well liked. We haven't been here that long and I was worried about him adjusting in a new town like this. But with both of you looking out for him and being so kind to him I'm sure he'll be just fine. He's felt so rejected since his father and I divorced. His father won't have anything to do with him."

About this time, Ted and I both felt about two inches tall. We both knew why we came over here. And it didn't really have anything to do with little Jimmy. We sat for a few moments not saying a word, then I broke the silence and looked at Ted and said, "Connie said she's been looking for a job but nobody seems to be hiring. Do you and Landen need anyone over at your office?"

"No. Landen takes care of all the paper work," said Ted, "but I do seem to recall Bill Montgomery saying something about needing a person at his law office."

"Why don't you try over there?" I said to Connie. "It might be the break you've been looking for."

She smiled at me and said, "I'm going over there the first thing Monday morning. What time do they open?"

"Nine o'clock," said Ted.

"Great! I'll be there at nine o'clock sharp," Connie said. "Maybe it will be my lucky day."

"I sure hope so," Ted said.

With the radio playing softly in the background, we talked about different music groups we liked and the songs that we liked to listen to. When I took another sip of my beer, Connie smiled at me and said, "Can I have another sip?"

I handed her my beer and she took another swallow. I could see Ted looking on in jealousy wishing it were his beer she was putting her lips on. About an hour later and a few less beers left in the refrigerator, the radio volume was getting pretty loud. Ted and I were taking turns dancing with Connie. Although Connie hadn't really had that much beer to drink, she was starting to get a little giddy like she said she would if she drank too much. I honestly don't remember whose idea it was but between the three of us we all decided it would be a good idea to go down to Sadie's Bar and Grill and do some real dancing.

"There is only one problem. I can't drive," I said. "I've been drinking."

"That goes double for me," said Ted.

As we looked at Connie she said, "Boys, don't expect me to be driving around anywhere smelling like beer!"

Ted said, "Why don't we just walk down there. It's only a couple of blocks."

That's a good idea," I said.

Connie said, "Let me go freshen up and I'll be right with you boys."

When Connie went into the other room, I looked at Ted and said, "How many beers have you drank, anyway?"

He said, "Just two."

"Are you sure?" I asked. "You look kind of tired. Maybe you should just go home and call it a night."

"I don't think so," Ted said, "besides I think Connie has the hots for me."

"Don't kid yourself," I said. "She's just being nice to you because you brought little Jimmy's canteen back for him. I'm sure you've seen whose beer she's been drinking out of."

"Get out of town!" Ted said. "She's just toying with you."

Connie came back in the room and said, "Are you boys ready to go?"

We both nodded and the three of us went out the front door and started walking toward Sadie's Bar and Grill. After a short walk of about ten minutes, we went into the front door of

Sadie's. The place was pretty crowded with a lot of country folks having a good old time.

When we walked in, Ted said, "I'll see if I can get through this crowd and go on over to the bar and get us a few beers. Would you like one of your own, Connie?"

"Sure, why not," Connie replied.

While Ted was making his way over to the bar to get the beers, the live band started playing a country rock song. Connie grabbed my hand and said, "Come on, Jason, let's dance."

We went out on the dance floor and started kicking up our heels, bumping elbows and booties with just about everyone on the crowded dance floor. When the song was over we worked our way through the mass of people over toward the bar area. I saw Ted waving three beer bottles in the air trying to get my attention. Connie said, "Where's Ted?"

I said, "I don't know. Maybe he went home or something."

Just then she saw him waving the bottles and said, "He's over there." She grabbed my hand and pulled me through the crowd over to where Ted was standing.

As he handed us the beers I said, "I've been looking all over the place for you. Where did you go?"

"I just went over to the bar," he said, "but it sure is crowded in here."

We stood there drinking our beer and trying to talk over the noise. The band cranked up another hot country rock song. Ted said, "Connie, may I have this dance?"

Connie flashed him a brilliant smile and said, "Let's go."

She handed me her beer to hold. Ted gulped down the rest of his beer and sat the empty bottle on a table by the wall. Out onto the dance floor they went. Ted was a pretty good dancer but he did his own kind of dance. He picked his knees up, left, right, left, right and bounced from side to side. Kind of like the mashed potato dance they used to do in the sixties.

Well, every crowd has one and this crowd was no different, except this big guy was named Gus. Big Gus, as a matter of fact. While Ted and Connie danced back and forth and side to side, every so often Ted's knee would come up and bump someone by accident. While Big Gus was dancing close to Connie and Ted, Ted's knee came up and smacked right into his big backside. As Gus kept dancing he turned around to look at who kneed him. Ted smiled as if to say, *Sorry about that.* As Gus turned back around and continued to dance, Ted's knee again came up unexpectedly and, unfortunately for Ted, it thrust right into Big Gus' hindquarters again. About this time, Big Gus figured this was no accident. This guy that smiled at him was doing this on purpose. So he stopped dancing and swung around and with a forceful blow struck Ted in the eye knocking him down onto the floor. The people on the dance floor all backed away as Ted jumped to his feet. Connie came running over to me. A couple of Gus' buddy's came over and stood by Gus.

Ted called out, "Hey Jason! I need a little help over here!"

I told Connie to go stand by the front door while I rushed over to Ted's side. The music had stopped and the crowd was quiet as we all stood there facing each other. Suddenly, the lead singer for the band spoke into the microphone, "Take it outside! Take it outside!"

Then the crowd started it softly, "Take it outside. Take it outside." Then louder and louder until the place was actually roaring with the chant, "Take it outside!" The five of us headed for the front door. Once we stepped outside and stood facing each other, I could see that the odds weren't in our favor. Although Ted was quite muscular and a good six feet tall, Gus was a few inches taller and outweighed him by at least a hundred pounds. Big Gus's two buddies were both about six feet and didn't look like they had missed any meals either. Although I was the shortest one in the bunch, I still stood five foot eleven inches and was in excellent physical condition.

As we stood there, Gus glanced down at me with a *Born to Kill* look on his face and said, "What's your name, boy?!"

I looked back at him with the meanest look I could muster on my face and said, "Jason T. Harmony."

He said, "Jason T. Harmony, huh? What's the T stand for?"

I said, "Trouble," and a big smile broke out on my face.

He looked at me sternly then his lips started to part and a smile came to his face. He turned to his friends and said, "I like this boy."

About that time Sheriff Arby came driving up in his squad car. As he got out he said, "What's the problem here, gentlemen?"

"Nothing, Officer," Gus replied and we all started nodding our heads in agreement.

Sheriff Arby took one look at Ted, whose right eye had already started turning black and blue and was beginning to swell, and said "Nothing, huh? What happened to your eye, Ted?"

Ted said, "I tripped on the stairs."

Sheriff Arby said, "There ain't no stairs in this joint." We all started laughing then Arby said, "Ted, you get on into the front seat of my squad car and I'll drive you on home. I don't want you tripping over any more stairs tonight, and Jason T, why don't you call it a night, too. By the way, where is that report you two investigators were supposed to be doing on that hawk attack for me?"

"You'll have it first thing Monday morning," Ted said.

"Good," said Sheriff Arby. He looked over at Gus and his two friends and said, "You boys go on back inside and behave yourselves. I don't want any more trouble out here tonight."

As they walked toward the door, Gus turned and said, "No hard feelings, boys."

Ted and I both nodded and said, "No hard feelings.

Ted got into the front seat of the squad car and I walked back into Sadie's and got Connie. When we came out we could see that Sheriff Arby was driving away with Ted. "I sure hope Ted is OK," she said.

While we walked back to her house I said, "Ted will be just fine. He's made out of good stock." When we got to Connie's house, I walked her up to the front door and said, "Well, thanks for a most enjoyable evening."

She smiled and said, "I sure had fun but I feel so sorry about Ted."

Yeah, I do to," I said. While I looked into her eyes, she leaned forward and touched her lips to mine and we kissed deeply. I thought to myself, *Alright!* After kissing for a minute or so I broke away and said, "I better be getting on home. It's getting late."

When she opened her front door she turned to me and softly grabbed my hand and led me inside and closed the door.

CHAPTER FOUR

Early Sunday morning I woke to the sound of my cell phone ringing. As I fumbled around trying to find it, I followed the sound to a table by the side of the bed.

"Hello?" I said, with one eye open.

"Jason. Where are you?" the voice asked on the phone.

"I'm here at home. Who is this, Ted?" I replied.

"Yeah, this is Ted. If you're home, how come you don't answer your regular phone?" he asked.

"Because it didn't ring," I said.

"Sure it rang," Ted said. "I've called it five times now and all it does is ring."

"Well it must be broken then," I said. "I'll have to get a hold of the phone company and have them repair it." Just then I opened both eyes and slowly sat up in bed. On my left side lay Connie, sound asleep.

"Are you still there?" asked Ted. "Your cell phone is breaking up."

"Yeah, I'm still here," I said as I looked around the room. *This is strange.* I thought to myself. *This isn't my room.* Then it all started coming back to me about what had happened the night before. "Hey, Ted, I guess I'm not at home after all. I must have spent the night at Connie's house."

"Well, that just figures," said Ted. "Here I wake up with a headache and a swollen black eye and you wake up in la la land with a beautiful woman."

"What can I tell ya?" I said. "I guess that life isn't fair some times."

"Boy, that is sure the truth," Ted answered.

"What time is it?" I asked.

"About six o'clock in the morning," he said. "The reason I called is that Landen wants us all to meet at the office at 8:30 this morning."

"What for?" I asked.

"He wants to go over the pictures he took yesterday and put together a report for Sheriff Arby."

"Sounds good," I said, "I've got some pictures on my cell phone camera that I haven't had a chance to look at yet. Maybe we can see if any of them came out."

"I need you to do me a favor, if you would," asked Ted.

"Sure. What is it?"

"Well, it seems that in all of the excitement last night I left my car over there at Connie's house," Ted said. "Do you think that you could drive it on over to the meeting and I'll give you a ride back home when the meeting is over?"

"I can do that," I said, "but there's only one problem."

"What's that?" asked Ted.

"I don't have the keys," I said.

"Oh, that's not a problem," said Ted, "there's a magnetic key holder stuck on the frame of the car under the driver's side door. It's got a spare key in it."

"OK, then," I said, "I'll see you at 8:30."

"Thanks, Jason," Ted replied as he hung up the phone.

About this time, Connie was starting to wake up from all the noise I was making talking on the phone. She opened her eyes sleepily and stared at me for a few moments. Then, when she became fully awake, she got a shocked look on her face and said, "Jason! What are you doing here?!"

I smiled at her and said, "Connie, don't you remember? You wanted me to stay with you last night. As a matter of fact you insisted on it."

"I guess I must have had a little too much beer," she said weakly. "It makes me do things I normally wouldn't do."

"I thought that might be the case. You were acting awfully giddy. I just can't believe I went to bed with you the first time I met you. You must have been overcome by my charm," I said with a smile.

As I got out from under the covers and sat up to put my shoes on, Connie replied with a shocked tone in her voice, "Jason, you're fully dressed?"

"I know," I said, "and so are you."

Connie swung the covers off of herself and could see that she still had all her clothes on. I looked across the bed at her and said, "I would never take advantage of a woman that's had a little too much to drink. Don't you remember? I told you I'm trustworthy."

She smiled, then reached over and grabbed my hand and pulled me to her. As she looked into my eyes she said, "I'm not giddy now," and touched her lips to mine. As we kissed we fell back onto the bed.

About seven o'clock, I was out at Ted's car looking for his key as Connie made coffee and scrambled up some eggs for breakfast. When I came back in, Connie had a cup of coffee waiting for me on the counter. "The eggs are done. I'm just waiting for the toast to pop up," she said. "Go ahead and have a seat at the table. I didn't put anything in your coffee yet because I didn't know how you liked it."

"Oh, this is fine," I said as I sat down at the table. "I like my coffee black. I figure if a guy wants something sweet and creamy in the morning he'd be better off just going down to Baskin Robbins and getting himself a dish of ice cream."

Connie laughed and said, "I never really thought about it that way before." She brought the breakfast plates over to the table and sat down.

As we started to eat our breakfast I asked Connie how the wounds on Jimmy's back were. "Oh, they're fine," she said. "I took him down to the medical clinic after the paramedics called me and Dr. Benstowe gave him a shot of penicillin and said he should be just fine. They aren't really anything but scratches but I wanted to make sure they didn't get infected."

"Well, it's always better to be safe than sorry," I said as I ate my eggs and toast.

"Yes, I agree," Connie said. "Jimmy means too much to me to lose over some silly scratches."

"Why in the world did you let him go to Wild Cat Ridge in the first place?" I asked as I sipped my cup of coffee.

"Oh, I didn't let him go," she said defensively, "the boys snuck off. Jimmy was supposed to be playing over at Billy's house and Billy told his mother he was going to be playing over here."

"Oh, I see," I said. "The old *'pull the wool over the parents' eyes'* trick. Kids are like that."

"Yeah, I know," she said, "and Jimmy's got quite an imagination too. When we were coming home from the medical clinic he kept telling me that Billy and him saw a baby unicorn running along with the wild mustangs out by Wild Cat Ridge."

"Wow! He sure does have quite an imagination," I chuckled.

After we finished breakfast and had cleaned off the table we said our goodbyes. I went out and got into Ted's car, waved and left for the meeting. I decided to stop off at my apartment to change my clothes before I went to the meeting. When I walked in the door, I went over to my answering machine and sure enough, I had inadvertently pushed the wrong button yesterday afternoon when I had gotten home and checked my messages. It was left off. No wonder the phone just kept ringing when Ted called this morning. After resetting it and making sure it was on, I went in and changed my clothes, spruced up a bit, walked on out and got into Ted's car and proceeded on my way to the meeting.

I drove out of the complex, turned left down Oak Park Drive, then pulled out onto Main Street. About a block down Main Street I came upon a smaller mid-size pick-up truck and when I looked closer, I could see the brake lights were on. *Must be slowing down,* I thought to myself. But no, it was moving right along with the flow of traffic. I sped up and moved closer to the pick-up truck. That's when I realized it was old Mrs. Willcon. She was probably on her way to church driving along about forty miles an hour with her foot pressed down on the brake pedal. Now this would explain why her brakes were completely worn out with only 2000 miles on the odometer. Sometimes when people get older they become a lot more cautious and scared of the traffic around them. The way they counteract this fear is to keep one foot on the brake pedal ready to stop at all times. *I guess I'm going to have to have a talk with that woman and let her know what I saw her doing the next time she comes in for a brake job. I'll have to tell her that she's going to have to pay full price for the next brake job.* I thought to myself as I continued to watch her. That's what we in the repair business call driver abuse and it cost parts companies millions of dollars a year replacing parts that weren't defective. As I drove on by her I honked my horn and waved at her. The sound of the horn must have scared her because the next thing I knew she had slammed on her brakes and was skidding to a stop. Well, at least it was good to know that the brake job that I had performed was working well.

When I got to the Meade brother's office, I parked Ted's car out front and walked on into the office door. Landen was sitting at the computer desk looking at the screen on the monitor and Ted was lying on the couch with his eyes closed.

"Good morning," I said cheerfully. "How's everything going?"

"Well it would be going pretty good if my eye didn't hurt so much," said Ted.

"That's what you get for going out and gallivanting around," said Landen.

Ted replied, "I was just dancing."

"Yeah," said Landen, "and I suppose dancing got you that black eye?"

"Well, actually it did happen that way," I piped in. "He was just dancing when it happened. You see…"

"What you boys do on your own time is your business," Landen snapped as he interrupted me. "Let's get busy. We've got a report to finish."

Landen got up and walked on over to the chalk board in the center of the far wall, behind the work table, as Ted and I grabbed some chairs and sat down at the table. "Now," said Landen as he wrote down six words on the blackboard, "what we need to know the answers to are, *where, what, who, how, when and why*. What happened?" he said, looking directly at Ted.

"A boy was attacked by a hawk," Ted answered.

"Good," said Landen as he wrote it down on the chalkboard. "Where did it happen?" he asked as he looked at me.

"At Wild Cat Ridge," I answered.

"OK," he said, as he continued to write down the information. "Who was attacked?"

"Jimmy Fowler," said Ted.

"What about me?" I asked.

"Yes," Landen replied. "You were attacked also." When he came to the last word, *why*, no one had an answer. After a few moments Landen said, "What are the characteristics of a hawk?"

Ted answered, "Let's see, they hunt smaller animals."

"They protect their area and their offspring," I said.

"They also fly, mate and the female of the species lays eggs in the spring time," said Ted.

"OK, then," said Landen. "The bird wasn't hunting when it attacked. It wasn't protecting its offspring when it attacked, so it must be protecting its area."

"If that's the case, it's carrying it a little bit overboard when it starts attacking people," I said

Ted said, "There must be a reason. But what could it be?"

"I got some pretty good pictures of the hawk yesterday," said Landen. "I've down loaded them into the computer and enlarged them. I got them on the screen right now. Come on over and take a look."

We got up and walked over to the computer and looked at the pictures as Landen clicked through them. "Wow! That is one fierce looking bird!" I gasped, while looking at the computer screen. "Its wing span has got to be every bit of five feet or more."

"Notice it's claws?" said Landen. "They could have easily ripped the skin off your body while you were on the side of that ridge but instead it chose to lightly strike your back. Almost as if it were trying to scare you away."

After looking through most of the photos, he brought up a picture where the hawk's legs were fully visible. When he was ready to click to another photo, I yelled. "Wait! It looks like there's something on the bird's left leg."

"Wow! It sure does look like there's something there," Landen said. He enlarged the picture as big as he possibly could.

"It looks like some kind of a round band, but it could just be a shadow. Is there some way we can enlarge the photo even larger?" I asked.

"Not with this equipment here," answered Landen. "But there is a company in Davis, California that has an imaging processor that's capable of enlarging photos up to two hundred times their original size."

"What's the name of the place?" I asked.

"It's called Larger Than Life," he answered. "I'll give them a call tomorrow morning and see if I can email a copy to them."

"Won't it come out distorted and grainy? You know, not really viewable?" asked Ted.

"No. That's the beauty of this place," said Landen. "They can enlarge the photos in such a way as to filter out the impurities and bring out the positive qualities of the picture."

"Speaking of photos," I interrupted, "I got a couple of shots on my cell phone camera yesterday while I was on the ridge. I'll go ahead and email them to you right now and maybe we can pull them up on your computer screen so we can have a look."

"That will work out great," said Landen. "Go ahead and give it a try."

Out of seven attempts I'd made of trying to get a picture while I was hanging onto the side of the ridge, one picture actually showed the part of the ridge where I'd seen the sun reflecting on a small shiny green object. The trouble was that this picture was of very poor quality and not very much help in my attempt to identify exactly what it was I had seen. The more Landen enlarged the picture, the worse the picture became. Finally Landen suggested that we send this picture along with the other one to Larger Than Life and see if they could do anything with it.

"Sounds like the best idea I've heard all day," I said. "If they are as good as you say they are, the pictures should come out as easy to see as the black eye on Ted's face."

Everyone started laughing. Then Ted said, "OW!! It hurts my eye when I laugh."

Landen walked back to the table and said, "OK, gentlemen. Let's get this report done so we can give it to the Sheriff tomorrow morning."

I interrupted again and said "Landen, can I ask a favor of you?"

He said, "That depends. What does it have to do with?"

"Well, you know Bill Montgomery pretty good," I said, "and I was...."

Landen interrupted, "I know him as an acquaintance. I've worked for him from time to time but he's not a close friend of mine. Why? What is it you want me to do?"

"Well, I have this friend who does secretarial work and she's been looking for a job and I understand that Bill Montgomery has a position open in his office."

"What's the woman's name?" he asked.

"Connie Fowler"

"Is this some kind of joke? Wouldn't that happen to be little Jimmy Fowler's mother?"

"Well, yes it is," I said. "But that has nothing to do with it. She's very good at what she does."

"It sure sounds like it," Landen said with a smirk on his face.

"Give her a chance," Ted piped in. "She's a good secretary."

"OK," said Landen. "I'll give Bill a call tomorrow morning and see what I can do. Now let's get back to this report."

After filling out all the information and facts that we had on the incident, the written conclusion at the end of the report read, *Hawk appears to be very possessive of the particular territory in the Bureau of Land Management area known in slang terms as Wild Cat Ridge. Although this bird has been credited with the attack on two individuals on two separate occasions, both attacks were minor in comparison to what the bird is fully capable of. At this time it is our opinion that this hawk poses no threat to human life. The incident should be treated in a secondary manner. Investigation is pending.*

With the report completed, Landen said, "I'll get these pictures out first thing in the morning. Hopefully we'll have something back by the middle of the week. Now let's get out of here and go home."

We all got up and headed out the door. Ted and I got in his car and drove to my apartment. When he dropped me off, we said our good-byes and I walked in my apartment. The answering machine light was blinking, so I pushed the button and listened to the message. It was Connie telling me what a wonderful time she'd had last night and asking me to give her a call if I got back before noon. I looked at the clock and it was twenty minutes to twelve, so I picked up the phone and dialed her number.

"Hello?" said Connie.

"Hi Connie. This is Jason. How are you doing?"

"I'm great, thank you for asking," she said. "Now, I have a question I want to ask you."

"What's that?"

"Jimmy and I would like to invite you to come on a picnic with us to Miller's Park. I've packed a picnic lunch with enough food for three people. Would you like to come?"

"That sounds like fun," I said, "I haven't been on a picnic for years. What time are you leaving?"

"Just as soon as you're ready," she said.

"Give me about twenty minutes and I'll come by and pick you up," I said.

As soon as I hung up the phone I walked over and turned on the radio to listen to while I got ready to go. Our local station, 92.1 FM, always had a wide variety of songs, mostly soft rock music that I enjoyed listening to, plus they had local news with *Andy Hall, The Voice of the Town*, so he claimed. While I was cleaning up and getting ready to leave, the news came on. Andy was talking about a local couple that was celebrating their sixtieth wedding anniversary. The man was 84 years old and his lovely wife had just turned 82 years young. Then he said, *"On a sad note, an unidentified body was found by a motorist at the side of the road on Highway 88. That steep section of the road sometimes called* No Pay Grade *by the people who drive those big rigs for a living. It was the body of a male in his late twenties or early thirties. Cause of death has not been determined yet pending a coroner's report. We'll keep you on top of any new developments in the case. And that's the news and how we see it here on ninety-two point one. Now, back to Sweet Jill Marie for those hits from the seventies and eighties."*

Wow! I thought to myself, *I bet Sheriff Arby is going to be happy about that. It's not like he doesn't already have enough stuff to keep him busy.* I grabbed a bottle of water out of the refrigerator, turned off the radio and headed out the door to Connie's house.

CHAPTER FIVE

When I was a boy I used to love going on picnics. The fresh air, the excitement of eating outside, everything about it was special. The picnic I'll always remember was when I was eight years old. My Uncle Lester and Aunt Minnie had just bought some property up by Truckee and they were so proud and excited about it. They couldn't wait to get my parents and us kids out to see their "Little Piece of Paradise" that they had purchased. They had planned an all day picnic with their kids, my parents, and us kids. We took two cars loaded down with all our supplies and necessities for the day. My Dad and I drove in Uncle Lester's car with Lester and his son, Freddy. Aunt Minnie drove in our car with my mother, my sister Cathy and my cousin Linda. While we drove along, Uncle Lester talked about how lucky he was to have found this property and how reasonable the price was that he had paid for it. When we came to the turn off from the main road, we got onto an old logging trail and followed it for what seemed to be miles. Finally we arrived at Uncle Lester's "Little Piece of Paradise."

As everyone piled out of the cars, Uncle Lester said, "OK, everybody listen up! Before you kids run off there are a few things I want you to know. First, there are hiking trails, fishing, tree climbing, swimming," he continued with a smile on his face, "and just about anything and everything you have ever wanted to do. Second, we have the buddy system here at our property.

Everybody has someone else with them wherever they go so if something happens to one of you the other person can get help. Now, any questions?"

My little sister raised her hand, "Yes, Cathy? What is it?"

"I have to go to the bathroom."

He gave her a disgusted look and said, "Number one or number two?"

"Number two," she replied.

"Are you sure you know what number two is?" he asked.

"Yes, it's poop."

"Why didn't you do this before we left?" he said, with his eyebrows tilted down toward his nose.

"Because I didn't have to do it then but now I do," she answered innocently.

Uncle Lester looked at Aunt Minnie and rolled his eyes. "Honey, could you get the shovel out of the back of the car and show Cathy how we go to the bathroom out in the woods? The rest of you kids help unload the stuff out of the cars and if any of you sneak a piece of that fried chicken your life won't be worth a plug nickel."

After everything had been unloaded, Freddy and I started to get ready to go to the river for a swim. All of the sudden everyone heard a blood-curdling scream. "What was that?" my Dad asked Uncle Lester.

"I'm not sure," he replied.

About that time Aunt Minnie came running by, dragging my little sister who was trying to run with her pants wrapped around her ankles. "BEAR! BEAR! BEAR!" my aunt was screaming at the top of her lungs.

Not far behind came a big black bear waddling along after them. Freddy and I ran for a couple of low hanging branches in a big pine tree, jumped on them and then began climbing our way up the tree. Meanwhile, Aunt Minnie made for an open car door and pulled my sister inside the car with her and shut the door. Everyone else scattered. My Mom and Cousin Linda jumped in the car with Aunt Minnie. Dad jumped in Uncle Lester's car and Uncle Lester, grabbing the picnic basket, jumped in the back seat of his car. The bear waddled into our little picnic area and stopped. The bear held its nose in the air and started to sniff. In between sniffs it slowly worked its way over to Uncle Lester's car. Uncle Lester shoved a piece of fried chicken through his partially opened window. When it hit the ground, the bear gulped it down. I could see by the look on my dad's face that he had thought of a plan. He slid into the driver's seat and started up the car and began driving off slowly. As the bear followed the car, Uncle Lester would stuff a piece of fried chicken out of the window every so often to keep the bear in pursuit. When they were far enough away, Freddy and I climbed down out of the tree and started to run for my parents' car. When we got to the car, Aunt Minnie yelled for us to go back and grab the folding chairs and the table and to put them in the trunk as quick as we could. With that done, we crawled into the car as fast as we could while my Mom began to drive away. About a mile up the road we caught up with my Dad and Uncle Lester. When they saw us coming, Uncle Lester threw the rest of the fried chicken out of the window to keep the bear busy while we drove off and made our way back to the main road. We ended up having our picnic lunch at a place called Fast Fry Hamburger Joint. I'm not sure whether Uncle Lester and Aunt Minnie ever ventured back to their property but I do know that they sold it not too long after that.

When I got to Connie's house, little Jimmy was on the porch by the open front door and as I pulled up to park I heard him yell, "Mom! He's here!" and he raced in the front door.

I got out of my car and walked on up to the door, "Hello" I said talking into the open door.

"Come on in," said Connie from the kitchen, "I'm just finishing up the fried chicken. Have you and Jimmy met?"

"No, I don't think I've ever had the pleasure," I replied.

Jimmy came walking out of the kitchen shyly. I held out my hand. His small hand grasped mine and we shook hands. "Hi Jimmy. I'm Jason. Jason T. Harmony."

Connie called out from the kitchen, "You can call him Mr. Harmony, Jimmy."

"Hi," said Jimmy. "You work down at that auto repair shop, don't you? I saw you the other day. Thank you for helping me and Billy."

"It's Billy and me," yelled Connie from the kitchen.

"Yeah, that too," said Jimmy with a smile on his face.

"You're very welcome," I said. "Are you healing up alright from the hawk attack?"

"Yeah. It really didn't hurt me any but I had to go and have a stupid shot at the Doctor's office. My mom made me do it. But that's OK, I'll get even with her."

"Jimmy, I did that because I love you and I don't want anything to happen to you," Connie said softly from the kitchen.

"My Mother used to do the same thing to me when I was a kid," I said with a chuckle. "I think there's some kind of law someplace that says that our Mothers have to worry about us."

"I need someone to test the potato salad," called Connie.

"I'll do it!" yelled Jimmy as he ran into the kitchen. I followed him and watched as he sampled a spoonful of potato salad that Connie held out to him in her hand. "Boy, Mom, I think that's the best potato salad I've ever tasted."

"Well, thank you, Jimmy. I'm glad you like it," she answered.

"Everything sure looks delicious," I said giving Connie the once over and then glancing into her eyes.

"I mean to please," she said glancing back at me with a sly smile on her face.

On the kitchen table sat an old picnic basket from years past. The kind we used to use when I was a kid. "Where in the world did you find one of those?" I said looking at the basket.

"I got it down at the church rummage sale a few months ago," she replied, "and it doesn't look like it's ever been used. Everything looks brand new inside. See?" She opened the lid so I could take a look. What I saw was surprising, neatly folded napkins, plastic plates and even the knives, forks and spoons were still wrapped in the original plastic.

"It looks like this needs to be broken in," I said.

"Yeah, Mom, it looks like this needs to be broken in," said Jimmy.

"Well, why don't you two good looking men give me a hand and we'll pack it full of food and take it out for its first picnic," Connie replied.

After the basket was packed, Jimmy and I carried it out to my car and we put it in the trunk. As we were walking back in the house Jimmy said, "Mr. Harmony? Do you like to play football?"

"Sure. I used to play it all the time when I was a kid. Why do you ask?"

"Well, I wanted to bring my football with us to the picnic but my Mom said it would be rude because you might not want to play football," Jimmy said.

"I'll tell you what," I said, "let's you and I go talk to your Mom and see if she'll reconsider your request. "Alright?"

Jimmy jumped up and down shaking his head in agreement saying, "Alright!!" as we started to walk back to the house.

When we got back inside Connie was picking up in the kitchen and getting ready to leave. "Beg your pardon, Madam," I said with a smile on my face, "but we two gentlemen would like your permission to bring a pigskin with us on the picnic."

From the look on Connie's face I could tell she's never heard of a football described like that before. "You want to bring a what?" she asked.

"We want to bring the football, Mom," Jimmy chimed in hopping from one foot to the other.

"Oh," she said. "That's fine with me as long as Jason doesn't mind.

"Heck, I don't mind. We can play a little bit of three man pass," I said.

"What's that? Jimmy asked.

"I'll show you when we get to the park," I answered.

"Do you mean three man pass or two man and one woman pass?" Connie asked.

"To make it politically correct we'll change the name to three person pass," I said laughing.

$\infty\!\diamond\!\infty$

When we got in the car and were ready to drive to the park I thought to myself about all of the things I liked to do when I was a kid on drives out to the country with my parents and sister. The first thing that came to my mind was singing car songs, as I used to call them. "Anyone know a good car song?" I asked glancing at Connie and Jimmy.

"What's a car song?" Jimmy asked with a quizzical look on his face.

"I believe it's a sing along song," said Connie. "Like people sing when they're traveling down the road."

"That's exactly what it is!" I said. "Anyone know a good one?"

"How about that new song by Taylor Swift?" Jimmy said, looking around for approval.

"How about not!" said Connie with a grin on her face.

"What we need is a good old standard song," I said. "Something like *Old McDonald Had A Farm*.

"What about *She'll Be Coming Around The Mountain?*" Jimmy shouted.

"That's a good one," Connie said.

"OK. Is everybody ready?" I asked as I put the car in drive and proceeded to drive down the road.

"She'll be coming round the mountain when she comes, She'll be coming round the mountain when she comes. She'll be coming round the mountain, she'll be coming round the mountain…"

Although the park wasn't that far away I took a few side streets and backtracked just a bit so the trip seemed longer and gave us more time to enjoy our newfound singing abilities. When we pulled up to the park we did the grand finally of the song, *"She'll be coming round the mountain when she cooooooomes!"* As we finally came to the end of the song we all broke out laughing.

We got out of the car and I spied a good picnic table under a nice shady tree. Jimmy and I carried the picnic basket over to the table and sat it down on top of the table. I looked around and found a small tree limb on the ground. I picked it up and stuck it in between the slats on the picnic table and said, "I, Sir Jason T.

Harmony, do here by claim this table in the name of Queen Connie and Prince Jimmy of the Fowler Crest!"

Connie smiled at me, curtsied and said, "You're my knight in shining armor."

I bowed and said, "At your service, my Queen."

Jimmy yelled, "Come on, let's play some football!" Then he ran out to the open field and kept throwing the ball up in the air. Connie and I came strolling up to him and he threw the ball in the air. As it was coming down I reached up and grabbed it while it was over his head.

"OK, listen up everybody. I'm going to explain how to play three man, I mean three person, pass. One person starts off as the quarterback and two people form an offensive line in front of him or her, whoever the person is. One of the people on the offensive line is the hiker and they will hike the ball to the quarterback. The other person is the receiver. They take the kneeling position along side of the hiker. The quarterback stands directly in back of the hiker and counts to three slowly. On the count of three, the hiker snaps the ball and the quarterback reaches in and grabs it. The hiker and the receiver immediately run down field. The quarterback starts counting out loud. When the quarterback reaches the number eight both people turn around. The quarterback passes the ball. The receiver tries to catch it. The hiker tries to block the pass or intercept the ball. The first person who catches a pass becomes the new quarterback and we start all over again.

"That sounds like fun!" yelled Jimmy jumping up and down in excitement.

"Yeah, it does!" Connie says with a big smile on her face.

"OK, I'll be the first quarterback," I said, "Who wants to be the receiver?"

"I'll be the receiver!" yelled Jimmy.

"And I'll be the hiker," Connie said.

"Alright then, let's get started."

They both took the kneeling position and Connie held the ball on the ground ready to hike it. I walked up in back of Connie and began to count "One, Two…"

Just as I got to three and was going to reach for the ball, Connie swung around and yelled, "Watch it, Buster!"

"What?" I asked quizzically as I stood up.

"Just putting you on notice that I'm watching you, so you better watch where you try to put your hands, Mister!"

The defiant look on her face really tickled my funny bone because I started laughing so hard that I couldn't have caught the ball if I had wanted to. While Connie stood there waiting for me to answer her and assure her that I was still a gentleman, I finally managed to stop laughing and then explained that I was always first and foremost a gentleman.

Connie said, "Well, see that you remain one. No accidents, do you hear me?"

"Honest. Scout's honor," I said still laughing.

"OK. Let's get the game going now that the ground rules have been set." Connie replied with a firm look on her face.

So with ground rules set, we started the game and I was extra careful to keep my hands to myself at all times. I grabbed the ball and passed it to Jimmy. Although Connie tried to block the pass, Jimmy managed to catch it.

This time when we lined back up, Jimmy was the quarterback, I was the hiker and Connie was the receiver. Jimmy passed the ball to Connie and I was able to intercept it and I became the quarterback again. We played for an hour or so and it seemed that I was the quarterback for more than my share of turns. My passing ability that day was phenomenal or at least I thought so. As we played, I noticed an older couple had claimed the picnic table across from ours. They were eating their lunch and watching us as we played.

When we were finally worn out from playing, I grabbed the football and said, "Do we want to keep playing or do we want to eat lunch?"

"Let's eat lunch!" Jimmy shouted.

"I'll second that," said Connie.

"All right then, let's go," I said. I tucked the football under my arm and then took off running like I was going for a touchdown. Jimmy ran after me laughing and we acted like we were still playing the game.

We returned to our picnic table and Connie opened the picnic basket to get out a tablecloth that she had put in the top of the basket. Jimmy and I spread the tablecloth out on the table and Connie put the plates and utensils around the table then we all sat down to eat. In-between bites of fried chicken and potato salad, we talked about picnics and how much fun they are. I told Connie that her fried chicken and potato salad were as good if not better than what my mom used to make.

"Thanks for the compliment," she said. "I learned how to make both of them from my Grandma. She used to tell me, *'Connie, if you want to have a good down home picnic you have to bring the right food'*. She grew up on a farm in old Kentucky. They raised chickens and grew their own corn, potatoes, green beans, and every other kind of vegetable you could think of. She said that fried chicken and tater salad had been going on picnics ever since man was knee high to a June bug."

"Sounds like she's quite a woman," I said.

"She was quite a woman. She died a few years back."

"Oh, I'm sorry to hear that," I said. "I bet you miss her."

"Oh, yes I do. I have been thinking about her a lot lately. She taught me so many things."

While we were talking I heard the older couple at the table across from us debating over something. The lady said, "I'm right and you're wrong."

"No, I'm right and you're wrong," he replied.

Finally they both got up and started walking toward our table. When they reached our table the man held his hand out to me and said, "Hi. I'm Harold Blackerd and this is my wife Sally."

I wiped my hands on my napkin, halfway stood up, put out my hand to shake his and said, "Glad to meet you."

Before I could introduce Connie or Jimmy he continued on, "My wife and I were watching you throw the football around out there and you're real good at passing. Excellent as a matter of fact and you're a dead ringer for Morrie Phillips, the quarterback for the Green Bay Packers. Are you indeed Morrie Phillips? Sally says you are but I'm not quite sure."

"Well, thank you for the compliments" I said, "but no, I'm not Morrie Phillips. My name is Jason. Jason T. Harmony."

Harold looked at Sally and she looked back at him. Finally she asked me in a curious voice. "What does the T stand for?"

With a straight face and a twinkle in my eye I said, "Touchdown."

She giggled and then she said, "Well, that certainly fits."

I looked at both of them and said, "Let me introduce my friend Connie and her outstanding son, Jimmy."

They nodded and said, "Glad to meet you."

Connie smiled and said, "Won't you sit down for a while and join us?"

"Don't mind if we sit for awhile but we have already eaten lunch. We bought a couple of burgers from The Burger Pit across the way there and ate them as we watched you play football," said Harold.

As they both sat down I asked, "Are you from around here?"

Sally answered, "No, we're just passing through."

"I retired last year," Harold said, "and we bought a motor home. We decided that we'd travel the country and just take our time about it. You know, stop and smell the roses, so to speak. Everything was going pretty good. We went through Arizona, crossed through into California for a ways. We then decided to cross into Nevada for a while. We had just started coming down that big hill outside of town when the engine started sputtering and stopped running. If that wasn't bad enough, when the engine stopped running, the power steering stopped working along with the power brakes. It was all I could do just to get it to the side of the road and bring it to a stop before I started to pick up speed from that steep grade. If that wasn't enough to ruin my whole day, what happened next was."

"What was that?" Jimmy asked while he continued eating his potato salad.

"Well, I put on my emergency flashers and I got out and opened up the storage compartment of the motor home to get out the reflector triangles so I could place them at the front and rear of our vehicle so people would be careful not to run into us. I walked about a hundred feet to the rear of the motor home and set up one of the triangles. At the edge of the road as I was getting up, I noticed a boot sticking out of the bushes. I walked over to take a look and that's when I saw that there was a leg sticking out of the boot along with the rest of the body."

"Oh my God!" exclaimed Connie. "Was the person alright?"

"Well, at first I thought that he might be sleeping or passed out from consuming too much alcohol but when I saw his hands I knew that he was dead." Harold said.

"Why? What was wrong with his hands?" Connie asked with her hands clutched to her chest.

Just then Sally interrupted, "Harold! Maybe you'd better save this story for later. These people are trying to eat their food."

"I suppose you're right dear," he answered, "besides it's getting close to three o'clock and we'd better check into that motel across the street so we'll have a place to sleep tonight."

Sally smiled and said, "The tow truck driver was nice enough to drop us off here after he towed our motor home to that repair shop down in town."

"Henderson's Auto Repair?" I asked.

"Yes, that's the place," said Harold. "Why do you ask?"

"Well, it just so happens, I work there" I answered. "I'm one of the mechanics."

"Well, not only can you pass a football but you fix vehicles as well," said Sally. "If I were twenty years younger I'd latch onto you in a second." She turned her head and gave a big wink at Connie. Out of the side of my eye I saw Connie wink back at her.

"I know that you guys are probably pretty busy down there at the auto shop," said Harold, "but do you think you could pull a few strings and get our motor home repaired first thing tomorrow morning?"

"I'll sure see what I can do," I said.

"What was wrong with his hands?" asked Jimmy looking at Harold intensely. "You can tell me. I'm all done eating."

Harold looked at Connie. Connie smiled and nodded her head. "Well the reason I knew he was dead is because his hands were turning black. Now, I'm no doctor or nothing, but I fought during the war and I've seen dead bodies. I know what it looks like when gangrene sets in."

"You know, I heard something about this on the news" I interrupted. "He was a Hispanic male in his twenties or thirties."

"That's right," said Harold. "I called 911 on my cell phone to report it. When I went back into the motor home and told Sally, she got pretty upset. She didn't like the idea of a dead person lying right outside of our motor home."

"I don't blame her," I said.

"Neither do I" Connie said leaning forward listening intently.

"When I finally got a hold of a tow truck company with a tow truck big enough to tow our motor home I noticed that the paramedics were pulling up. I guess the 911 operator didn't believe me when I told her that the person was dead." Harold said.

I replied, "I think they have to send the paramedics anyway. It's some kind of county protocol."

"Well," said Harold with a deep hearty laugh, "I can tell you this, it didn't take them but a few seconds to see that he was dead. While the paramedics were talking on their radio a squad car pulled up and out stepped this great big Sheriff."

I interrupted again, "That must have been Sheriff Arby."

"I guess," said Harold. "I didn't really catch his name. Anyway he talked to the paramedics for a minute or so then he comes over to our motor home and pounds on the door."

"I thought he was going to break the door he was pounding so hard," said Sally with a smirk on her face.

"Well, I opened the door," continued Harold, "and he says, *The show's over! You people pull back on the road! This here is a crime scene!* I looked at him and said, *Our motor home is broken down. The engine quit running. Didn't you see the reflective triangles I placed on the road in back of us?* He replied *What reflective triangle?* I stepped down from the motor home and pointed toward the rear. When I took a glance it wasn't there. *It was right over there,* I said to him.

'Right about where your squad car is parked.' I got down on my hands and knees and looked under his car. *'There it is. Right there under your car,'* I said. He looked at me and said, *'Well, I sure didn't see that triangle when I pulled up here and parked. You sure you didn't just put that thing under my car when I wasn't looking?'* Then he broke out in a big smile and said *'Well, I guess I'll have to buy you a new one of those things some day.'* With that he walked over and got into his car. He stuck his head out of the window and yelled, *'You got a tow truck coming?!'* I shook my head yes. He yelled back, *'Try to stay out of the way of the crime scene!'* and then he pulled back out onto the road and sped away. I walked over and picked up the reflector triangle. It was a little worse for wear but it still worked. I set it back up and walked over and got back in the motor home. Not long after that the tow truck arrived. When he got our motor home all hooked up and was beginning to tow us away I looked back and noticed a white van pull up beside the paramedics vehicle and then a distinguished looking man stepped out and started talking to the paramedics."

"That sounds like it must have been the coroner," I said. "He must have come out there to pick up the body."

"Yeah, that's probably who it was," Harold answered. "So anyway, the tow truck driver towed our motor home to the repair shop and then he was kind enough to drop us off here."

"That was nice of him," Connie said.

"Yes. He seemed like a nice young man," Sally replied.

"And that's how our day has gone," Harold continued. "Full of mishaps and excitement."

"I'm sure glad we had a chance to meet you folks," I said holding my hand out to shake hands with Harold again.

"The pleasure was all ours," Harold said.

"Yes, it was very nice to meet all you nice folks," Sally chimed in.

Connie said, "I sure hope everything turns out alright for you two."

"Oh don't worry about us. We'll be just fine," Sally answered.

Both Harold and Sally waved as they walked off. We picked up our dishes and cleaned off the picnic table. Jimmy and I carried the picnic basket back over to the car and put it in the trunk.

"Do you think his hands were really black?" Jimmy asked me as we were waiting for Connie to come to the car.

"I'm sure they weren't black like the color black," I said, "but they were probably pretty dark."

Connie walked over with a small bag of trash left over from our picnic lunch and threw it in the public wastebasket then joined us. We all got into the car and started for home. As we pulled out of the parking lot I started singing *"Old MacDonald Had A Farm E I E I O!"* Both Connie and Jimmy joined in singing, *"And On His Farm He Had A ...... Hippopotamus!"* Jimmy yelled, *"E I E I O..."* We sang all the way back to Connie's house. While we were singing I thought to myself about how so much of this picnic had been about doing things I hadn't done since I was a lot younger. Things like throwing the football around. Heck, I hadn't done that since I was in High School. It's funny how things you like to do and patterns you get into in your life change from time to time without you realizing it. Things that were so important to you at one point in your life become secondary the older you get.

We pulled up to Connie's house and got everything unloaded. I was preparing to leave when Connie asked Jimmy, "Don't you have something you want to say?"

"Oh, yeah," said Jimmy. "Mr. Harmony, thank you for coming on the picnic with us."

I looked at Jimmy and said, "Jimmy, you're quite welcome. And thank you and your mother for inviting me to come. I had a great time with you and your Mom."

Connie smiled and said, "I sure had fun today too. I hope that we can do this again sometime soon."

I looked back at Jimmy and asked him, "Jimmy, could you do me a big favor?"

His eyes opened wide and he answered, "Sure. What do you want me to do?"

"Stop calling me Mr. Harmony and maybe just call me Uncle Jason?"

He shook his head up and down, smiled and said excitedly, "OK, Uncle Jason!"

They both stood at the door watching and waving as I got in my car and left.

CHAPTER SIX

I walked into my apartment and went over to check my answering machine for messages. The light was blinking. I pushed in the button and I heard my mother on the phone, *Hi Jason. This is Mom. I've got some bad news for you so you had better sit down. This morning your Uncle Lester passed away. He died in his sleep. He was only 57 years old. Your Father and I are flying to Arizona for his funeral. We'd like to have you be there if you can arrange it. Also, it would mean a lot to your Aunt Minnie. I'm not sure yet when the funeral's going to be but I'll give you a call back when I find out the details. I love you, Son. Bye, Bye.*

Wow! Uncle Lester dead? I didn't know what to say. Heck, I was just thinking about him today. What a shock. The last I had heard anything about Aunt Minnie and Uncle Lester, they had moved to Arizona because of his asthma. The dry weather was supposed to be a lot better for his condition. Seems like it was just a few years ago, but now that I think about it, it's been close to 15 years now. They'd moved to a town called Tucson. I always meant to go there and visit with them but I never really got the chance. It seems kind of sad to have to visit at a time like this.

After a nice long day full of fun, good friends and exercise. I decided that a nice warm bath would probably be the best thing for me at this time so I walked into the bathroom and turned on the water in the tub. While the water was running into the tub I went in the bedroom and got undressed and returned to the bathroom. After soaking in the nice warm water for awhile and thinking about family and good times that I have had, I got out, dried off and went into the bedroom, got dressed for bed then went into the kitchen to fix myself something to eat. Looking over my selection of TV dinners in the freezer I decided that tonight would be Mexican Dinner night. I put the dinner into the oven and set the timer then I turned on the TV set and sat down on the couch. I surfed through the TV stations for something good to watch. On the Comedy Station I found a show with my favorite comedian, Jim Follsworth, on it. He was saying, *If you cut your grass and find the wagon you lost when you were a kid, you could be a hillbilly. If your little brother's name is Bubba, you might be a hillbilly.* While I watched, chuckling at some of his jokes, the phone rang. It was Mom.

"Hi, Jason. The funeral for your Uncle Lester will be this Wednesday at 2:00 P.M. at the Golden Hills Chapel on 1624 Main St. in Tucson Arizona. Do you think you'll be able to make it?"

"Well I'm not sure, Mom. I'll have to check with my boss tomorrow and see if I can get some time off. I'll certainly be there if I can. When are you and Dad leaving?"

"We're going to leave tomorrow so we can get there early and keep your Aunt Minnie company. We'll be there to help her any way we can."

After talking for a few more minutes we said our goodbyes. The timer went off so I got my dinner out of the oven and then sat down to eat it. I finished watching the comedy show and part of a movie. When a long series of commercials came on I decided I'd just go ahead and call it a night, so l got up and brushed my teeth and went on to bed.

CHAPTER SEVEN

Monday morning found me pulling into the Henderson's Auto Repair shop parking lot. It was about 7:30 a.m. The shop didn't open until 8 a.m. but I liked to get there early so I could get a heads up on what the work schedule looked like for the day. I saw the motor home that belonged to Harold and Sally parked by the side of the shop. I walked on into the shop, opened my toolbox then slipped into my coveralls. I grabbed my coffee cup and walked over to the coffee pot that we had for all us hired hands and poured myself a cup of coffee. Mr. Henderson always liked to have the coffee ready for us as soon as we came in.

Mr. Henderson's door was open so I stuck my head in his office and said. "Good morning, Bill. I'd like to talk with you when you get some time."

He looked up at me and smiled, "Jason, I always have a minute for you. What can I do for you?"

"Well, there are actually two things that I wanted to talk with you about. First I wanted to see if I could get Wednesday off. My Uncle died and I'd like to attend his funeral in Arizona if at all possible."

"Jason, it's not that I don't need you this week because I do. Family is very important and if you need to take some personal leave time I can work around it for a day or two."

"I sure appreciate it, Bill, but I think if I fly out Tuesday after work I can be back here for work on Friday morning."

"Well, that's fine with me, Jason and if you find you need more time just call me and let me know."

I thanked him and started to walk out of the office when he asked, "Didn't you say there were two things that you wanted to talk to me about?"

"Oh, yeah, I almost forgot. I met a nice couple yesterday. A Mr. and Mrs. Blackerd. It seems their motor home broke down on them and they had it towed to our shop. They're staying in a motel for now. They asked me if I could talk with you and see if we could work on it first thing this morning."

"Jason, that would be great. That big old bucket of bolts is blocking half of our parking area. We need to fix it and get it out of here. We can use all the space we can get. I put the key on the front desk. The tow truck driver dropped it through our mail slot. The sooner we get it out of here the better off we'll be."

I walked on out and grabbed the key off the desk, got my tool tote tray out of my tool box and went out to take a look at the vehicle. After running a few tests I traced the problem to a defective fuel pump. Unfortunately the fuel pump on this particular model was in the fuel tank. This meant that the fuel would have to be drained from the tank in order to remove it from the vehicle to access the fuel pump. Checking the fuel gauge, it showed that the tank was half full. They make the fuel tanks on these vehicles a lot bigger. With larger a capacity, it enables the owners to drive longer distances without having to stop at a gas station every two hundred miles or so. This tank held fifty-two gallons. Our shop had a handy system for draining fuel tanks. It was a clean fifty-five gallon oil drum with an inlet tube welded into the topside of the drum and an outlet tube welded at the bottom of the drum. It had hoses connected to each tube and an electric fuel pump that could be used to suck the fuel out of a tank or to pump fuel back into a tank. I went in and told Bill we needed to order a fuel pump for the motor home and let him take care of that part of the job while I got the drum and equipment and prepared to drain the gas out of the vehicle. I got everything outside to the vehicle and hooked it up to start draining the fuel.

It was shop policy to stay by the equipment while the fuel was being transferred, just in case something was to go wrong and fuel started to spill, so I kept a careful watch on the operation. After about twenty minutes the electric fuel pump started to sputter which was an indication that it was sucking up the last of the fuel. I immediately turned off the pump and unhooked it from the system. Now it was time for me to go to work. I rolled under the motor home on my creeper and began loosening the fuel tank mounting straps so I could drop the fuel tank down and remove it from the vehicle. That's when I noticed a plastic bag that was stuck on the right rear shock absorber. I pulled it off and was surprised to see it said Bowman Ice Company on it. Then written with black marker it said Willy's Pit Stop. It must have been blowing around on the road and got stuck under the Blackerd's vehicle. What in the world was a bag of Slick Willy's ice doing stuck under their motor home? It didn't make a lot of sense. I continued loosening the fuel tank straps and, with the help of a floor jack, I was able to drop the tank down and roll it out from underneath the motor home. I removed the fuel pump from the top of the tank and covered the tank with shop towels so the vapors wouldn't spew out into the air. After settling everything under the motor home I walked back into the shop and got another job from Bill, working on a car, while I waited for the fuel pump to arrive from the parts house.

My cell phone rang and when I answered it, it was Connie. She was very excited. "Jason! You'll never guess what happened!"

"You won the Sunday night lottery." I answered.

"No silly! I got the job at the Montgomery Law Firm!" she screamed with joy and excitement. "He was so impressed with me that he hired me right on the spot!"

"Wow! That's great. When do you start?" I asked.

"I start the first thing tomorrow morning," she replied. "That will give me the rest of today to go shopping and pick up some new clothes so I'll look nice on my first day of work."

"Connie, you don't need new clothes to look nice," I said. "You look great in whatever you wear."

"Thank you Jason," she giggled, "but I think you'd even like me if I wasn't wearing anything.

That was a loaded statement and I figured maybe I should be careful how I replied to her so I simply said, "Connie, when God made you he made an extremely beautiful woman." There was silence on the phone. After a few seconds I asked, "Are you still there Connie?"

Finally, in a quiet voice she said, "Thank you, Jason. No one has ever said that to me before." Then she said louder, "Oh, I am so excited. I just wanted to let you know about the job. Thank you so much for telling me about the law firm. I never would have had the courage to try there if it were not for you. I'm on my way to the department store now. I'll talk to you later."

We said our goodbyes and I continued working on the car.

About 9:30 a.m. the new fuel pump arrived for the motor home so I switched back to working on it. I got everything completed and was just preparing to pump the fuel back into the tank when the Blackerd's came waking up to the motor home. "How is it going?" Harold asked.

"Well, if everything goes right," I said, "it should be done in fifteen or twenty minutes."

"That would be wonderful. What did you find was wrong with it?" he asked.

"The electric fuel pump quit. I installed a new one and now I'm pumping the fuel back into your tank."

"You had to take the fuel out?" Sally asked. "That sounds like it was quite a job."

"Well, it's not the hardest job I've ever done but it wasn't the easiest either."

Looking over at the empty bag of ice I had pulled off his shock absorber Harold said, "This ice company must be pretty popular around this area."

"Why do you say that?" I asked.

"Because I saw a few of these bags lying around the area where our motor home broke down."

"This one was stuck on your shock," I said. "It's kind of odd because the only place that sells this particular brand of ice around here is a store called Willy's Pit Stop just outside of town and let me tell you, it's not the cheapest place you'll ever buy ice."

"Yeah," said Harold, "we got a place like that back home. It's called Friendly Freddie's. The guy could sell raincoats in the desert."

"That sounds just like Slick Willy! Maybe they're related" We both laughed then I said, "You know, I've been wondering, instead of spending the night in a motel room, why didn't you just stay in the motor home?"

"There's two reasons," Sally answered. "First, the *No Loitering* sign that's posted at the front of the building and second, we like to get out of the cramped quarters of the motor home every so often and stretch out and take baths instead of showers and that type of thing."

"I can see where it would get a little bit irritating after awhile," I replied.

When the fuel was back in the motor home tank I turned the engine over and it started right up. Both Sally and Harold let out a cheer. After I checked to make sure everything was tight and I hadn't left any loose ends, they went into the office to settle up their bill with Mr. Henderson. Before they left, Harold came over, shook my hand and thanked me for all the work I had done on the motor home. Sally gave me a big hug. I told them that if they ever passed through this way again to be sure to come and look me up. I waved as they pulled away, then went back into the shop to finish the other job I was working on.

Right about lunchtime I got another call on my cell phone. When I answered, it was Landen. "Hello, Jason. I've gotten a hold of some pertinent information about the pictures we took on Saturday out at the B.L.M. land. We need to get together and go over it."

"What exactly is it?" I asked.

"I don't wish to discuss it over the phone," he said. "Can you meet at the office when you get off work?"

"Sure. About what time do you want me there?"

"Ted will be here at about 5:30 this afternoon. Will that time be good for you?" he asked.

"That's fine with me," I said. "I'll see you and Ted there at about 5:30 then. By the way, would you like me to stop at *Fast Fry* and pick up some hamburgers and fries?"

"That would be excellent," Landen replied. "Can you see to it that my burger only has mayonnaise and lettuce on it?"

"You've got it," I said. The rest of the day I couldn't stop thinking about what information he could have gotten and why he couldn't tell me over the phone.

CHAPTER EIGHT

When quitting time rolled around I jumped in my car and headed on over to Fast Fry. After picking up the food I went straight to the Meade Investigations office.

Ted was just pulling up when I arrived. "Hey, Jason! What did you get for me?" he yelled out of his car window.

"Burgers and fries!" I yelled back.

"Great," he replied, "I'm so hungry I could eat a horse or at least a small pony." He helped me carry the bags inside and we sat them down on the conference table.

Landen was sitting at the table with a folder in front of him. "Were you able to get one with mayonnaise only?" he asked.

"You bet I was," I said. "The girl at the counter didn't care for the idea too much but I told her it was for my boss, an eccentric old coot that would chain me in his dungeon if I didn't return with his request."

"Hey, whatever it takes," chimed in Ted.

As we sat at the table munching on our food, Landen opened up the folder and took out some pictures. "I was able to get in contact with Larger Than Life out of Davis, California. With their image processor they were able to enlarge the pictures we took on Saturday. Through their special process the pictures were blown up over a hundred times their original size. I asked them to concentrate on the bird's left leg. When they emailed me back their results I down loaded them and printed them out in picture form." He passed around the pictures for Ted and me to look at while he continued on, "There is a band on the hawk's leg. From looking at the different angles of the pictures I've been able to make out some lettering on the band, perhaps some type of name or I.D. number. If you study the pictures closely you'll see there's an ARK on the top line followed by an IRD FA on the second line. On the bottom line is an AZ with a number 2407 and the rest is not legible. What we need to do is make some kind of sense of the lettering. I believe the AZ probably stands for the state of Arizona. The rest of the lettering is anyone's guess."

As I studied the picture I tried to keep in mind that this bird was not a normal Red Tail Hawk. By its actions of attacking humans, I knew that it was something Red Tail Hawks seldom do. Also to be able to control the intensity of its attacks was another thing a wild bird would never be able to do. The fact that it had a band on its leg meant only one thing; the band could only have been put there by a human. I noticed that there was a small space between IRD and FA. Could the letters on the second line possible be two words? I brought this up in a question to Landen and Ted.

"That's an excellent thought," said Landen. "Let's start with that theory. If that's the case then the IRD would be the end of the front word. So we simply use the letter elimination process. Adding a letter at the start of the word and working through the alphabet."

It wasn't long before we figured out the first word was BIRD. But the second word took a while longer. When we were done we had figured out the lettering on the band, or so we thought. It seemed to read ARK BIRD FARM. "What a weird name," said Ted. "It must be short for Noah's Ark, after the story in the Bible. We need to go on the internet and see if we can locate the exact address."

"Yeah," I replied. "Arizona is an awfully big place."

"Before we do that," said Landen, "there's something else I want to show you." He reached in the folder and pulled out one more picture. "This is a blow up of the picture you took on the side of the cliff, Jason. If you look closely you'll notice that shiny object you saw is perfectly round."

I gazed at the photo and was surprised to see the shiny object had a circular shape to it. "What in the world do you think it is?" I asked Landen.

"I'm not exactly sure," he answered, "but I will say this, I'm almost certain it is not a rock."

After examining the photo a little longer we decided to log onto the Internet and see if we could locate Ark Bird Farm under the section Bird Feather to Bird Houses. We were finally able to locate farms but there was only three places listed. The only one that was in Arizona was a place called Clark Bird Farm. Landen's face lit up when he saw the name.

Ted said, "What are you so pleased about? The place we're looking for isn't listed."

Landen smiled and answered, "Oh, but it is listed. Don't you see we've been under the assumption that the ARK was the complete name but it's just the last three letters. If you add CL to ARK you have the full name, CLARK."

"This is it! This is the place we're looking for. Brilliant piece of detective work!" I said. "That hadn't even crossed my mind."

"I'm sure we would have gotten it," Ted added, "but it would have taken us a little longer."

"I'll take that as a compliment," Landen answered. "That's probably about as close as I'll get from you, Ted."

Ted smiled and gave him a pat on the back, "Good work!" he said.

Viewing the Clark Bird Farm web site, we discovered that the farm was located in Oro Valley, Arizona. Along with a few pictures of the layout of the farm was an advertisement that read, *We breed and train exotic birds of all types.* I wondered to myself how in the world could a Red Tail Hawk with a band on its leg from an exotic bird farm in Arizona get to be in the wild lands of Nevada? Could it simply have escaped from the farm and flew away then ended up here? The whole thing didn't make a lot of sense. There was an email address to contact the place so Landen sent an email asking for more information about the farm and the types of birds available for purchase. As we waited for a reply I asked if anyone knew where Oro Valley was located in Arizona.

"I think it's somewhere over by Phoenix," said Ted.

"Let's look it up on the 'net while we're waiting for a reply," Landen said.

When we viewed the map and located Oro Valley, we found out that it was near Phoenix. Ted smiled and shouted, "Am I good or what!?"

"Just a lucky guess," Landen answered.

"Lucky guess? NOT!" Ted replied. "I know my geography."

"Too bad you don't know your limitations," Landen said as he laughed. "You can't even pronounce the word correctly."

I was looking at the computer screen and saw at a closer glance that Oro Valley wasn't too far from Tucson either. In fact it was probably a little closer. "I haven't told you guys yet," I spoke up and interrupted their lighthearted arguing, "but I have to go to my Uncle's funeral on Wednesday in Tucson, Arizona. If need be, I might be able to visit this farm and maybe talk with the owner. Maybe we can get some more information that might help in our investigation."

"Well, if it's possible for you to do that," said Landen, "it would work out great. Let's figure out the distance from Tucson to Oro Valley. That would give you a better idea of how many miles you'll have to travel and also give you some idea about the amount of time it will take to get there."

We did a rough calculation and came up with ninety-eight miles, depending on the road conditions. "It would probably take about two hours to drive. It looks like the best route to take out of Tucson is Highway 77" Ted said.

After printing out a route map from the MapQuest site on the internet we went back to see if we had gotten an answer to our email. There was a reply saying we can train and equip any type of bird you wish. Our farm is a thirty-two acre facility just outside of Oro Valley. Our prices are negotiable depending on the particular bird, the degree of training and if you want the bird equipped or not. At the bottom it said, Regards, Devon Clark.

Ted glanced at me and asked, "What in the world does he mean when he mentions equipped?"

Landen spoke up and said, "I'm thinking it would probably be some type of a restraining device so the bird is easier to control. I'll write back to him and ask if it would be possible to meet with him later this week at his farm and get a closer understanding of his methods of training and take a tour of his facilities. You did say that you will be in Tucson on Wednesday, right?" he started typing the email and then asked, "Could you stop by his farm late Wednesday afternoon or Thursday morning?"

"Either time would be fine with me," I answered. "My boss said I could take a couple of days off if I needed to."

After corresponding back and forth through emails, Landen set up an appointment for nine a.m. sharp on Thursday morning. Devon gave strict orders not to be late. Landen printed out the directions off of MapQuest and handed them to me and said, "I'll talk with Sheriff Arby and let him know that we're following up a lead on the Hawk investigation. For now we'll just continue on our normal schedules."

"Hey, I almost forgot," Ted interrupted, "the coroner's report came out on that guy that they found up on No Pay Grade."

"What did he find was the cause of death?" Landen asked.

"He determined it was shock," Ted answered. "Evidently all the guy's internal organs had shut down."

"That's odd," I said. "I talked with a guy yesterday who found the body and he said the guy's hands were black. He said it looked like gangrene had set in."

"Couldn't that accompany the shock condition?" asked Ted.

"I'm not sure," Landen answered. "But I guess it must, otherwise the Coroner wouldn't have diagnosed it that way. It's not like our Coroner's ever made a mistake, now is it?"

We all started laughing thinking about a something that happened a few years back when Clarence Osborn was found dead in his bed. It started out looking like an open and shut case.

The Coroner said he died of a heart attack. But then it was discovered that just six months before he had inherited a large sum of money. The Sheriff found out that there were at least three people who stood to profit from his death. His darling wife, whom he had fought and argued with since the day they were wed. His loving son, Farley, who hated his dear father's guts and he didn't care much for his mother either, mostly because of what they named him. It was bad enough going through life with a name like Farley but his middle name, Ferdinand, was even worse. If you were to say both names rather swiftly it sounded like a dish you would order at a French Restaurant. The third person was Clarence's own mother. Although she had never been close to her own son she had developed a close relationship with his wife, her loving daughter-in-law and her grandson. Clarence had no sooner inherited this large sum of money, $500,000 dollars from a man in Boise, Idaho whom he had helped around his potato farm when he was growing up, when his mother, wife and son started conspiring between themselves to get every last cent of it.

Their plan was to have a will drawn up dividing the money equally between all three of them. Once they copied his signature from an old bar tab he'd finally paid off they transposed it to the will. Now there was only one thing left to do, get rid of him, and rub him out. Clarence liked to drink his beer every chance he got so the three of them figured they'd stick something in it. But what could they get? They came up with a drug called Lopressor. It was used to treat high blood pressure. It slowed a person's heart rate down. When the heart beat slowed the flow of blood through the veins and arteries was considerably less causing the pressure to drop. If they put enough of this drug in Clarence's beer sooner or later his heart would stop completely. The brilliant thing about the plan was that Clarence was already taking a small dose of this medicine daily so if it were found in his system nobody would think anything about it.

The best way to accomplish this task, they decided, was to have a party, just a small one with some of Clarence's old drinking buddies. Farley acquired the medicine from a friend he had who worked at a pharmacy in Twin Peaks, a small town about a hundred miles away. The wife and mother picked up several of cases of beer and a few bags of pretzels. Clarence had recently bought a plasma wide screen TV so the three of them figured that the theme of the party would be *Friday Night Boxing Live On HBO*. They sent out invitations to a few of his friends with instructions that it was a surprise party for Clarence and not to let him know about it.

That Friday, at about six p.m., his good old buddies started showing up at the door. It wasn't long before the plan was put into effect. The first beer Clarence had wasn't spiked because he had opened it himself but after that one the rest were loaded with pills.

"Here's another beer for you, son," his mother said as she gave him an opened can of beer.

Not long after that his son brought him another open beer, then his wife, then his mother again and on and on. Heck, at one point he was drinking one beer and had an open one waiting for him on the table in front of him. By the time the main event was over on the Friday night fight program he had consumed nine beers, each one containing three one hundred gram tablets of Lopressor. With the amplified effects of the alcohol he had washed them down with it would be enough to kill a horse.

When his friends left, Clarence announced that he was feeling a little weak so he thought that he would go ahead and hit the sack. A few hours after that his wife called 911 to report that her husband was not breathing. When the Paramedics arrived and found no pulse and that he was not breathing, they called for the Coroner to come. When the Coroner arrived Clarence's wife told the Coroner that her husband had been complaining of chest pains but refused to go to see the doctor to get it checked out. After conferring with the Paramedics for a few minutes the Coroner himself took a quick check of the body and pronounced Clarence dead. He then announced that the official cause of death was a myocardial infarction or, in layman's terms, a heart attack. He asked the wife if she had any preference for a funeral home.

When she said no, he told her that the closest one is Peace On Earth. Then he said, "Would you like me to arrange to have them pick the body up?"

"Yes, please," she answered in a meek little voice. Then added quite strongly, "ASAP."

The Coroner gave her a strange look then opened up his brief case and took out a list of emergency numbers for mortuaries throughout the area. He dialed the number and talked with the person on call. They said they'd be right over.

Meanwhile, the Coroner took the legal papers out of his briefcase and began to fill them out. When he was done he said, "Mrs. Osborn, I've completed the death certificate. Come to my office on Monday and I will supply you with a copy."

Farley spoke up, "There's a copy making device on the fax machine. Can't we just go ahead and make a copy of it right now?"

The Coroner was taken aback by this comment. "That's highly unusual," he said with a concerned look on his face. "Why are you in such a hurry?"

"I'm just thinking of my poor Mother," Farley replied. About that time his mother put her head in her hands and faked some high pitched wails then started moaning and rocking back and forth. Then he continued, "I don't want her to have to deal with any more than she has to in her time of grief and sorrow."

"Well," answered the Coroner, "I suppose that it would be OK."

After the copy was made and the Coroner was preparing to leave, that was when the person from the funeral home arrived. The body was loaded into the back of his van and then the Coroner and the person from the funeral home left at the same time.

The next morning at ten a.m. sharp, the mother, wife and son were waiting outside the funeral home door until it opened for business. They were escorted in and sat down in solemn dignity with the funeral director to discuss the business at hand. The director started the proceedings showing them the different types of coffins or housings that were available for purchase. He started off with a $60,000 Cadillac of coffins. All three of the grieving family shook their heads, no. Then he worked his way down the line of coffins he had and telling the advantages of each until he came to the cheapest one.

The funeral director said, "This one here is a very fine coffin. It's priced to be more affordable and it's made of durable long lasting materials. I can let you have this one for just $3,500 plus tax."

Farley shook his head and with a loud voice of discontentment said, "Hell, we're not looking to buy a damn car here. All we want is something we can stick the body in so we can burn it. Don't you have something for a few hundred bucks?"

"Oh, I see," said the director, "you're going to have the deceased cremated. Well, we do have what we in the business call the Soap Box Derby model."

'What's that?" Farley asked.

The director explained, "Well, it's a coffin made entirely out of pinewood. Nothing fancy mind you. Just a basic box shape."

"How much is that one?" Farley inquired.

"Let me see," he said. After doing some figuring on a piece of paper he announced, "I can let you have it for just $1,500 plus tax."

"Fifteen hundred dollars?" Farley shouted. "Hell, I could go down to Cabinets 'R' Us and have the same thing built for four hundred dollars!"

After bickering back and forth over the price they finally settled on seven hundred and fifty dollars. There would be no funeral or services. The body would be placed in the coffin and transported to the crematorium to be cremated the next morning. With that taken care of they all three left the funeral parlor and went home to have a quiet celebration.

CHAPTER NINE

On Monday morning when Clarence didn't show up at work, his boss got concerned. Clarence was never one to miss a day of work in all of the years he had worked there. Finally, at nine o'clock, he decided to call the house to see if everything was all right. When Clarence's wife answered the phone he told her who he was and asked if he could please talk with Clarence.

She answered, "Clarence isn't here."

"Well, where's he at?" he asked. "He's supposed to be at work."

"He's gone," she answered.

"When will he be back?" he asked.

"He's gone and he ain't never coming back," she said.

"I'm not sure I understand what you're saying."

"Clarence died of a heart attack on Friday night," she replied with no emotion.

"Heart attack?!" said the boss. "He just had his company physical last week and they said he was in excellent physical health. My God, what terrible news. How are you holding up?"

"I'm doing fine," she said in a whiny voice. "My son and mother-in-law are staying with me so they can help out."

"When are the services and the funeral going to be?" he asked.

"Everything's been done," she said. "He was cremated yesterday."

The boss started getting a little suspicious. Clarence had told him about the large sum of money he had come into a few months ago and now he was dead and cremated, all in one weekend. It just didn't seem like it was on the up and up. He said his goodbyes and told Clarence's wife that if she needed anything to give him a call. She said that she didn't need anything.

After thinking about everything that he had heard on the phone he decided to give his good friend Arby Fillmore, the Sheriff, a call and voice his suspicions about the demise of Clarence. The Sheriff said that he would look into it for him and assured him that he would get to the bottom of it. The Sheriff called the coroner and asked about the cause of death. When the Sheriff got off the phone he got in his squad car and drove on over to Clarence's house to ask the next of kin a few questions.

Meanwhile, the coroner thought it might be a good idea if he took a closer look at the body so he called the funeral home and talked with the mortician. After finding out that the body had been scheduled to be cremated on Sunday, he gave a quick call to the crematorium. When the phone was answered he asked the man on the phone about the remains of Clarence.

"Oh, it hasn't been burnt yet," he said. "Our incinerator operator has been sick for the last two days. He just came back to work this morning." After that all you could hear was the man talking while the receiver dangled from the phone base as the coroner made a mad dash to his vehicle and rushed to the crematorium.

The Sheriff arrived at Clarence's house so he could begin talking with the next of kin. When the widow answered the door, the Sheriff could tell that she was highly nervous. He asked the widow if he could come in and the son spoke up and said, "I don't think that would be a good idea. My mom's in mourning and she doesn't want to answer a bunch of intimidating questions."

"This won't take long," Sheriff Arby answered. "Just a minute or two."

The son looked at his mother and then at his grandmother sitting on the sofa, then said, "Well, OK. But just for a minute."

When the Sheriff walked into the house the first thing he noticed was an empty bottle of champagne sitting on the kitchen counter. The son, noticing where the Sheriff was looking, quickly announced that he'd opened that bottle to give his mom a glass so as to try and calm her nerves.

"She's really broken up about my father's passing," he said.

About that time the mother let out with a loud cry and his grandmother joined in. "I think they're just too upset to answer any questions right now. I'll try to answer your questions for you, Sheriff," he continued.

"OK. That's fine," the Sheriff said. "Exactly how did your father die?"

"He died of a heart attack in his sleep," answered the son.

"Did he have any preexisting conditions such as high blood pressure?"

"Yes he did," Farley said.

"Was he taking any medication for it?" The Sheriff directed this question directly to the mother and grandmother. Both started crying louder when they heard the question.

"Yes," Farley answered for them. "He was taking Lopressor. 50 milligrams a day."

The Sheriff thought it was rather odd that the son knew exactly what dosage his father was taking when he didn't live at home and hadn't lived at home for ten years. "I understand," said the Sheriff, "that your father had just inherited a large sum of money."

The mother and grandmother started crying uncontrollably. "That's true," said the son, "but I think you really better go now. You're upsetting my mother and grandma."

"That's fine. I'll leave. I think I've got all the information I need."

When the Sheriff left, the son and two mothers waited and watched for him to drive off and then they got the will that they had made and jumped into the their car and headed for Mr. Montgomery's office.

When the Coroner arrived at the crematorium he ran inside yelling, "Where's it at? Where's it at?!"

The man at the counter said, "Calm down, sir. I can't make heads or tails out of what you're talking about. Now say it slowly so I can understand."

The Coroner said, "I want you to put a stop order on the remains you received from Peace On Earth over the weekend."

"Oh my goodness!" said the man. "It's already out in the incinerator room waiting to be burnt. We'd better hurry!" When they got to the room there was no coffin to be found. "It must be in the firing temple already. We can't go in there. It requires protective gear but I can speak to the operator through this intercom system. He picked up the microphone and said, "Nelson. Could you please bring out number POE62507?"

After a few minutes the door for the firing temple opened and our stepped Nelson with a large metal container of ashes. "This is POE62507," he said. The Coroner's face turned pale.

"I guess we're too late," the man said. "Nelson, thank you for your trouble. That's all we need for now."

As Nelson went back to work the two men started to leave the incinerator room when suddenly the outside door blew shut. "Oh, my God!" said the Coroner. "We're not locked in here are we?"

"No, no," said the clerk. "The door can always be opened from the inside. It's a state requirement for burning facilities." When they got outside, the Coroner thanked him for his trouble and then left.

The Sheriff drove to the District Attorney's office after he left the Osborn house. The D.A.'s name was Donald Stevens. He and the Sheriff had known each other for years. They'd worked on a lot of cases together. The Sheriff walked right into the

D.A.'s office and began to tell him about what he had found and the suspicions that he had concerning the three relatives.

Meanwhile, the Osborn family arrived at Mr. Montgomery's law office. After talking with the receptionist for a few minutes, they were led into his office. He stood up from his desk and smiled then said, "Have a seat please. Now what is it I can do for you today?"

Farley answered, "Well, my dear father passed away Friday night..."

"Oh, I'm so sorry to hear that," interrupted the attorney.

"Thank you," said the mother.

"Anyway," Farley continued, "we found this will of his that he left in his important papers lockbox at the house." Farley handed the will to Mr. Montgomery. As he looked it over he asked if he had this filed with an attorney.

"No," said the mother. "He just made it out a few weeks ago when he was having chest pains. He said he wanted to make sure his loving family was taken good care of if he were to die."

"I see," Mr. Montgomery said. "Then you witnessed him making this will out and signing it?"

"Yes I did," she said.

"Well that should be sufficient," he remarked, "as long as no one tries to contest it. That shouldn't be a problem though. I see all three of you are beneficiaries. Are there anymore next of kin?"

"No," said the grandmother. "We're the last of the Mohicans," and as she said this, a smile broke out on her face. Mr. Montgomery gave her an odd look then continued looking at the will.

"How long do you think it will take to execute the will?" Farley asked.

"Let's see," said Mr. Montgomery. "If we petition the probate court this week we can probably have the matter taken care of in nine to ten months."

"Why so long?" asked Farley.

"Well, you have to give all his creditors a chance to file a claim on what they are owed," said Mr. Montgomery.

"Isn't there a less time consuming way to handle this?" asked the mother.

Mr. Montgomery thought for a minute and then said, "Well, I suppose we could have you post a bond. Did your husband have a lot of outstanding debts?"

"Nothing to speak of," answered the mother. "The house is paid for. We still owe a little on our car but that's about it."

"What about credit cards?" he asked.

"We have a few but we seldom ever used them. When the bill came in Clarence always paid them off. He never let them build up."

"Then I think I can bend the law a little bit," Mr. Montgomery said. "Let's see, I believe if you were to post a twenty-five thousand dollar bond we can get away with not filing in probate court. Now, as far as the inheritance goes, your name is on the house deed and the automobile title so that part of the estate will naturally go to you, Mrs. Osborn. The rest of the estate, his private bank account with the five hundred twenty three thousand, nine hundred sixty three dollars and fifty seven cents, will be divided into three equal shares after we take the money out for the bond. The bond will stay in effect for one year from when it is posted. At the end of that year whatever monies are left will be divided into three equal shares and be distributed to the three of you. Do you have any questions?"

"Yes, I have one," said Farley. "When do we get the money?"

"First we'll need the death certificate," he answered. "That usually takes a few…"

At that point the mother interrupted him, "I have it right here" she said.

He turned and looked at her in amazement. "How in the world did you get that so quickly?" he asked.

"The Coroner made a copy for us on our fax machine copier," Farley chimed in.

"That's highly unusual," Mr. Montgomery said.

"That's the same thing he said," answered Farley.

After looking the certificate over Mr. Montgomery said, "Well, it looks like everything's in order. I'll fill out the legal papers and file them. You might see your money by the end of this week."

After thanking him they all three left his office and headed back to the house for another celebration.

Meanwhile, after forty-five minutes of discussion, the Sheriff and the D.A. came to the same conclusion; there was definitely enough suspicion in this case to hold it over for a possible murder case. The D.A. called Judge Murdock and had him issue three bench warrants, one for the mother, one for the wife and one for the son. Then he scheduled a preliminary hearing for the next morning at nine a.m. The Sheriff stopped by the court and picked up the warrants and went to the Osborn home.

When he pulled up the three suspects were just getting out of the car. Farley had an unopened bottle of champagne in his right hand while he was shutting the car door with his left. The Sheriff stepped out of his squad car and walked over to where the three were standing and said, "I have warrants for your arrests. You have the right to remain silent…" he continued on advising them of their rights until he was finished.

"What are we being arrested for?" asked Farley.

"For suspicion of murder," answered the Sheriff as he took out his handcuffs.

"Have you lost your mind!" said Farley. "Do we look like criminals? There must be some mistake!"

"No mistake," said the Sheriff. "We have reason to believe that you all three conspired to murder your late father."

"That's absurd!" said Farley. "We haven't murdered anyone. The mother and the grandmother both started crying hysterically. "Now see what you've done, you insensitive bastard!!!" shouted Farley. "Here we are in a state of mourning and you come over here making false accusations! I'll have your job for this!"

"Sorry, ladies," said the Sheriff, "but this has to be done. If you promise me you'll behave yourselves I won't handcuff you."

They stopped crying long enough to agree that they'd behave. The Sheriff ushered them into the back of his squad car. As he turned around he told Farley to put his hands behind his back.

"But you said if we behaved you wouldn't handcuff us," Farley said.

"I was talking to the ladies," answered the Sheriff. "You, I'm handcuffing!"

He put the cuffs on him and sat him in the squad car with his mother and grandmother. As he drove them to the jail house the Sheriff kept trying to get them to admit to the murder but not a word came out of their mouths. They were sworn to secrecy. After booking them into the County Jail they were each given one phone call. All three calls were made to their attorney, Mr. Montgomery.

Meanwhile, the Sheriff got a search warrant and went back to search the house. In a small town like Jeffersonville City, word spreads quickly and by suppertime everyone in town was talking about it. After searching the house and coming up with nothing at all, the Sheriff decided to look in the trashcan outside. After pulling out and going through most of the garbage he found what he'd been looking for. It was an empty prescription bottle. There was no name on the label but under medication it listed Lopressor, 100 milligrams, quantity 25 tablets. *BINGO!* went off in his mind. He hurried back to the station house to book it into evidence.

When nine a.m. Tuesday morning came the courthouse was packed tight with people from all over town. This was the biggest thing that had gone on in Jefferson City since the gold rush days.

The bailiff said, "All stand for the honorable Judge Murdock!" The Judge walked in and set down. "Please be seated. Judge this is case number 351 Jefferson County preliminary trial.

Will the attorneys please stand and introduce yourselves to the judge?"

The attorneys rose. "Yes, your honor. I'm Donald Stevens, the District Attorney. I'll be prosecuting this case. I believe we've met."

The judge smiled and said, "Yes, I believe we have."

"Good morning, your honor. I'm William Montgomery. I'll be representing the defendants in this preliminary hearing. I believe we've also met."

The Judge smiled and said, "Well, it's certainly a pleasure having two such distinguished attorneys in my court room today. Let's begin the hearing. Mr. Stevens, are you ready to call your first witness?"

"Yes your honor. I call Mary Jenkins to the stand."

When she was sworn in and took the stand Mr. Stevens asked, "What's your profession, Miss Jenkins?"

"I'm a paramedic for the city of Jefferson City."

Mr. Stevens continued, "And how long have you worked as a paramedic?"

She replied, "For almost eight years."

After a lot of basic questions he established that she had responded to the Osborn house when Clarence passed away. "In your professional opinion what was the cause of death?"

Mary sat up straighter and replied, "By all indications it appeared to be a myocardial infarction. We could detect no pulse or heart beat. There were no visible vital signs."

Mr. Stevens asked, "Could this have been caused by an overdose of medication?"

"I'm not sure," she said. "I suppose it could have been."

"Objection, your Honor!" Mr. Montgomery said. "Speculation on the part of the witness."

"Objection sustained," said the Judge.

"Thank you, Miss Jenkins," said Stevens. "Your witness counselor."

"No questions," Montgomery answered.

After going back and forth with several witnesses and establishing the motive and the Sheriff testifying about the medicine bottle he had found in the trash can it was time to call the key witness in the trial, the Coroner.

The prosecutor started in, "Sir, is it true you've established the cause of death as a heart attack?"

"Yes. Mr. Osborn died of a myocardial infarction," the Coroner answered.

"How did you determine this?"

He answered, "I examined the body and medical history of the deceased. I also talked with the paramedics at the scene of the death"

"Would it have been possible that this death could have been caused by an overdose of a medicine called Lopressor?"

The Coroner answered, "That would be highly unlikely. I'd have to say no, it was not caused by an overdose of medication."

"Are you sure?" asked the Prosecutor.

"Yes I'm quite confident."

The Prosecutor looked directly at the Coroner and asked, "Did you take a blood sample at the scene and test it for any irregularities?"

"No, that was not necessary."

The Prosecutor shouted, "Not necessary!?... Not necessary!?... I'm sure you are aware that the deceased was cremated shortly after his death!"

"Yes, I'm aware of that!" said the Coroner who was starting to shout back his answers.

"Don't you think," continued the Prosecutor, "that it would have been a good idea to take a blood sample of the deceased!?"

"It wasn't needed!" shouted the Coroner. "Sir, I'm a professional at what I do!"

"So you're 100% sure the deceased wasn't poisoned!?"

"The man died of a normal heart attack!!" shouted the Coroner. "I'll stake my reputation on it. The Lord himself would not doubt my word!!!"

About that time there was a rattling at the back of the courthouse. Everyone turned around to see what it was. Suddenly the courthouse door swung open and in stumbled good old Clarence. The audience gasped. The Coroner fainted straight away. The three Osborns on trial stared at him with their mouths wide open.

"Well, lordy be," said the Judge, "Could that be Clarence standing there?"

"It's me, Judge," said Clarence. "Does anybody have a bottle of water or something? I'm powerful thirsty and I don't seem to have my wallet or any change on me."

It seems that all the Lopressor medication hadn't killed old Clarence after all. It slowed his heart rate down so low it only beat once every minute or so. His breathing had been so shallow it was clinically undetectable for lack of another word. He was in a state of hibernation. It had been blind luck for Clarence that Nelson, at the crematorium, had taken off sick. Otherwise he wouldn't have survived the ordeal. When he finally did stir early Sunday morning and raised the lid on his coffin it was all he could do to find his way out of the door in the incinerator room before he collapsed in the back of a mulberry bush just outside the building where he hibernated for another twenty hours or so. The Coroner was reprimanded by the City Officials for his lack of professionalism but under the unique circumstances he was allowed to keep his position. In turn, for agreeing to sign divorce papers and signing the house over to him, Clarence never pressed charges against his wife or the other two.

"No, our Coroner never makes any mistakes," I said to Landen. Then we all started laughing out loud.

CHAPTER TEN

After I left the detective office I stopped by Connie's place to see how her day went. When I knocked on the door Jimmy answered and yelled, "Uncle Jason! Mom! Uncle Jason is here!"

"Just a minute," Connie yelled from the other room.

"Come on in," Jimmy said as he left the front door open and walked over to the sofa and set back down to watch the rest of the Hannah Montana Show on T.V.

"You're not a Hannah Montana fan are you? I asked Jimmy.

"Not really," he said. "I just like to watch her dance and sing."

About that time Connie came walking out from the hallway in a tight black dress with high heels on.

With a smile on my face I said, "Hellooooo, Connie. Wow! You sure look nice!"

"Well, thank you," she said with a confident look on her face. "This is one of the new dresses I bought today for work."

"Wow! If you wear that to work," I said, "I don't think Bill Montgomery will get anything done."

She giggled and asked, "Then you think I'll be a hit?"

"Oh, yeah. If you type as good as you look you'll be a huge success," I answered. "Let's go in the kitchen and sit down at the table and talk for awhile."

When we sat down I told her about my Uncle Lester passing away and having to travel to Arizona for the funeral. I also talked about the bird farm and stopping by to view the operation.

"But I don't want you to go," she said with a sad puppy dog look on her face.

"I know, but I owe it to my Aunt Minnie and my cousins," I replied. "I'll only be gone for a couple of days and I'll call you every night and let you know how everything's going and you can tell me how your new job is going."

"OK," she said. "But I'm going to miss you." She leaned over the table and gave me a long tantalizing kiss. "Besides, we won't be able to kiss over the phone. You sure you don't want to just forget about going and stay here with me instead?"

Still smitten by her luscious kiss, I had my doubts about going to Arizona at all. But after a few moments I came back to my senses and said, "We'll be able to kiss when I get back home."

"Promise?" she asked.

"Yes, I promise," I answered. "Now I better get going. I have to go home and pack my suitcase and make some traveling arrangements."

∝◇◇◇∽

When I got home I called and booked a flight for six p.m. the next day. I called Ted and he agreed to take me to the airport. After getting off the phone I packed my bags and took a quick shower and went on to bed.

CHAPTER ELEVEN

Tuesday afternoon at about three-thirty Ted stopped by the auto repair shop to pick me up. With Mr. Henderson's blessings I left work an hour early so I could make it to the airport on time to check in for my six o'clock flight. I took my luggage out of the trunk and locked up my car and gave the keys to the boss in case he might need to move it for whatever reason while I was gone. I put my luggage in Ted's car and we left for the airport.

"I'm sure sorry to hear about your uncle," Ted said. "Were you two pretty close?"

"Not really," I replied. "Our families used to do a lot of things together when I was younger but I haven't seen him for quite a while now. I was always going to visit them when they moved to Arizona but I just never got around to it. Other things kept coming up."

"I know what you mean," Ted answered. "Time flies when you're having fun. You always mean to do something but you never get the time and when you do get the time you never have enough money."

As we drove along I figured I'd better give Connie a call and let her know I was on my way. I dialed the number where she was now working and heard her answer, "Montgomery Law Offices. This is Connie. How may I help you?"

"Hi, Connie, this is Jason. How's the new job going?"

"Oh, it's going great!" she answered. "Bill said I'm doing such a good job that he wants to take me out to dinner tonight to celebrate."

"Well, that's fantastic!" I said. "Are you going to bring Jimmy with you?"

"No. He's going to go to Billy's house tonight for dinner then they're going to watch a movie his mother rented at the video store. You know that new one with Harrison Ford in it where he plays *Indiana Jones* again."

"Oh, yeah. I heard it's a really good movie," I said.

"I know," she laughed. "Those two boys have been talking about Indiana Jones ever since they saw that first movie *The Raiders Of The Lost Ark*. They must have watched them all a dozen times or more. They're so excited. I told Billy's mom that I wanted Jimmy home by 8:30 so we'll see how that goes."

"Well, I guess that just leaves you and Mrs. Montgomery to enjoy dinner with the boss," I said.

There was a slight pause on the line and then she said, "Mrs. Montgomery is out of town visiting her sister. That's one of the reasons Bill asked me out to dinner. Why..."

I interrupted, "So his wife won't know about it?"

"No. No," she answered, "because she isn't home to cook him dinner. He says he knows nothing about cooking. He doesn't even know how to boil water."

"Well, you have fun but be careful. He might be up to no good."

She giggled, "Don't worry about me, you just have a safe flight and be sure and call me when you get there and get settled in."

"OK, I sure will. I guess I'd better let you go. I'll call you soon." When I got off the cell phone I looked at Ted and asked him. "What do you know about this Bill Montgomery? Is he on the up and up?"

"Are you kidding me, Jason? He's probably the most trusted man in town, with the exception of Judge Murdock. Why do you ask?"

"Well, I'm sure you heard that Connie just started working for him," I said.

"Yeah, I heard about that," he answered. "What about it?"

"It's just that he seems to be coming on to her a little too strong."

"How so?" Ted asked taking a quick glance at me.

"He already asked her to go out for dinner and she hasn't even worked there a full day yet."

"Oh, come on, Jason, he's probably just being kind to her."

"Yeah, you're probably right. Besides he's got to be a good fifteen years older than she is," I replied.

When we got to the airport, Ted pulled up in front of the terminal into an unloading zone and I jumped out of the car and grabbed my luggage, told Ted thanks and then I headed for the ticket check in line. Once I got on the plane and it took off it didn't take any time at all to get to Tucson, Arizona. After we landed I waited for my suitcase to be unloaded and then preceded on to the car rental booth to get a rental car that I could use while I was visiting.

After leaving the airport I headed straight for Aunt Minnie's house. I figured I would stop by and visit for an hour or so then check into a motel someplace close by. When I arrived at Aunt Minnie's house I noticed that my parents were there along with my cousins, Linda and Freddy. My sister Cathy was also there and all of their kids, running in and out of the house reminding me of the way the four of us use to be when we were younger. Two of the kids belonged to my sister and the other three belonged to by cousins. My father was in the dining room talking with my sister's husband, Rick, and my mother was sitting on the sofa consoling Aunt Minnie who was sitting beside her.

As I walked in everyone was happy to see me. Aunt Minnie motioned for me to come over to her and she stood up and gave me a big hug. With tears in her eyes she said, "Jason, you've gotten so big."

"It sure is nice to see you again, Aunt Minnie. I'm so sorry to hear about Uncle Lester. Is there anything I can do to help?"

"Just being here at this time with my family is help enough."

Then my cousin Freddy came over and shook my hand and said, "Long time no see, Jason. You sure are looking good."

I replied, "You're looking pretty good yourself."

He leaned over and whispered in my ear, "Can I talk with you in private for a minute?" and then led me into the kitchen. When we got into the kitchen he said, "Jason, I need to know if you'll be a pall bearer at my father's funeral tomorrow? I think my dad would have wanted it that way."

"You know I will, Fred. I always thought a lot of your father. It would mean a lot to me to be able to honor him that way," I answered.

After talking with Freddy, or Fred as he was now called, I found out that the other pall bearers were to be Fred, my father, Linda's husband Gary, my brother-in-law Rick and a very close friend of Uncle Lester's named Rex Smith. We were to be at the funeral home at 10 o'clock because the services were to start at 10:30 a.m. From the funeral home we would proceed to the cemetery where we would carry the coffin to the site for burial.

After getting the information from Fred and visiting with all the folks it was time for me to go and find a motel. I'd seen several motels in the area when I drove in. Some were pretty rundown looking, others I could tell would be way too expensive. I decided to stop at a Holiday Inn about ten miles up the road from Aunt Minnie's.

When I walked inside the clerk said, "Cómo estás, amigo."

I'd seen a lot of Hispanic people while I had driven through town on the way to Aunt Minnie's house but it didn't dawn on me that the businesses in town would speak Spanish as their first language.

"Hello," I answered. "I'd like to get a room for a couple of nights. Do you have anything available?"

"Yes, we do," he answered in English. "Would you like a queen or king size bed?"

"A queen size would be fine."

"I have a non-smoking room on the first floor for ninety-six dollars a night. Would you like that one?"

"Yes. That would be fine," I answered.

He stamped up my credit card and had me sign the invoice then gave me the room key. "When you go out this door, turn to your right. Your room, she is at the end of the hallway."

I thanked him and walked out the door. I saw a Mexican señorita standing down the walkway. As I came close to her she said, "Hey, hombre. You want to have a little fun tonight? For twenty dollars I make you feel so good."

"I'm sure you would, sugar," I said as I looked her over quickly, "But I've got a long day tomorrow and I have to get to bed early tonight."

As I continued to walk to my room she said, "Hey! You so cool maybe I do you for free."

I looked back at her and smiled as I made my way to my room.

When I got inside and got settled in, the first thing I did was take a nice warm bath. I got out and got dressed for bed and looked at the clock sitting on the end table. It was already quarter to ten. I picked up my cell phone and dialed Connie's number. When she answered I asked her how dinner went.

"I had a fantastic time," she said. "He took me to Manchester's Manor and…"

"Wow," I interrupted. "That's the swankiest place in the county. How was it?"

"It was just unbelievable," she replied. "We started off with caviar appetizers and champagne while we decided what we wanted to order. Then when they started bringing our seven-course meal, Bill ordered a bottle of red wine dated *1952!* It cost over eighty dollars a bottle!"

"Sounds like it must have been some pretty good wine," I said.

"Oh, it was the best wine I've ever tasted!" she said excitedly. "Then when we were all done and getting ready to leave, Bill left the waiter a hundred dollar tip on the table. Everybody kept looking at us like we were the most important people in the place. It was like a dream. I couldn't believe it was happening!"

As I was listening while she was talking I thought to myself, either this guy has a lot of money to burn or he's putting on a big show. When she was done talking I asked her if he'd been a gentleman and hadn't tried to make a pass at her.

"Of course he was. He was a perfect gentleman," she answered. "We did kiss goodnight but that was just his way of thanking me for going out to dinner with him so he didn't have to spend the evening alone."

"Well, I'm glad you had a good time. Now you better get some sleep because you have to get up and go to work tomorrow and I've got to get up early and get ready for my Uncle's funeral tomorrow. I'll give you a call tomorrow and let you know how everything went."

We said our goodbyes and I got off the phone. After watching the TV for a short period of time I turned off the light and went to sleep.

CHAPTER TWELVE

I was awake by six a.m. and after shaving and brushing my teeth I got dressed in my suit and headed over to Arizona Flaps for some of their famous flapjacks and ham for breakfast. After breakfast I drive over to a AAA office in town and got some maps of the area so I could plan the route I would take *to Clark's Bird Farm* the following day.

By ten o'clock I was at the funeral home ready for the services. When the pastor talked about Uncle Lester's life and the things he had done one of the things he mentioned was the picnic at the property with the bears. Everyone had a good laugh and it seemed to help ease some of the sorrow we all felt about his passing. From the funeral home we followed the hearse to the cemetery and placed Uncle Lester in his final resting place. After that everyone went to Aunt Minnie's house to celebrate Uncle Lester's life. There were platters full of all kinds of different foods, salads, ham, chicken, cakes, pies and plenty to drink. The refrigerator was packed full of beer and sodas. There was whiskey and vodka on the kitchen counter along with bottles of Seven-Up and a large container of ice.

As I walked in the front door Cousin Fred handed me a cold can of Budweiser beer. "Here," he said. "This is a time to be happy, not sad. My father would have wanted it this way."

My mother came over and gave me a big hug and said, "Jason, you sure look handsome in that suit. You look a lot like your father when he was your age."

The house was full of people, all friends and family of Uncle Lester and Aunt Minnie. My dad was standing at the dining room table cutting a baked ham into slices with a carving knife for people to put on their paper plates when they were ready to eat.

I walked over to the table and asked Dad, "Is there anything I can do to help?"

He smiled and answered, "Son, just being here for your Aunt Minnie and their kids in their time of need is help enough."

We talked for a while and I told him about the case I was working on with the Meade Brothers and about going to visit the bird farm the next day. He looked at me sternly and then said, "Jason, you really love doing detective work, don't you?"

I nodded my head and said, "You bet I do."

"Well, then, why don't you quit your mechanic job and do it full time?"

I started laughing and said, "Do you want me to starve to death?"

"Son," he said, "I've always heard that if a man's going to work all his life at a job to make a living then it better be doing something that he loves to do. I think this applies to your situation. You're a good mechanic and you like working on cars and trucks, but that's just it, you like it, you don't love it. On the other hand you love this detective stuff. Why don't you go for it?"

"Dad, let me think on it."

About that time Aunt Minnie motioned for me to come over to her. She was holding something in her hand. I worked my way past the people and when I got to her she handed me a small carving of an elephant made out of ivory that I had always admired when I was growing up. Every time we would visit Uncle Lester and Aunt Minnie in their home I would ask Uncle Lester if I could look at the elephant and he would take it down from the shelf of the china cabinet and let me hold it and examine it. I was always truly amazed at how someone could have made something so beautiful with their own two hands.

With tears in her eyes, Aunt Minnie said, "Jason, your Uncle Lester always told me that if anything ever happened to him he wanted me to make sure that you got this elephant. He always loved this thing and it made so happy to see that you loved it just as much as he did."

As I held it in my hands I said, "I don't think I'll be able to take it on the plane trip home with me because it's too fragile and it might break."

Aunt Minnie said, "Here, use some of this to wrap it in." She walked over and picked up a local town newspaper that was lying by the couch and began wrapping the elephant with its sheets of paper. When she was done she found an old shoe box and put it inside the box. She tied a piece of string around the outside of the box to hold it shut.

"There," she said. "That should keep it safe and sound for your plane trip back home."

I thanked her, gave her a big hug and told her that I would always treasure it. While the rest of the day went by with everyone trying to be happy on such a sad occasion, the weather was changing outside. The dry crisp sunshine had slowly changed to dark clouds. By the time I left for the motel at about 8:30 that evening it was starting to rain. There were bright flashes of lightening followed by earth shattering bursts of thunder.

When I got back to my room at the motel, the sky had opened up and the rain was coming down in buckets. I gave Connie a call to see how things were going back home. We talked for a while about how her day had gone then she told me that there had been a warning on the local radio station about a flu virus going around. She said that a few cases had been reported and a medical report said that they had not identified the strain of flu virus at this time. They were cautioning everyone to cleanse their hands after being out in public and to use hand sanitizer when at all possible.

"Are you and Jimmy feeling alright?" I asked.

"We're fine, Jason. Don't worry about us," she replied.

We talked for a while longer then said our goodbyes. When I got off the phone I heard a loud burst of thunder outside. *Wow! What a miserable night out there.* I thought to myself. I had planned the route I would take to the bird farm the next day and I figured it would take me a good two hours of driving time. If I left at about six thirty in the morning it would put me there by eight thirty. That would make me a half hour early for my appointment. After taking a shower and brushing my teeth, I got ready for bed and set the alarm clock on the nightstand for five thirty a.m. I figured that it would give me a good hour in the morning to get dressed and have breakfast before I had to leave. As I lay in bed trying to get to sleep, the burst of a loud clap of thunder jarred me back awake and somewhere between the thunder and the heavy rain, I fell fast asleep.

CHAPTER THIRTEEN

When I awoke the next morning the sun was shining through the curtains on the window. I glanced over at the alarm clock and it was flashing the 12:00 digits on its screen indicating that the power had gone out, probably from a lighting strike. I reached over quickly and grabbed my cell phone, opened it up to check the time. It was 7:05. *Oh, my God! I've overslept!* I thought to myself. This can't be happening. Devon, the manager at the bird farm, made it pretty clear that if I wasn't there precisely at 9:00 a.m. that I shouldn't even worry about coming. I jumped out of bed, got dressed in a flash and was out the door in less than a minute. I stopped by the motel lobby and grabbed a quick cup of coffee and a donut. I ran back out to my car, got in and took off for the highway.

Traffic was moving pretty slowly all the way out of town but once I got on the open highway it moved along quickly. Every chance I got I sped up to 75 and 80 mph to try and make up for some of the time lost. I only hoped that I could get there as soon as possible. I didn't want to miss out on the meeting just because I was late. Once I pulled off the main highway it was impossible to make any time. The road had too many curves. My average speed was between 50 and 55 mph. When I finally reached the turn off for the bird farm the check engine light in the rental car I was driving started flashing on and off. *Boy, this is all I need to make this miserable morning complete* I said to myself. When the check engine light went out completely I breathed a sigh of relief. But it didn't last for long because the light flashed back on a minute or two later and this time it stayed on. It wasn't too much longer after that when the engine began to lose power and finally stopped altogether.

With the car stopped, I pulled the hood lever and got out of the car to take a look under the hood. As I looked at this brand new engine I realized that I was helpless without a diagnostic machine to plug into its computer. I knew the problem was a sensor of some type that had failed but there were numerous sensors that could cause this problem. I looked for tell tale signs like wires that were disconnected but nothing was visible. I checked the oil and it was fine. I could see through the plastic reservoir tank that the coolant level was fine. I got back into the car and tried to start it but the engine just kept spinning over without actually starting. I got back out of the car and reached for my cell phone that I always had in my left front pocket, so I could call AAA road service for a tow truck. That's when a cold chill went down my back. In my rush to get going this morning I must have left it on the nightstand at the motel.

I looked up at the sky and said in a very loud voice, **"GOD, WHY ME!!!"** Here I was out in the country on some desolated road miles from anywhere with no cell phone and a car that doesn't run. The sun was creeping overhead and I could tell it was going to be another hot summer day in this part of Arizona. I found a bottle of drinking water on the front passenger seat that I had bought at the airport but never drank. I grabbed the water bottle and locked the car and started on my way walking down the road. I figured the bird farm wasn't too far away but I didn't really know how far, maybe a couple of miles, maybe farther. The further I walked the hotter it seemed to get. There was really no shade to speak of along the road. Although there were trees off in the distance they didn't help shade the road.

After walking along for what seemed to be every bit of an hour I started hearing something off in the distance. It was a rumbling sound that appeared to be getting closer. When the noise was almost right in back of me I turned around to see an old pick-up truck approaching. It appeared to be a Chevrolet from the late forties or early fifties. Sitting inside the cab of the truck were two Hispanic men. The one who was driving was very obese and large. The other was a very slender man. In fact you could say he was as skinny as a rail. The large man looked like he hadn't shaved for a few days. The skinny one was clean-shaven and much better kept. The old truck they were driving sounded like it was missing on several cylinders and judging from the loud exhaust noise it was making it probably had a large hole in its muffler, if it had a muffler at all.

They came to a stop by where I was standing. The large one yelled out, "Hey, hombre! Where might you be walking to?"

As I turned to look at them I thought to myself, *Well, when it rains it pours. Everything else this morning has gone wrong. Now I'm probably going to get beat up by a couple of Hispanics and robbed.* Finally I said out loud, "I'm looking for the bird farm. I'm supposed to meet Mr. Devon Clark."

"Señor Devon?" said the heavy set one, "We work for Señor Devon. I am José and this is my cousin Manuel. We are going to the farm to clean the cages. If you would so like you can drive with us. You will have to sit in the back of the truck. There is no so much room in the cab."

I said, "Gracias," and crawled into the bed of the truck. Off we went bouncing down the road.

It wasn't long before we came to a large fence made out of stone. It stood about 10 feet high and looked like it went on forever.

"This is Señor Devon's hacienda," José yelled out his window.

The large metal gates were open so the truck pulled on through and drove up to the front of a huge Spanish style house.

"You will find Señor Devon inside," José continued.

I jumped out of the back of the truck and thanked them. I walked to what looked to be the front doors and lifted the large knocking ring and struck it soundly against the door three times. In a few moments one of the doors opened slightly and a beautiful señorita appeared and asked, "Sí? What is it you wish?"

"I'm supposed to have a meeting with Mr. Devon Clark," I said.

Before I could tell her my name or that I was late for my appointment she said, "Just one momento," and she pushed the door slightly shut. She reappeared and said, "Mr. Devon wants to know if you are Señor Jason T. Harmony?"

I said, "Yes, I am."

She turned and yelled, "Yes, it is he!"

I heard a deep gravelly voice from inside say, "Well, the asshole is over an hour late for our appointment. Ask Mr. Jason T. Harmony what the T stands for in his name!"

She turned back to me and said, "Señor Devon is no so happy with you. He wishes to know what the T stands for in your name."

I smiled and told her that the T stands for *tardy*.

She smiled back then turned and yelled, "He says the T stands for *tardy*!"

I heard a bit of a chuckle inside then he said, "Tell Mr. *Tardy* he can come in."

She turned back to me and gave me an inviting smile and said, "Señor Devon say for you to come in."

When I walked in the door Mr. Clark was standing to the right in a large room just past the door. I held out my hand and said, "Hi. I'm Jason T. Harmony. I'm so sorry I'm late."

He shook my hand and said, "It's not often I meet with people who are late for appointments or *tardy*, as your middle name suggests, but I'll make an exception in your case because you made me laugh. This world would be a very miserable place if it weren't for laughter. What in the world happened to make you so late, anyway?"

As I began to tell him all about how my morning had gone he began to laugh. The more I told of the troubles I had, the harder he laughed. When I was done he motioned for the señorita that had met me at the door to come over to us.

"Jason," he said, "this is my maid, Maria."

I smiled and shook her soft hand and said, "It's nice to meet you."

She smiled back and said, "It is so much nice to meet you, too."

"Jason," he continued, "it sounds like you've had a rough morning. Can I have Maria bring you something, anything at all?"

"Well, I sure could use a strong cup of coffee," I answered.

"Maria makes the best coffee," he said. With that, he told Maria to bring me a cup of fresh coffee and to bring him a cup also. As Maria walked off to get the coffee he said, "Jason, come over here and let's have a seat at my guest table."

He led the way into the next room, which was a dining room with a large table and chairs. There was a lovely antique china cabinet off to the side of one wall and on the other side of the room was a beautiful antique buffet.

"Wow, Mr. Clark, this furniture is breath taking!"

"Thank you. But don't call me Mr. Clark. It's much too formal. Just call me Devon."

As we sat down at the table waiting for Maria to bring our coffee, I started thinking to myself about how could a man like this amass such wealth. He looked very ordinary. He stood about 5' 9" tall, a little overweight but not by much. I would guess that he was in his middle to late forties. His balding head shined as if it had been buffed with a polishing cloth. He had a well-groomed goatee beard and very normal facial features.

"So you like my furniture?" he asked.

"Yes, I do. It's beautiful. Is it antique?" I asked.

"Yes. It's 19th century," he said. "My knowledge of birds and my creativity with birds has paid for all of this, my house, my furniture, my cars, my ranch. I am the only man in the world who does what I do with my birds. There is no other bird farm like it. Kings, sheiks, dictators and yes, presidents come to me for my birds."

Maria came walking in with a tray holding two cups of coffee and a container of cream and a bowl of sugar.

"Thank you, Maria," he said. "Just set that down on the table." As we drank our coffee he asked, "Are you looking to purchase one of my birds?"

"Well," I started, "I could lie to you and tell you that I'm very interested in purchasing one of your birds but instead I'm going to be quite honest with you. I'm working on a case with Meade Investigations out of Nevada. It is a case that involves a bird attack."

He interrupted, "So, you're a detective?" he asked.

"Just part time," I said. "I'm still new at it."

"Well, I'll tell you, I've always dreamed of being a detective," he said. "It seemed like such an intriguing type of life."

"I don't know about intriguing," I said, "but it is definitely not your normal nine to five job. Anyway, the bird that attacked was a very large Red Tail Hawk. It didn't seem to go in for the kill. It just seemed to want to warn people away. It was almost like it was protecting its nest or something."

"That sounds like one of my birds," he interrupted once again.

"Yes, we're sure it is," I said, "because it had a band on its leg that says Clark Bird Farm."

"Oh yes, that's one of my birds. I band all my birds when they're a week old. That way there leg grows into the band and it can't be removed. What is it you're actually looking for from me?" he asked.

"I'd like to take a look at your bird farm operation and maybe go over your records to see if I can figure out who would have purchased this particular Red Tail Hawk," I asked.

"I'll tell you right up front that you cannot go over my records. Any birds I sell fall under what I call a seller client category. Once I sell a bird I never divulge whom I've sold it to. That's the way I like it and that, in most cases, is the way my clients like it. But I will show you my entire bird farm operation, if you'd like."

"I'd like that very much," I said.

"Well, come on then," he said gaily. "Let's get started. He led me to a rear door that opened up into an immaculate four-car garage. Sitting in the first stall by the door was a brand new John Deere Quad Runner. He pushed a control button to open the garage door and we both got into the quad and he drove it out the door.

While we drove along he turned to me and smiled, "This is my little bit of paradise. It is my piece of God's wonderful earth." The long path leading to the bird operation area was black topped and lined with trees and green bushes of all types. After driving for a few minutes we came to a metal gate lined with fine mesh wire. Devon got out and pushed a button on a post at the left side of the gate. The gate slowly slid open as he got back into the quad and then we drove inside and parked in a little area by the front. There were rows upon rows of cages, some smaller in size and some large enough to walk in. As we walked by the cages he would point out the different type of birds in each one.

"I have over one hundred different species of birds," he said. "Each species is unique in its own rights. I have lovebirds, flamingos, swans, and every type of soft beautiful bird you can think of. I even have the true homing pigeon. I know, it is extinct you say, but I am here to tell you that it is not. I have the last pair in existence. Down here are my more aggressive birds." He motioned for me to follow him. As we walked along the cages got much larger. "Here are my bald eagles. They're such forceful hunters and truly beautiful birds. Over here are my ravens and next to them are my crows. Crows are actually very friendly birds and very humorous at times. Down here I have ten different species of owls. And over in this next section are my hawks. These hawks are the Doberman Pinschers and German Shepherds of the bird world. I train them to be extremely diversified. They can be delicate enough to fly over and softly put a grape in your lips or deadly enough to rip the eyeballs right out of your head. It all depends on the command."

"These are the birds over here you are enquiring about," he continued as we strolled down to a huge cage that appeared to be the size of a small house. Devon opened the door and we walked inside. There were large nesting boxes hanging down from the twenty-foot high ceiling with cables and chains. "This is my Red Tail Hawk section. I have ten pairs of breeders which produce anywhere from twenty to twenty five chicks a season. The nests you see are suspended in the air by cables that are connected to a small one-ton crane system that I designed myself. I can lower each nest individually and examine the young chicks and band them. I start their training sessions when the chick reaches three to four weeks of age, depending on the chick. The young males are neutered and the females have their reproductive organs removed. This way I have their undivided attention. They also grow much larger and stronger. When the young birds are weaned from their parents they each get their own nesting box. They are trained to always return to their box, somewhat like a Homing Pigeon. When the bird is purchased, their nesting box will go with it."

"How do you train the birds?" I asked.

"The precise methods that I use are my secret. I will tell you that it involves food and discipline. Let's step out of here for a moment and I'll show you my laboratory where I operate on the birds."

We walked past the nesting boxes and out of a door at the end of the building and into another door off a short walkway. Inside was a complex that looked like a veterinarian's office. "This is my medical laboratory," he continued. "It's stocked with veterinary supplies and any and all of the equipment I need to treat my birds if they are ill and also to perform the surgeries that are required to transform my birds."

As he talked I thought back about the email he had sent asking if we wanted the bird equipped. So when he paused for a moment I asked, "How exactly do you equip one of your birds?"

He turned and looked at me for a short time as if to decide whether or not to let me into his confidence then he said, "Well, Jason, all my birds are trained by voice command. Whether it is to perform some type of trick, as a lot of my friendlier breeds of birds are, or to attack and defend, as I teach my more aggressive types of birds to do. Through years of trial and error I've developed a unique system for my birds that enable the masters of these birds to control their creatures without even being present or close to where the bird is located at any particular time."

"Wow! That's fascinating!" I said. "How in the world is that possible?"

"It takes quite a sophisticated system of microscopic receivers and surveillance cameras. If the customer requests that their bird or birds be equipped I surgically install a tiny receiver in the left outer ear of the bird. Then on its forehead I install a small surveillance camera about the size of a pinhead. The camera is part of a computer program I have designed. It allows the owner to have a bird's eye view from their computer screen. The receiver in the bird's ear is activated by a transmitter system where you simply talk into a microphone of some type to give your bird its orders. There is a bigger system available that will accomplish all of this from a base station but the most convenient and accommodating is the iPhone. With this portable system you can control your bird from wherever you are. You have your computer screen and your microphone all in the same instrument."

"So I could conceivably control one of these birds from a thousand miles away?" I asked.

"It would be just like talking on your cell phone," he answered. As long as you have reception you're good to go."

"That is truly unbelievable," I answered. "I would have never thought that anything like this could be possible."

"This is the best security system in the world," he replied with a slightly crazed look on his face. "Unlike security dogs, or even security guards, that get hampered by walls and fences or any other obstacles on the ground, this is all done from the air above and knows no boundaries. Would you like to see a demonstration?"

"That would be great," I answered.

"Here, follow me," he said.

We walked back into the nesting complex and out yet another door that opened into a huge dome covered area. It was much larger than a football field and looked a lot like a sports arena. The only difference was it had a few trees and bushes. There was a clearing in the center with beautiful green grass that was so well kept it looked like carpeting. The top of the dome was constructed of some type of wire mesh screen that appeared to be made out of stainless steel. In the middle of the clearing were three mannequins placed about twenty feet apart. Over to the side of the arena I saw two familiar figures hard at work trimming the bushes. It was José and his cousin Manuel. They looked up at us where we were standing which was about twenty feet above the clearing and José gave a quick wave and went right back to work.

"This is my training complex," said Devon. "It is perfect for my needs. The platform we are standing on is built on the side of the hill slopping down to the arena below. Underneath this platform are my birds in training. I have twelve in this particular class. They each have their own nesting box or homing box, as I like to call them. The boxes are secured to the platform by a series of cables and small electric cranes and are the same as the nesting boxes you saw inside. Ten of these birds have been ordered equipped by customers throughout the world. The other two birds respond by voice command only and have been purchased by a circus in Canada to perform as part of their show. Each of these birds has completed their training course and need only to be tested for a few more weeks to assure their perfection."

"What is the difference in price between a bird that has been equipped and one that hasn't?" I asked.

"Well, a bird that's equipped sells for eighty thousand dollars. If the customer buys two birds at the same time, which most customers do, then I let them have the pair for one hundred and fifty thousand dollars," he answered. "The birds that are not equipped I sell for fifty thousand a piece or two for ninety thousand dollars."

"You've got to be kidding me," I said. "People actually pay that much money for birds?"

"Yes, they do," he answered. "And these birds are worth every penny of it because when I'm done with them they are precision instruments."

"Well, it's plain to see that I'm in the wrong business," I said with a grin.

"Come, Jason, there is more to show you."

To the right side of the platform was a small room. As we walked inside he pointed to a desk that completely lined one side of the wall. On the desk were computers and all kinds of different modern technology.

"This is my base control station," he said. "The birds that I have equipped I eventually end up controlling from here. Once I establish the program for each individual bird I record him or her in my records and notes and then transfer each program to an iPhone for that particular bird. Watch closely and I will show you something that you won't soon forget."

With the push of a few buttons the sky over the arena was full of Red Tail Hawks, twelve to be exact.

"We'll use bird number five today," he said.

"How will I know which bird is number five?" I asked.

"Watch through the open window and in a few moments you'll know which bird is number five," he answered.

From the small control room you could see everything that was going on in the arena by simply looking out a series of windows to the front of the room or looking up at a closed circuit TV screen he had mounted above the desk.

"All my birds are trained with simple control words such as left or right, circle or land," he continued. "The calmer birds such as flamingos and cranes I teach to do tricks and bow. The crows I train to run in circles and flap their wings and even do somersaults. There are six basic command words I use for all my birds but my Red Tail Hawks have a vocabulary of twelve words, these extra six words are what make them so magnificent and amazing. The words alone make no sense to the normal person because I scramble them. For instance I might use the word apple for left or cherry for right and so on and so on. Only the person who purchases the bird knows the proper control words."

At this point I was quite sure he was deliberately trying to throw me off the track. For him to use different words for each single bird would be much too confusing. I was sure he used some type of scrambling system but it would only make sense to use the same system for each bird. As I watched out of the window, suddenly one of the hawks dove straight down for the center mannequin and hit its head with such force that the mannequin fell to the ground. The bird then flew back up into the air and circled for a moment then dove for the mannequin again, this time sinking its claws into the back and actually picking the mannequin up into the air with it. The whole time this was happening I heard Devon speaking into one of his small microphones. When the bird reached about fifteen feet in the air it let go of the mannequin and the mannequin slammed to the ground with tremendous force.

"That is a sample of a kill!" yelled Devon from his control panel.

José and Manuel had been watching all of this from the side of the clearing where they were trimming bushes and shrubbery. Suddenly the hawk flew straight over to José and began to circle. José looked up and dropped his clippers and began to run. As the bird dove closer to him he began to cry out, "No, Señor Devon! Please don't do this to me! No, Señor Devon!"

Manuel quickly crawled into one of the bushes and hid. As José ran I could see the look of terror on his face and the tears that fell from his eyes. The closer the bird came the faster José tried to run. I never saw a man the size of José run quite so quickly.

"Please, Señor Devon! No! No! No!"

The bird dove hard and fast and when it came within a few feet of him something strange happened. I heard Devon say 'balderdash' into the microphone and the bird slowed as if putting on some type of braking system. When it did strike José it wasn't much more than a strong tap on the shoulder. The bird flew back up into the air and circled a few times then flew off. I thought to myself, *That's exactly what I saw happen to little Jimmy and Billy.*

From the control panel Devon yelled, "That's a sample of a warning."

Through the open window I heard José yell to Manuel, "We go. I no more work for this chorizo of a Señor." Manuel crawled out of the bush and quickly followed José out of the gate.

"I think they're quitting," I said to Devon.

He began laughing hysterically, "They'll be back," he said between all his laughter. "They always come back."

CHAPTER FOURTEEN

After sizing up everything I had just witnessed with the way the hawk had bumped José on the back and not actually hurting him, I figured that the Case of the Red Tail Hawk was pretty much solved, or was it? I knew how the hawk attacks had happened, but who was actually controlling the hawk? Or was it more than one hawk. Devon had said that he usually sells two hawks to a customer and for God's sake, why would this bird be out on the B.L.M. land that's owned by the Federal Government? What could it possibly be used for? None of it made a lot of sense.

When Devon had let the hawks exercise their wings for about an hour or so. We left the hawk section and walked back thru the complex to the quad runner sitting by the gate. As we crawled in and drove out the gate Devon said, "Well, have I answered all your questions for you Jason?"

"All except one," I said.

"Which one is that?" he asked.

"The one about who purchased the bird," I replied.

"Now, Jason," he said, "I told you that's all top secret information. It's a seller client privilege. Besides if I told you it would probably just get you into some type of trouble."

Well I did know one thing, I thought to myself. Who ever bought the bird wasn't exactly poor. At one hundred fifty thousand dollars a pair they didn't come cheap.

"How about a late lunch?" Devon asked.

"What time is it?" I asked.

He looked at his watch and said, "About three o'clock."

"It couldn't be that late. I'm supposed to be on a flight back to Nevada at 3:30," I said.

"Well, I'm afraid you'll have to reschedule," Devon said, "because there's no way you'll be able to make it."

I realized that he was right. I was just hoping that the airline would work with me on rescheduling my flight so I wouldn't lose the money I had already paid. Another thing I realized was that I hadn't had anything to eat all day except for a donut that I had grabbed this morning in the motel lobby.

"A late lunch sounds great to me," I answered.

"Good," he said. "I'll have Maria whip us up something."

When we pulled back into the garage, Maria was standing out in front of the house watering some plants.

"Maria!" Devon hollered. "Could you make us up a bunch of your world renowned tacos?"

"Sí, Señor. Right away," Maria answered. She turned off the hose and hurried into the kitchen.

"Maria makes the best tacos I've ever had the pleasure of tasting," Devon continued. "I'm sure you'll fall in love with them as I have."

"Well, if she cooks as good as she looks I'm sure they're quite tasty," I replied.

"Come this way my friend. Let's get washed up," he said. "There's a small wash room just inside the door. I'm sure you'll find it very accommodating."

I thanked him, walked in and found the washroom. I washed my hands, freshened up and got ready for some real Mexican tacos. When I came out I caught a glimpse of Maria in the kitchen preparing the tacos for our lunch. The smell of freshly cut vegetables and the meat cooking on the stove made my mouth water. As I glanced at her she suddenly turned her head and looked at me. She then smiled and gave me a seductive wink.

"Cómo estás, Jason T. You look like a much hungry man," Maria said.

Judging by the look on her face I wasn't quite sure if she was talking about the food she was preparing or her herself and for once in my life I was at a loss for words. When I finally thought of something to say, Devon walked in from another room.

"Jason, come on in the dining room and we'll have a quick martini before lunch," Devon said.

I walked in and looked around the room before I took a seat at the table. I noticed a fabulous trophy sitting on the buffet. It had playing cards going across the top of it in a half circle to form an arch. Under the arch, in bold letters, it said *MGM GRAND*. Under that, in smaller letters, it read *First Place*.

As Devon busied himself with the liquor bottles I said, "Wow. That's some trophy you've got there."

He turned around and walked over to the trophy and picked it up. "Yes. It is pretty impressive, isn't it," he said. "I won this in a poker tournament in Las Vegas. Do you play cards?" he asked.

"Not really," I answered. "I just play for fun once in a while."

"Well you don't know what you're missing," he said with a faraway look in his eyes. "Oh, the feeling you get when you draw that fourth ace or when you fill that inside straight. It is so exciting. Add to that the lights and the charisma of Las Vegas itself. It's just an unbelievable combination. I go every chance I get." He sat the trophy down and walked back over to finish mixing up a batch of his concoction. When he had everything ready, he took a couple of crystal glasses out of his china cabinet and filled them to the top, then stuck an olive on a toothpick into each glass.

"Drink up," he said as he sat down at the table.

After talking about his beautiful ranch for a few minutes I remembered the thing that had been pressing on my mind all day. I had to get back to the motel and pack for my flight back to Nevada. I also do something about the trusty rental car that had left me stranded in the middle of nowhere.

"Excuse me, Devon," I asked. "Do you mind if I use your phone to call the rental car company?"

"Jason," he answered, "I wouldn't mind at all but I don't have a phone. I don't believe in the constant hassle of the ringing and wrong numbers, not to mention the telemarketers. The fact that there's no phone cable coming out this far from the city was the final factor in by decision. My computer is my only communication to the outside world. I use a satellite dish to link me up to the highest speed internet connection in the world. It's even faster than fiber optics."

"What about a cell phone?" I asked. "You've got the iPhones. I do know that."

"You're right," he answered. "I do have the iPhones but I use them strictly for programming my birds, not for my own communication. I know you must be worried about the car and how you're going to get back to town but I've already solved that problem for you."

"You mean that you've gotten hold of the car rental company?" I asked.

"No. No," he said. "I've devised a simple plan. You see Maria goes into town on Thursday afternoons to pick up supplies and visit with her mother. You can simply drive into town with her. She'll be leaving in a little while so that should work out perfect. It will give you a chance to enjoy your lunch."

"That sounds like a great plan," I said.

After we talked for a while longer, Maria brought in a plate of taco fixings and some warm taco shells covered with a steaming cloth.

"Here you go, Señores. I hope you much like them," Maria said.

"Thank you, Maria," Devon replied. "They look delicious."

"Would you like something to wet your blower?" she asked.

"You mean whistle," said Devon. "Yes, I'll have a Michelob. What about you, Jason?"

"Yes, that sounds fine to me," I said.

After eating three tacos that I had stuffed full of everything that the poor tortilla could hold, I could eat no more.

"Maria, that was delicious," I said. "Where did you learn to make such food?"

"I learn from my Mamacita," she said. "She make everything taste too good."

When we were all done with lunch and Maria had put away the dishes, she got cleaned up and was ready to leave for town. I thanked Devon for his hospitality and he told me that the next time I was in Arizona to make sure I stopped by to see him.

Maria grabbed some car keys from a key box by the rear door and said, "Come, Señor Jason. We go now."

She led the way out to a beautiful Mustang convertible sitting in the far stall of the garage.

As we got into the car she smiled and said, "You come with **me** now!"

As soon as we began to drive off I told her that I needed to stop by my rental car and leave the key somewhere on the car so the tow truck driver would be able to open up the car and operate the steering wheel.

Before long we arrived at the car. I got out and unlocked it and tried to start it one last time but it was a hopeless case. It just turned over and over but would not even try to start. I stepped back out and locked the door then put the car key on top of the left rear tire for the tow truck driver when I was able to get to a phone and call for one. I crawled back into the convertible with Maria and we left.

As we drove along she said. "Mr. Jason T. it's so hot today. You look oh so much warm. I take you to my most nicest place I like in the land."

Before I could say a word she slowed down and turned onto a narrow dirt road.

"You will like this you will see," she said.

"But I really have to get back to town," I said trying to summon all the resistance that I could muster up. She was a very lovely and sexy woman and she was controlling the car so I figured I'd just sit back and find out where this adventure would take me.

After driving for a few minutes Maria pulled to the side of the road and parked by a big clump of trees.

"You like to take a swim with Maria?" she asked with a tempting look on her face.

The only word I could say was, "Yes."

"This is my little oasis," she said. "I come here when I'm happy or sometimes when I just want to think."

I could see a large pond of water in the distance surrounded by trees. It looked just like an oasis out here in the middle of all this dry dusty terrain. As we got out of the car she led the way down a small trail through the trees. The closer we came to the pond you could actually smell the fresh scent of the crystal clear water. From the looks of things there appeared to be some kind of an artesian spring that supplied the large pond with its water. We walked to the side of the pond and there was a small beach like area with a little sand and rocks.

Maria smiled and said, "We can no swim in all these clothes. Maybe we take them off, sí?"

I sat down to take off my shoes while she scampered behind the trees. Suddenly she reappeared with nothing on but her underwear and a smile.

In a poetic verse she yelled, "Oh, Jason T! Come and get me!" and then she ran off and jumped into the water.

I hurried to get my clothes off and when I'd finally stripped down to my boxer shorts I jumped in after her. She swam out a few feet and disappeared under the water. When I began to wonder if she was OK or not she shot up from under the water in front of me, wrapped her arms around me and gave me a long kiss. Then she pushed away and swam back out toward the middle of the pond. I quickly swam after her and grabbed her by the waist. She stopped and fell into my arms and we kissed again.

After frolicking around in the water for quite some time we got out of the pond and lay down on the sandy bank in the warm sun and kissed as we held each other tightly. The warm sun gave way to our romantic desires and shortly after we both dozed off and fell soundly asleep.

CHAPTER FIFTEEN

I awoke to someone shaking me. It was Maria and she was saying, "Jason. Jason. We're so much late. We're so much late. Señor Devon, he no be happy with me."

When I opened my eyes the warm sun was setting and about ready to go down behind the hills on the horizon. I jumped up, grabbed my clothes and got dressed in a flash. Maria dressed quickly and we both ran for the car. We got in and Maria got the car turned around and heading in the right direction then we took off for town. Judging by the sun, or the lack of it, I figured it had to be close to eight o'clock. My biggest concern at that time was getting to a phone so I could reschedule my flight back to Nevada and I also needed to do something about the rental car.

The longer we drove, I started to realize that my skin was beginning to hurt. I didn't know how long I'd been lying asleep in the sun but I did know that I had one heck of a sunburn. That was all I needed to end this day that had started off so hectic. When I was younger, if I rationed my time in the sun from day to day and did it slowly, I was able to get a nice tan after a few weeks. But if I spent too much time in the sun the first few weeks of summer I would always turn bright red. I should have given some thought to this before I lay out in the hot sun unprotected. But, as they say, fools rush in where wise men never go. I might have acted foolish but the time I spent with Maria was worth every inch of sunburn that I had received.

As we got to the main road I could tell that Maria was worried. "What's the matter?" I asked. "Are you alright?"

"I'm just so much worry about Señor Devon," she answered. "I no have his dinner for him he be much mad at me. He maybe fire me." After she said that she started to cry.

"I've got an idea," I said. "Pull over to the side of the road."

When she pulled over, I got out of the car and asked her to open the trunk of the car. She stopped the engine and took the key out of the ignition, stepped out of the car and walked back and opened the trunk.

"What is it you wish to see?" she asked as she sniffled.

"I'm looking for the spare," I said.

"What is despair?" she asked.

"Not despair," I said. "The spare tire is what I'm looking for."

She gave me a dumbfounded look and said, "I'm not sure I know too much about these things."

After I removed some covering from the bottom of the trunk there it was. "Bingo!" I said out loud. "A full sized spare."

Maria smiled at me and said, "I'm so happy for you, my Jason."

As I looked at the tire my plan fell into place. The tire had been used before. Perhaps Devon had his tires rotated regularly as the car manufacturers suggest.

"Everything will be fine, baby," I said.

She smiled and said, "I am your baby, no?"

"You are my baby, yes," I said. "Now here's what we're going to do," I explained as I let the air out of the spare tire. "You will tell Señor Devon that the reason you are so late getting back is that you had a flat tire on your way home and you didn't know what to do. After sitting at the side of the road for quite some time, some nice amigos stopped and changed the tire for you. I'll take the hubcap off of the left rear tire so it looks like it's been changed and I'll take the car jack and lug wrench out of the holder and throw them back in the trunk all awry with the spare tire laying on top of them."

She threw her arms around me and gave me a big kiss. When she was done she said, "Jason T., you're my guardian hero."

"I think you mean angel," I corrected.

"Sí," she said. "You an angel too."

When the air was finally drained out of the tire I rolled it around in the dirt a few times and bounced it on the ground to give it a worn effect. Then I put the jack, tools and tire in the trunk and placed the hubcap at the side of the tire. After glancing at it one more time it looked perfect. Nobody would be able to doubt her story. Everything would add up. I shut the trunk and we got back in the car and we continued our drive to town. On the way to town I rehearsed with her the story she would tell Devon until she told it so well I almost believed it myself.

We got to town and I showed her where my motel was. She pulled into the parking area, then looked at me with a sad puppy dog look on her face and said, "Jason, do you really have to leave Maria?"

"Yes, I have to leave. I really don't want to since I've met you but I have obligations that I must return to," I answered.

"Will you call me?" she asked.

"Call you? How can I call you? You have no phone at Devon's home," I replied.

"Sí, this is true. But you can call me on my cell phone," she innocently answered.

"Cell phone?" I said in a surprised voice. "You have a cell phone?"

"Sí. It is right here." She then reached into her purse and brought it out to show me.

"Why in the world didn't you tell me that you had a cell phone?" I asked.

"Well, you no ask me if I have a cell phone," she answered. "If you ask me I tell you yes."

I thought to myself about how much I could have used a cell phone in the last six hours but she was right. I had never asked her if she had a cell phone. I just assumed that she didn't. I wrote down the number on a paper she had in the glove box and stuck it in my wallet. After kissing good-bye I walked over to my room. I waved to her as she drove away.

When I got into my motel room I immediately got on the motel desk phone and got the number for the airport. After talking with the airline ticket agent for close to thirty minutes he was able to book me on the next flight to Nevada at five a.m. the next morning. I was also able to get a partial refund from the flight I had missed and it was credited to my new ticket.

By now it was close to ten p.m. and I knew I probably wouldn't get much satisfaction from the rental car agency but I called the number just for the heck of it. After telling the woman on the phone about how my day had started off and about the rental car breaking down I could tell that she was trying to hold back her laughter. But when I came to the part about the old truck with the Mexicanos in it she could hold back no longer. She began laughing hysterically.

"Ma'am," I said in a stern voice. "This isn't funny."

She gained her composure long enough to say, "I know, sir." Then she burst out laughing again.

"Ma'am? Ma'am?" I said again and again.

"I'm sorry, sir," she finally said still giggling. "But that's just about the funniest story I've ever heard in the seven years I've worked here. Please excuse me for laughing."

"Oh, that's OK," I said. "Now that I've had a chance to think about it I guess it is rather amusing."

After telling her where the rental car was left and about leaving the key on the rear tire she said, "Well that's not important right now. We can get that picked up tomorrow. The important thing right now is getting you back into a rental car."

When I explained that the only thing that I'd need it for was to get to the airport in a few hours she said, "Just a minute sir. Let me see if I can get a hold of my supervisor and work something out for you. Can I put you on hold?"

"Yeah, sure. Go right ahead," I answered thinking to myself, why not? Just about everything else has gone wrong today. Now watch me get cut off. While I was waiting for her to come back on the line I remembered I was supposed to call Connie, but now it was much too late. She'd probably be asleep. I reached over and grabbed my cell phone from the end table where I'd left it this morning and checked it for messages. There were five.

The first one was from Ted. As I played it back he said, "Jason. Where are you? I'm here at the airport and your flight has arrived but I can't find you. I'm standing by the baggage pick up area. Can you see me?"

The second one was from Connie. "Hi Jason. I was just wondering if your plane made it in yet. Give me a call when you can. Love ya."

Just then the woman came back on the phone from the rental car company. "Hello, Mr. Harmony?"

"Yes, ma'am," I answered.

"I've talked with my supervisor and after explaining the ordeal that you went through with our rental car we've decided to wave all your rental car fees."

I replied, "That's great! But how am I supposed to get to the airport tomorrow morning?"

"That's the best part," she answered. "We're going to send a taxi cab out to pick you up and bring you to the airport free of charge."

"Wow!" I said. "That's fantastic!"

"I thought you'd be happy about that," she said. "And I think it's the least we can do after all the trouble you've had, a lot of it caused by our own rental car." She then asked me what time she should have the cab come by to pick me up.

I told her, "About three-thirty in the morning should be fine."

After getting the name of my motel and the street address, she confirmed the time and then asked if there was anything else she could do to help me. I told her no and thanked her for all the help she had given me.

When I hung up the phone I went back to the messages on my cell phone. The next one was from Ted, "Jason. It's now seven o'clock. I've checked with the ticket counter and after doing some checking they said you weren't on the flight so I'm going to go back home. Please give me a call because I'm starting to get a little worried about you. Let me know. Thanks."

The next message was from Connie again. This time she wasn't so pleasant. "Jason. Where in the world are you? I've talked with Ted and he told me you weren't even on the plane. What's going on? Have you forgotten my number? It's 850-706-7737. Give me a call, buster!"

Wow, I thought to myself. It sounds like she's pissed off. When I listened to the fifth and final message it was Connie again. This time she was crying. "Jason, I'm sorry I yelled at you. It's just that I'm so worried about you. I haven't told you this but I think I'm in love with you. From the first time I caught a glimpse of you working at the auto repair shop I was hoping that sometime I would meet you. Then that evening when you came knocking on my door I couldn't believe my eyes. Jason, please call me. Please! I'm sooo worried about you."

After listening to her message I felt like a real heel. I was very attracted to Connie and I liked her immensely but I wasn't sure if I loved her or not. I know I had deep feelings for her, but was it love? More important, where do I tell her I've been all day? She knew I had to go to the bird farm but I was supposed to be back by two. I can tell her the rental car broke down. That's the honest to God truth. I can tell her the bird farm had no phones. That's the truth also. I can tell her Devon's maid gave me a ride back to my motel room. That actually happened. But I can't say anything about the pond and the beach or Maria. Now, I was late getting to Devon's house and she won't know exactly how late I was so I can lead her to believe I was a lot later that I actually was. Although it's late, I thought to myself, I better give her a call and let her know I'm OK and that I've changed flight plans.

I dialed her number and when she answered I said, "Hi Connie."

She immediately said, "Jason, are you alright!?"

Before I could answer I heard a man's voice in the background say. "Is that him?"

I told Connie I was fine then I asked her who was there with her.

"Oh, that's Ted," she answered.

"Ted?" I asked. "What's Ted doing at your house at this time of night?"

"Well," she explained, "We were both worried sick about you. We kept calling each other to see if the other one had heard from you. Then we realized that our phones would be busy if you tried to call. Ted thought that it would be better if we were here together. That way if something had happened to you we would be able to comfort each other"

"Well, that was sure thoughtful of him," I replied. The whole time that Connie was talking I was thinking that this guy is a real slime ball for trying to move in on Connie the minute I haven't returned a few phone calls.

After telling Connie about the alarm clock not going off, the car breaking down and forgetting my cell phone, I asked if I could talk with Ted for a moment. When she handed him the phone he immediately said, "Jason, you're OK! We were so worried about you. You weren't on the flight. What happened?"

"I'll tell you all about it when I get back," I said, "but right now I need to know if you can pick me up at the airport tomorrow morning about seven o'clock?"

"Sure," he replied, "but I'll need to get some gas on the way back. I'm down to a little over a quarter of a tank." I knew this was his way of telling me he wanted me to buy him some gas.

"I'll fill your car up on the way home," I said.

"Oh, you don't need to do that," he answered.

"Yes I do," I said. "I owe it to you for as many times as you've been out to airport for me this week."

I talked to him for a short time longer then he gave the phone back to Connie. When we were done talking I told Connie that I'd give her a call tomorrow morning when my plane got into the airport.

When I hung up the phone I walked down to the motel lobby and settled up my bill. I asked the man at the desk if he could schedule a wakeup call for me at about a quarter to three in the morning.

"Why so early?" he asked.

After telling him about my alarm not going off which ended up causing me to miss my flight, he said, "You know, señor, I've told the motel owner that we need a backup generator system for this place but he says it would cost too much. Besides, he says the power don't go out enough to warrant a backup system. I guess he's right. He's the Boss, ya know. But it would still be nice to have something like that then we could have one of them slogans that say, *We'll leave the light on for ya even if the power goes out.*"

"Boy, that would be pretty catchy," I said thinking to myself, doesn't this guy ever stop talking?

Finally when he paused to catch his breath I said, "What was that?"

He said, "What was what?"

"That noise…" I said.

"I didn't hear any noise," he answered. "What did it sound like?"

"Kinda like a squeak, maybe a mouse or something."

He started to talk and I said, "Shhhh! There it goes again." I pointed toward the room just in back of the lobby and whispered, "It sounds like its coming from there."

He whispered, "Maybe I'd better get my broom."

I whispered back, "Good idea."

Then he reached over and grabbed a broom leaning on the side of the wall by the lobby desk and then tiptoed over to the room and slowly opened the door. When he creped in to take a look around I quietly walked out the lobby door and headed back to my room. It really wasn't too nice of me to make him think there was a mouse in there but sometimes a diversion is the only way you can get people to shut up. This guy would have talked all night and as it was I was only going to get a few hours of sleep before I had to get up and go to the airport.

I went back to my room and looked in the motel bathroom to see if there was something that I could use to help ease the pain of my sunburn. On the counter I found some skin lotion. I put it on and immediately it seemed to help take the burning feeling away. Hopefully I'd be able to get some sleep.

CHAPTER SIXTEEN

I awoke to the sound of the phone ringing. While I rolled over to pick it up I glanced at the clock sitting on the nightstand. It was fifteen minutes to three.

"Hi. This is a wakeup call for Mr. Harmony," said the person on the phone.

"Thank you," I said. "I'm awake now."

The taxi arrived right on time and I got to the airport in plenty of time to check my bags and grab a cup of coffee. While I was waiting to board my fight I decided to give Maria a call to tell her I was leaving for Nevada. I know that it was a little early in the morning but I was sure she'd like to hear from me. When she answered her cell phone she said a sleepy hello.

I said, "Hi, my lovely Chiquita. This is your Jason."

"Oh, my Jason, it's so much too early," she said.

"I know, Maria, but I wanted to call you to tell you that I'm leaving for Nevada and that I really enjoyed the time I spent with you."

"I enjoy you too, my Jason," she answered.

Just then my flight was called over the loud speaker to start boarding so I said my goodbyes and told her to go back to sleep.

The flight back to Nevada went smoothly and arrived right on schedule. Ted was there in the terminal waiting for me when I arrived.

The first thing he said to me was "How in the world did you get that sunburn?"

I replied, "That's what happens when your rental car breaks down and you have to walk ten miles in the hot sun without a hat."

"Wow," he said. "You had to walk ten miles?"

"Well, I don't know if it was ten miles or not but my rental car left me high and dry in the hot sun."

After picking up my luggage we walked to the terminal parking lot where Ted had parked his car. On the way he asked about what had happened in Arizona and why I wasn't able to call anyone. I told him most of what had happened but I never mentioned Maria and what had gone on at the pond. I told him we needed to meet with Landen so I could share all the information that I had gotten at the bird farm.

When we got in his car and headed back to town he reaffirmed what Connie had told me about some kind of flu virus going around.

"How many people have gotten it?" I asked.

"Well, not many people have caught it," he said, "but the Doc can't seem to figure out what strain it is. He's not having much luck treating it so he's called in a specialist from San Francisco Medical Center to help him isolate the strain so it can be treated."

"Wow," I said. "Sounds like quite a mystery."

"What makes it stranger," he continued, "is that two of our paramedics have it. The undertaker at Peace On Earth has it and the Coroner's got it. Oh, yeah, and that incinerator guy named Nelson at the crematorium has it also."

"It seems like some kind of a pattern," I said. "If those are the only people that have it then they must have all contacted it from the same place."

"I agree," replied Ted, "but where?"

As we drove along I remembered that I was supposed to call Connie, so I took out my cell phone and dialed her number.

"Hello?" she answered.

"Hi, Connie. I'm back in Nevada. Ted picked me up at the airport. We're gonna stop at the gas station and fill up his car then he'll drop me off at the auto shop."

"I'm so glad you're back," she said. "Do you want to have lunch together?"

"I'd like to," I answered, "But I can't. I'm going to be a little late to work so I figured I'd work through my lunch break to make up the time."

"OK. Well I'll see you tonight then," she said.

"Tonight?" I asked.

"Yes, tonight. Didn't Ted tell you that I want both of you to come over for dinner tonight? I'm going to be cooking my famous fried chicken."

I looked across at Ted who was staring straight ahead at the road and said, "No, Ted didn't say anything about that."

"Well, he probably forgot," she replied. "But you will come, right?"

"Oh, you bet I'll be there. You couldn't keep me away from your fried chicken"

"Good. Then I'll see you at about seven-ish."

When I got off the phone Ted gave me a sheepish look and said, "Oh, by the way, Connie wants you to join us for dinner tonight."

"Join you?" I said somewhat surprised. "I thought she wanted you to join us for dinner."

"Well, she'd like both of us to come over to her place for dinner tonight is what I meant to say. I was going to say something about it before," he said, "but we started talking about your Arizona trip and I forgot all about it."

I thought to myself, yeah, I bet you forgot all about it. And what's with this, saying Connie and you would like me to join you for dinner. Heck, I've only been gone for a couple of days. It's not like I moved away or something. I could see right now that I'd better keep my eye on good old Teddy Boy or he'd try to draw me out of the picture.

When we pulled up to the auto shop I took my luggage out of the back of Ted's car and then thanked him for picking me up.

"Are you going to set up a meeting with Landen?" I asked.

"Yeah, I'll talk with him later today and see what he wants to do," he answered. As he drove away he smiled and yelled to me, "I'll see you tonight!"

When I walked into the shop I could tell that Mr. Henderson was happy to see me. With a big smile on his face he said, "This place has been falling apart ever since you left. It's nice to have my ace mechanic back on board."

"Well thanks for the kind words," I said, "but I'm sure you got along just fine without me."

"Are you sure you feel up to working today?" Mr. Henderson said giving me a close second look.

"Of course. Why do you ask?" I said.

"Well it looks like quite a sunburn you have there," he said.

"Oh, it looks worse than it is," I said.

"Alright, if you're sure. Here," he said, "come on over to the desk. I've got a pile of work orders that we need to get started on."

By ten o'clock I had completed my third job and the boss was walking around humming a cheerful tune. I could tell he was quite pleased. The fact that today was Friday probably had a lot to do with it also.

Ted gave me a call at about eleven o'clock and said that Landen wanted to meet at the office at six that evening. The rest of the day went by pretty quickly although, toward the end of the day, my body started dragging from the sleep, or lack of, that I had gotten last night.

When the workday was done I drove to my apartment, unloaded my bags and took a nice warm shower then put on some clean clothes. At about twenty minutes to six I headed on over to the Meade's Detective Agency headquarters. I arrived and saw Ted standing out front talking on his cell phone. He immediately hung up and put his phone back in his pocket.

"Hey, Jason," he said, "Are you all ready for the meeting?"

"Let's do it," I answered.

When we walked inside Landen was sitting at the conference table finishing up a hamburger and some fries. "Just a minute, gentlemen. I'll be right with you," he said wiping his mouth with a napkin. He cleaned the wrappers off the table and got up and threw them into a small wastebasket sitting by his desk.

"Jason, are you sure you feel up to this meeting? Landen asked. "Ted said you had a sunburn but I didn't think it was this bad."

"Actually, it looks worse than it is. I am fine," I replied.

"OK," he said as he picked up a notepad. "Everybody have a seat. Jason, do you have a report for us?"

"I don't know if you'd call it a report," I answered, "but I do have a lot of interesting facts that I found out at Devon's, I mean, the Clark Bird Farm." I went on to explain how immaculate the Clark Ranch was and how high tech he ran his operation. Then I went into detail about the hawk section of the farm and how this man was able to train these birds to kill or warn off subjects with the mere mention of different words.

"That's all fine and dandy," said Ted, "but how could someone control a bird if it's out in the country? Someplace like our bird is?"

"I'm getting to that," I said. As I continued to talk, Landen walked over to his desk and picked up the envelope of pictures that had been blown up from the ones we'd taken last Saturday of the bird on the B.L.M. land. When I came to the part about surgically installing the receivers and microscopic cameras, Landen looked at me dumbfounded. Then I went on to tell them about being able to control the birds from an iPhone.

"That's truly incredible," he said. "It's almost unbelievable."

He took the pictures out of the envelope and placed them on the table. As he looked through them he pulled out one of the pictures I had taken with my cell phone from the side of the ridge right before I started to fall. He held it up so Ted and I could see it. "Now we know what this is," he said smiling."

"What is it?" Ted asked.

"I believe it is a lens of some type. A surveillance camera possibly," he replied. "Take a close look. It's perfectly round and it certainly isn't any type of rock. It's looks very much out of place in its surroundings."

"You're right," I said. "That's the only thing it could be. Whoever owns that lens controls that hawk!"

"But why in the world would anybody want a security system out there in the wilderness?" asked Ted.

"They must be protecting something," said Landen.

"Either that or hiding something," I responded. "Whatever is going on out there, I for one, think it's time to hand the case over to Sheriff Arby."

"No! No! No!" said Landen loudly. "Don't you see we're not absolutely sure that this is actually what is going on? We're mostly just guessing at this point."

"It seems to be pretty cut and dry to me," I said.

"Yes," he replied. "It seems like that but we need to make sure."

"Yeah," said Ted. "And besides, if it turns out we're wrong Sheriff Arby won't fill out a pay voucher for our work and we won't receive a plug nickel."

"Did this Devon guy say for sure this was one of his birds or who he sold it to?" asked Landen.

"No. He said that information was considered seller-client privilege. He treated it like it was top secret and would not release any names or dates what so ever" I answered. The only thing he would say is that they usually buy two of them."

"You mean there could be two of these birds out there?" asked Ted.

"That's a possibility," I replied.

"Listen, gentlemen," Landen said, "I think what we need to do is to take another trip out to the B.L.M. land tomorrow and do some snooping around."

"What good will that do?" I asked. "We've already been out there once. We know that when we get close to Wild Cat Ridge the bird appears and we're pretty sure that there's some type of security camera on the ridge."

"This is true," answered Landen. "So what we need to do is take a look around on the other side of the ridge."

"You mean go up by way of No Pay Grade and see if there's a way around it?" Ted asked.

"That's exactly what I mean," said Landen.

"Won't that be a little difficult?" I asked.

"It might be," he answered, "but everything worth achieving in life is difficult. Besides," he continued looking at Ted and I, "you two look like you could use a little exercise."

"Well, I guess it's worth a try," I said. "And if there are two hawks I'm sure we'll meet up with the second one. What time do you want to leave tomorrow?"

"Let's all meet down at the Wal-Mart parking lot at five in the morning," he said, "and bring a bag lunch with you because this might be an all day project."

When the meeting was over I followed Ted's car over to Connie's house on the other side of town.

CHAPTER SEVENTEEN

Dr. Benstowe shook hands with Dr. Lewis B. Abernathy who had just arrived from San Francisco. "Good evening, Doctor," he said. "Glad to make your acquaintance."

"The pleasure is all mine," replied Dr. Abernathy. "So why don't you give me a quick rundown on what exactly is going on and the tests you've run so far."

"Good. I'll do that. Let's go into the Medical Center and I can go over it with you in the laboratory," he said.

Once they got to the lab Dr. Benstowe said, "Now Doctor…"

Doctor Abernathy interrupted him and said, "Why don't we drop the formalities. Just call me Lewis."

"OK, Lewis. Why don't you just call me Fred? Now if you will look closely, I put this blood sample into our computer data base collection processor and compared it with all the computer bank data throughout the world for influenza samples. In each case it comes back, no data available. When I type in related samples available, it comes up with two. The configuration is close on both samples but not exact. If you look closely at the first one, which is labeled *Hong Kong Flu Virus* and match it to our sample it's identical in many ways but not an exact match. The second one that pops up is labeled *Asian Flu*. If you compare our sample to it you can see that it too resembles our sample in many ways but does not match exactly."

"Yes, I see what you mean," Lewis replied. "What precautions have you taken to prevent the spread of this strain of flu that you're dealing with?"

"Well, fortunately I'm the only one dealing with the five patients at the moment, myself and my staff, that is. The five patients all seem to have come down with it around the same time, all within the same twenty-four hour period." Fred then continued, "When I first suspected that it was something other than a common cold or upset stomach I was able to quarantine all five patients in our ward adjacent to this clinic."

"What seems to be their symptoms?" Lewis asked.

"All complain of stomach pain. They're having difficulty breathing. They don't seem to be able to urinate easily and they're complaining of weakness and dizziness," answered Fred.

"That is quite a list of symptoms," Lewis said. "How are you treating them at the moment?"

"I started off giving them a saline I.V. to keep a vein open for medicine," answered Dr. Benstowe. "But when the urination problem occurred I immediately stopped the saline. I've given them 10cc's of penicillin every six hours to fight infection."

"Is it doing any good? Have you seen any improvement?" Dr Abernathy asked.

"To be quite honest with you Lewis, they seem to be getting worse rather than better."

"Do you mind if I look at their charts and examine the patients?" Lewis asked.

"No! By all means, please do," Fred answered. "That's one of the main reasons I asked for your help. You are the leading authority in this area for this type of problem. There are facemasks and gloves in the medical cabinet and you'll find a clean smock in the linen closet by the front desk. Here, follow me."

CHAPTER EIGHTEEN

As we pulled in to park by Connie's house we saw Jimmy and Billy were out in front playing catch.

Ted got out of his car and Jimmy ran up to him and yelled, "Uncle Ted! Do you want to arm wrestle again?"

"Not right now, Jimmy," Ted answered quickly.

I thought to myself, that's strange. I wonder when Ted arm-wrestled with Jimmy?

Then Jimmy ran up to me and said, "Uncle Jason! I'm glad you made it back. We were all worried about you."

"Well it's nice to be back, Jimmy," I said.

Jimmy looked up at me oddly and asked, "How did you get so red?"

"It's a long story, Jimmy. Maybe I'll tell you later on this evening," I replied. I knew that I'd better not take my shirt off or for that matter, any other article of clothing. I had a long sleeve shirt on and I was planning on keeping my sleeves down if at all possible. From the front yard I could smell fried chicken in the air.

Ted looked at me and said, "Boy, that sure smells good."

"Yeah, it does," I responded. We both walked on in the house and found Connie in the kitchen frying up chicken.

She turned around and said, "Oh, it's my two favorite men," with a smile on her face. Then she looked closer at me and said, "Jason, what in the world happened to your face?"

"Sunburn," I said. "My rental car broke down and I had to walk. Remember, I told you about it last night?"

"Yeah, I remember. But you didn't say anything about getting a sunburn."

"I'm sorry," I said. "I thought I mentioned it."

"No, you didn't but I think you look even cuter with a sunburn," she said winking at me. Then she asked, "Would you boys like a beer? There's some in the refrigerator."

We both walked over to the refrigerator and Ted grabbed a couple of beers and handed one to me. It might have just been my imagination but he sure seemed to act a lot more confident around Connie than he had the last time we were here. Oh, it was probably nothing.

"Sure smells good," said Ted.

"Well thank you kind sir," Connie replied giggling. "So, Jason how was Arizona otherwise? Did your uncle's funeral go OK?"

"Everything went OK," I answered. "It was just a sad time for the family."

She put down the fork that she was using to turn over the chicken and came over and gave me a hug. I squinched when she touched my sunburn but tried not to show it.

Connie said, "Jason, I'm so sorry you had to go through this. I wish I could have come with you so I could have been there for you."

I gave her a kiss and said, "There's nothing you could have done."

"I could have hugged you and kissed you if you started to get too sad," she replied.

"Yeah, but if you did that," I answered, "I probably wouldn't have gotten around to going to the funeral." At that point we both laughed. She gave me another hug and patted me on my fanny playfully and then walked back over to finish cooking the chicken.

When the chicken was all done and the table was set, Connie yelled to Jimmy and Billy to come in and wash up for dinner.

"Is Billy staying for dinner?" Ted asked.

"He sure is," answered Connie. "It's Billy's turn to spend the night with Jimmy. They alternate back and forth. It's good for them to get used to being away from home. It will prepare them for when they get older and move out on their own."

"Yeah," I said jokingly, "and it also gives the parents a much needed night off every once in a while." We all laughed.

The boys came out from washing up and we all set down at the table. Connie asked me if I would please say grace. I said a short prayer thanking God for the food and said amen and then we started passing the food around. After everyone's plate was full we all began to eat.

Jimmy looked over at me and asked, "Uncle Jason, can you tell me about all the stuff that happened to you in Arizona? I mean, you know, how come you weren't able to call anybody and all that stuff?"

"Sure, Jimmy," I answered. I began telling about the bad lightening storm that had passed through the evening after my Uncle's funeral and how it knocked out the power in the middle of the night. When I got to the part about Devon's maid giving me a ride back to town, I inadvertently said Maria.

Connie immediately stopped me and asked, "Maria?"

I couldn't believe that I'd said the name. "I, oh, Maria? She's Devon's maid."

"What's she look like?" asked Connie.

"Well," I said as I dreamed up a description that I thought would meet with her approval, "She was an older woman..."

"How old?" Connie pursued.

"Oh, I'd say late forties, maybe early fifties."

"Was she attractive?" Connie continued.

"Lord no!" I answered. "She was very heavy set and had a great big nose that resembled a beak." Jimmy and Billy started laughing. "She was a Hispanic woman," I continued, "and she must have been as blind as a bat because she had thick rimmed glasses. But she sure made delicious tacos." I figured that my description of Maria should squelch and further interest Connie might have and it worked like a charm.

When I was finished telling my story, Ted was sitting quietly as though he was in deep thought. Then he said, "That doesn't add up."

I looked at him quizzically and said, "What doesn't add up?"

"Well, isn't it about a two hour drive from Tucson to Oro Valley?" he asked.

"About that," I answered.

"Then it would have to be the exact same from Oro Valley to Tucson yet you didn't call anyone until after ten in the evening. That would have to mean that you didn't leave this, Devon's house, until well after eight o'clock in the evening."

Oops! I'd forgotten that I was dealing with a full time detective. I smiled as though to say good point and show my air of confidence at the same time. The whole time I was grasping at straws wondering how I was going to answer this bit of logic that Ted had come up with. Everyone was staring at me, waiting for me to say something.

After what seemed to be hours, but it was only a second or two I said, "Well, I wanted to save the best part for last. You see, Maria is a very slow driver being as old as she is and with her vision problem and all. She doesn't drive much faster than thirty miles an hour."

"Thirty miles an hour?" exclaimed Connie. "It seems like the cops would pull her over and give her a ticket for going too slow."

"Why didn't you drive?" Ted asked.

"When I saw how slow she was driving I offered to drive" I said. "But she said that Devon didn't want anybody driving his car except her."

"I can go faster than that on my bicycle" said Jimmy with a mouth full of chicken.

"Cannot!" Billy replied with a mouth full of mashed potatoes.

"Can too!" said Jimmy.

"Cannot!" said Billy.

"Boys!" said Connie, "Stop that! You're starting to give me a headache."

I didn't like seeing the boys bicker back and forth but just this once it was a welcome sight. It threw the spotlight off of me and my cockamamie story that seemed to be getting better as I went along. "This chicken is absolutely delicious, Connie. You really out did yourself this time," I said.

"Yes, it's scrumptious," said Ted.

"Thank you," said Connie with a big smile on her face. "I'm glad you are enjoying it."

"Uncle Ted can we arm wrestle again when we get done with dinner?" asked Jimmy. "I want to show Billy how strong I am."

"When did you ever arm wrestle with Jimmy?" I asked Ted.

Connie gave Ted a concerned look. "Oh that," said Ted. "Well it was last night when I was, I mean we were, that is all of us were waiting to hear whether you were still alive or if something had happened to you."

"So you passed the time arm wrestling?" I asked looking at him suspiciously.

"Well, some of the time," he answered. "It seemed to help us a... a ..."

"What? Not think about me?" I asked.

"No! No! Of course not!" said Ted.

"Jason!" interrupted Connie. "I think you're being much too hard on Ted. We were all worried sick about you!"

I thought to myself, yeah it sure sounds like it.

Connie continued, "You need to apologize to him right now. After all he is one of your best friends."

At this point I could see that there was no sense in pursuing this conversation because with Connie on his side the deck was stacked against me so I said the only thing I could say, "Ted, I was just kidding around with you I hope you didn't think that I was serious, did you?"

He looked at me and smiled, "I really wasn't sure if you were or not."

"Well, I was just joking with you," I said. "It cracks me up when you get on the defensive."

"I'm proud to have you as a friend," said Ted with a bit of a tear in his eye. "Your friendship means a lot to me."

"The feeling is mutual, my friend," I said.

"I don't know what it is about men," said Connie. "But I don't care how old they are they always seem to act like little boys. It's just like your bodies grow older but your minds never quite mature beyond childhood. I guess that wasn't the best thing for a woman to say when she's sitting at a table full of males."

"What do you mean by that?" asked Ted.

"Yeah! Do you mean that me and Billy act like children?" Jimmy asked.

"First," said Connie, "it's Billy and I, and second, a woman is entitled to her opinion. And third, yes, Billy and you do act like children because you happen to be children."

I didn't say a word. I just took another bite of my mashed potatoes and grinned. Connie looked over at me and grinned back then, she said, "Don't you have a voice in this matter?"

I swallowed the food in my mouth and answered, "I think you're absolutely right. We do act like little kids sometimes but there's a reason for that. A man has a lot of responsibilities. Everything is usually piled on his shoulders. When something goes wrong it's always blamed on the man. A lot of times the only way a man can get rid of all the tension and stress is to revert back to when he was a child. When he was so secure, careless, footloose and fancy free. Oh, listen to me, I sound like a psychologist or something."

"No, not at all," said Connie. "You sound like a man who knows what every woman's been trying to figure out for years."

When we were all done with dinner and the table was cleared, dishes were put into the dishwasher and the leftovers put away we all went into the living room and sat down.

"OK," said Ted putting his elbow on the coffee table. "Who wants to arm wrestle?"

"I do! I do!" both Jimmy and Billy yelled.

Ted would put on a good show pretending that Billy or Jimmy just about had his arm all the way down almost touching the table, then all of a sudden he'd get a burst of strength and slowly lift his arm upward and all the way over to the other side and pin his challenger. As they wrestled back and forth Connie and I watched and laughed with each new endeavor. Then I asked Connie how her first week at work went.

"Oh, it was wonderful," she answered with her voice full of enthusiasm. "I got the phone introduction down to a science."

"I'm not sure I understand," I said. "What's a phone introduction?"

Connie said, "Here, let me do it for you. Pretend that you just called the office and the phone is ringing."

"OK," I said. "The phone is ringing. Now what?"

"Now I answer," and in a very sexy voice she said, "Hi. You've reached the offices of the *Montgomery Law Firm*. One of the most trusted names in legal services. This is Connie. How may I be of assistance to you?"

"Wow!" I said. "That was outstanding. You sound so professional."

"Thank you," she said glowing with pride. "It took a lot of rehearsing but I finally got it down pat. And another thing," she continued, "Bill has put me in charge of accounts receivable and accounts payable. His computer program is a little different than what I'm used to but I'm starting to get the hang of it."

"I'm sure that with your ability and determination you'll be a full partner in the firm in no time at all," I told her.

She squeezed my hand and said, "I think you might be just a little prejudiced when it comes to my accomplishments."

CHAPTER NINETEEN

Across town in the Medical Clinic, both doctors had put on their masks and gloves. With their medical smocks in place they had stepped into the isolation ward so Dr. Abernathy could examine the patients and go over their medical charts. When his examinations were completed, he studied the charts closely.

Finally he turned to Dr. Benstowe and said, "There seems to be some sort of pattern that your patients are following."

"How so?" inquired Dr. Benstowe.

Dr. Abernathy began, "Well, for instance, two of your patients, I'll call them number one and two and the rest I'll number up to five, they seem to have gotten the more serious symptoms first and at the same time. Then shortly thereafter, patient three came down with the exact same symptoms followed in unison by patients four and five. Patients one and two developed the urinary problem simultaneously. Then shortly thereafter, patient number three got the exact same problem. Then patients four and five developed the same problem within hours of each other."

"I see what you mean," said Dr. Benstowe. "It seems to be some type of pattern that they are all following."

"I think that the problem we're dealing with," continued Dr. Abernathy, "has far surpassed any type of flu or virus that is common knowledge within the medical community. It seems as though it leans more toward some type of edema. What's more

153

confusing is that the first two patients seem to be developing some neurological disturbances. Their speech is slurred and their reactions are slow and somewhat labored. None of these symptoms are of a contagious nature. It's almost like they were exposed to something..." then he paused for a moment and cleared his train of thought and said, "No. I'm sure that couldn't have occurred."

"Something?" asked Dr. Benstowe. "Something like what!?"

"Well it's almost like they were exposed to radiation," he answered. "Something that was radioactive. But I'm sure there's nothing around in this small town of Jefferson City that is radioactive."

"Nothing that I'm aware of," Dr. Benstowe answered. "But let's follow that thought. We can resubmit the blood samples into the computer data base system and look for matches under the heading of radioactive."

"Let's do that," Dr. Abernathy said. "Let's do that immediately. Another precaution we need to take is to prepare to set up a dialysis machine because if this is some type of radiation poisoning the patients might start experiencing kidney and heart failure. We'll need to stimulate the kidneys to excrete excess fluids."

"I'll have my staff prepare the machine right away," said Dr. Benstowe.

After alerting the staff both doctors cleaned up and went to the laboratory.

They programmed in the sample. It wasn't long before the computer came up with a match. Radiation poisoning.

"Just as I had suspected," said Dr. Abernathy. "The patients must have been exposed to some type of radioactive material. But it would have had to be somewhere in the category of a lighter dose, say maybe one to forty Grays, otherwise they would have been dead by now."

"I'm not sure I understand you when you mention Grays?" said Dr. Benstowe. "What exactly is a Gray?"

Dr. Abernathy explained, "A Gray is a way to measure doses of radiation. For example, one Rad is a very light dose of radiation. Hardly even traceable. Now if you take one hundred Rads and put them together they would make one Gray. As you can probably visualize a Gray is a much more serious dose. Most radiation poisonings between one Gray and ten Grays can be treated. But when the dosage gets higher it's sometimes hard, if not impossible to treat. The cut off for treatable radiation poisoning is usually about forty Grays. Anything over forty Grays usually causes death. In these five cases I think we have a good chance of saving their lives. I would think that one of the most important things we want to do besides treating them is to try and find out where they contacted this radioactive material. We need to find where it is and contain it so one else gets this dreadful condition. I'm sure that you are also aware that, as doctors, we are required to report certain information to the authorities pertaining to cases involving child abuse, communicable diseases and situations that pose a threat to the public. In this case we're not only required to report it to the State and Local Governments, but when radioactive material is suspected, we're also required to report it to the Federal Bureau of Investigation."

"Yes, I'm aware of that, Lewis," said Dr. Benstowe. "I just have concerns with getting the F.B.I. involved. It seems that they always end up making a mess of things."

"Well, Fred, let's just hope that won't be the case in this situation."

"I've got the emergency phone numbers in my desk," Dr. Benstowe said as he opened up the top drawer and took out a folder. Thumbing through the folder he stopped and said, "Here they are right here. I'll call the State and Local authorities but I would rather that you confer with the Federal Authorities."

Dr. Abernathy said, "As you wish."

CHAPTER TWENTY

Back at Connie's house the evening was winding down. The arm wrestling had pretty much come to a stop. Mostly because the boys had worn their arms out trying to defeat Ted who, by the way, had declared victory and bragging rights over both boys.

At a little after nine Ted and I both agreed that we better call it a night because we both had to get up early the next morning. When we were leaving Connie gave Ted a quick friendly hug and a kiss on the cheek.

"Bye Champ. I'm glad you were able to come for dinner," Connie said coyly.

"I wouldn't have missed it for the world," Ted said with a big grin on his face.

I thought to myself, what's with this champ stuff? Has he done something I don't know about? Finally I spoke up, "Champ?" I asked raising my eyebrows.

"Oh yes," said Connie. "He's our undefeated champion of the high stakes arm wrestling competition."

"Hey. That's right!" I said. "We'll have to get him one of those championship belts with a big buckle on it that says *Winner! Arms Down!* on it."

We all started laughing then Connie came over and gave me a big hug and a kiss. "I sure missed you," she said.

"I missed you too," I said, "but I was only gone two days."

"I know," she said, "but it seemed like a lot longer."

Ted and I left and I drove down the street to my apartment.

When I got home I went into my bedroom and got ready for bed. I walked back into the living room and I noticed the shoebox that Aunt Minnie had given me sitting on the table. I picked it up and sat down on the couch to open it. I opened the box and then I peeled the newspaper off from around the treasure inside. I found that the little elephant was still intact and looking exactly like I remembered it from years ago. What a work of art, I thought to myself as I held it in my hand. I walked across the room and placed it on a nick-knack shelf that I had in my front room and then went back to pick up the newspapers that had fallen on the floor. I picked them up and I noticed that it was the want ad section from the Tucson, Arizona paper that the elephant had been wrapped in. There on the front was a quarter page advertisement and in bold letters it said *MEXICANOS MAKE MUCHO PESOS IN NEVADA! TELEPHONE 1-800-882-6000! NO GREEN CARD NEEDED!*

Wow! I knew there were quite a few Hispanics in Arizona but now they're begging them to come to Nevada without green cards? I'm surprised that a respectable newspaper would allow that type of advertising. I took the papers and put them in the waste paper basket, walked over and turned off the light and went on to bed.

CHAPTER TWENTY-ONE

I awoke the next morning to the alarm clock buzzing. I got up and started some coffee, then took my ice chest out of the hall closet and brought it over to the refrigerator. I stuck some soft drinks and bottled water in it, then sprinkled the one tray of ice that I had in my small freezer over the top of it. I could see we'd probably have to swing by Willy's Pit Stop on the way and pick up some more ice if we wanted this stuff to stay cold. I went back into my bedroom and got dressed, then walked into the bathroom, shaved, brushed my teeth and combed my hair. When the pot of coffee was done I filled up a cup and poured the rest into a thermos. After I loaded the ice chest into the car, I drove to the Wal-Mart parking lot to meet Landen and Ted.

When I got to the parking lot, Landen and Ted were just driving up in the Meade Mobile. Ted saw me, and he turned on the flashing light on top of the van. As I parked my car I was quite surprised to hear a loud voice over a P.A. system say, "Get out of your car and keep your hands in the air!" It was coming from the Meade Mobile.

Ted parked the van and got out. "What do you think of the new system?" he asked.

"It sounds kind of loud," I answered.

"Loud?" he said laughing. "I only have the volume up to five. It goes all the way up to ten. Here, take a look."

He opened the truck door to show me the devise that was mounted onto the dash. When I glanced at the system I also saw that Landen was in the passenger seat with his eyes closed trying to get a few extra winks of sleep.

I looked at Ted and whispered quietly, "Watch this." I slowly turned the volume on the unit all the way up to ten. Then I picked up the microphone and spoke into it, "Landen. Wake up."

It was so loud you could have easily heard it a mile away. Landen jumped up and almost hit his head on the roof of the van. I quickly handed the microphone to Ted and looked at him shamefully. As Landen came to his senses he took one look at Ted holding the microphone and shouted, "That's it! You've lost your microphone privileges for the rest of the week! Now put the damn thing down and turn it off!"

"But I didn't do it," Ted pleaded. "It was Jason."

I gave Ted a disgusted look and said, "Don't try to blame your short comings on me. I don't even know how to work the contraption."

While Ted gave me a look that could kill I said, "Landen, can I pour you a hot cup of coffee from my thermos?"

Landen handed me his empty coffee mug and said, "Thanks Jason. I'd like that." Then he continued, "It's nice to see we have one civilized person besides me between the three of us."

I smiled at Ted as I walked over to my car to get my thermos. After pouring Landen a cup of coffee Ted and I loaded up my ice chest into the back of the van. When we were finished I locked up my car and jumped into the van.

"Is everybody ready?" asked Landen after swallowing a big sip of coffee. Ted and I both said we were ready, then Landen replied, "Let's go, gentlemen."

Ted started up the van, put it into drive and we were on our way. I glanced at my watch. It was now five minutes after six. We were right on schedule.

When we drove out of town and got on the main highway we turned off at Willy's Pit Stop to pick up a bag of ice. As usual,

Landen waited in the van as Ted and I went in to get the ice. Willy was sitting on a tall stool behind the counter drinking a cup of steaming hot chocolate.

"How may I help you fine men today?" he said, grinning from ear to ear.

"We just need this bag of ice," I said, setting the bag on the counter.

"Did you want some rock salt with that?" he asked.

"What in the world would we want rock salt with the bag of ice for?" asked Ted.

"Well, the only thing I can figure," he said as he took off his hat and scratched the top of his head, "is to make homemade ice cream with it. Somebody must be making a lot of ice cream," he continued, "because I've been selling a lot of it lately."

"I didn't know they still sold rock salt," I said.

"Well, you know, son," he replied, "I haven't sold a bag of that stuff in years. I had five bags sitting right on that shelf over there that I'd been carrying on my books for maybe ten years now. Then a couple weeks ago some guy comes in here and wants to buy all five bags. But that's not the good part," he continues, "not only did he buy all five bags but he puts down a tidy deposit and tells me he wants me to order twenty five more bags of the stuff."

"Did you order it?" asked Ted.

"Well, I sure did. I ordered those bags of salt," answered Willy. "But not only that, when the guy comes back to pick up the twenty five bags he orders twenty five bags more."

"Wow!" I said. "What would a guy do with all that rock salt?"

"Make ice cream is the only thing I can figure out," said Willy. "Now mind ya, this here's the same guy who comes in here and buys twenty bags of ice at the same time."

"That's all the guy buys?" Ted asked.

"Oh, shucks no," answered Willy. "He also buys about every container of Budweiser I have in the place at the time."

"Well, he can't be that bad if he drinks Budweiser," I said laughingly.

"No! No! He's a good customer!" said Willy. "And he always pays cold hard cash. Just the way I like it."

"What's the guy's name?" I asked.

"Don't know, son," Willy said, "but I don't think he's from around here cuz I've never seen him before this and I know everyone around these parts."

I said, "When we were here last week you were talking about some guy buying a bunch of ice."

"Yep," said Willy chewing on a toothpick. "Same guy."

"What's this guy look like?" Ted asked.

"Well, he's white," says Willy taking the toothpick out of his mouth. "He's got kind of dark hair. I'd guess he's about six feet tall or so. Looks like he's about the same age as you boys are. He's just your average looking kind of guy. Oh yeah, there is one thing that sets him apart from the rest of the crowd," he continued. "He's missing part of his little pinky on his right hand." Then he stopped and gave us a suspicious look. "Say, why are you boys so interested in this here guy anyway? Has he done something wrong?"

"Probably not," answered Ted. "We're just a little curious. It's not often that a person buys that much rock salt and bags of ice."

Yeah," I chimed in. "By the way, how do we know that you're not just making this whole thing up. It seems that lately, every time we come in here you tell us this same story and then turn around and try to charge us more money for a bag of ice. You say that because your ice is getting so scarce you have no choice but to raise the price."

"Well, son, you're right about one thing," Slick Willy said, putting his toothpick back in his mouth.

"What's that?" I asked. "You're making the story up?"

"No," he answered. "My ice is scarce and I'm forced to raise the price per bag." He looked at the bag of ice that I had set on the counter. "That will be five dollars, gentlemen."

"Five dollars?" I said, raising my voice. "There's no way we're going to pay five dollars for a two dollar bag of ice."

"We'll give you three dollars," Ted said rolling his eyes.

"Well, I'll tell you what I'm going to do," said Willy chewing on his toothpick, "you know I've kind of taken a liking to you boys, so out of the kindness of my heart, I'm going to let you have that there bag of ice for only four dollars. But you gotta promise me you won't tell anybody about it. If word got out that old Willy was giving away ice for only four dollars a bag then everybody would want to get in on the deal."

Ted looked at me and then looked back at Willy and said in a stern voice, "We'll give you three dollars and fifty cents. Not a penny more!"

Willy took his toothpick back out of his mouth and looked over at me and then looked back at Ted and said, "I suppose I could go that low, being as it's for you. But I'm still gonna have to charge you sales tax on that. You don't want to cheat your government, do you? Well, do you?" he asked looking at Ted and raising his eyebrows.

"No! No! Of course not," Ted answered with a perplexed look on his face.

After paying for the ice we walked back out to the van and put the ice into the cooler. Once we were back in the van we headed on out toward No Pay Grade to find a way to the area in back of Wild Cat Ridge.

In all the time I'd lived here, I'd never once seen the area in back of the ridge. I'd heard it was a series of hills and ridges with a few valleys in-between. I knew that parts of it were heavily covered with trees because, years ago, logging had been done up that way. But after only a few months the Federal Government shut down the logging operation because it was found, by some group called The Sierra Club, that the area was inhabited by a bird called a Spotted Owl, which at the time was on the endangered species list of the Federal Government. Landen was able to acquire an old logging plot plan map that showed where the company, which was Pacific Lumber, had planned to log and also what areas they had planned to build logging roads for their equipment. It was our hope that possibly the logging company had built a few of the roads before they were told to cease and desist their operation. Although the roads would certainly be overgrown by now, they would lead us on a clearer path to walk rather than climbing down the sides of hills and over uneven terrain.

The Meade Mobile did have a lot of different gadgets on it such as a rotation light and a microphone system, all of which would probably never be used. But it also had one very practical device that would hopefully help out in our attempt to navigate some of these old logging trails. It was equipped with four-wheel drive, the best thing to come along since the four-mule team in the olden days.

Our plan was to drive up No Pay Grade and turn around at the top and head on back down the side of the road that was adjacent to the area in back of Wild Cat Ridge. There was only one problem with this plan. There was no place close enough for us to accomplish this. The road had a divider strip in the middle so we would have to drive twenty miles past the top of the grade and exit at a place called Dell Ridge, then go on the overpass to enter back on the other side of the highway. Although there were two small sections of center divider that were purposely left open along this long stretch of road, they were put there for emergency use only. While the Meade Mobile had a rotating beacon on top of it, Sheriff Arby had made it quite clear to both Landen and Ted that it was not considered an emergency vehicle and any attempt to use it as one would result in the loss of their beacon privileges permanently.

When we reached Dell Ridge, we turned around, heading in the opposite direction. We headed back the extra twenty miles toward the top of the grade. About a mile before we got to the grade, Ted pulled over to the side of the road and stopped. Landen pulled out the logging map and laid it on the center console of the van.

Pointing to one section on the map, Landen said, "This is what we're looking for, gentlemen. It's an old logging trail that used to exit and enter this road somewhere down around the middle of No Pay Grade. It's most likely overgrown and, judging from the contour lines on this map, it's somewhat steep. It might not be readily visible from No Pay Grade so we'll have to drive slowly along the shoulder of the road and keep our eyes open for anything that resembles a road of any type. We're looking for something that used to be anywhere from twenty to thirty feet wide."

When we came to the grade, Ted pulled off to the edge of the road and slowed down to a crawl. Landen and I began looking out the windows for any sign of the old logging trail. It was now approaching seven thirty and the sun was on the rise. If for any reason we missed locating the old trail, it would throw our time schedule severely out of whack. This would mean that we would have to circle around and drive all the way back up the grade to Dell Ridge and come back down for a second try at finding the road. This was not an option. We needed to find it on our first try.

After we had traveled down the grade for approximately a mile, I began to notice something peculiar. There was a large clump of dead bushes piled up about four feet high and ten feet in width and length lying down off to the side of the grade.

"Stop!" I yelled.

"What is it?" asked Landen.

"Those bushes down there," I said pointing toward the pile.

"What about them?" asked Ted?

"They look kind of out of place," I replied. "Why would somebody pile bushes there?"

"Very good point," said Landen. "Very good point indeed. Turn off the truck and let's all go take a closer look."

Ted turned off the truck and we all three got out and walked off the side of the road down the slight grade to the bushes. We moved part of the pile and we could see what appeared to be the old logging trail.

"This must be it," said Landen throwing a bush off to the side. "It appears as though somebody was trying to hide it."

"It sure looks that way," said Ted.

Although the road was somewhat over grown with weeds and small brush it was easily accessible with a four-wheel vehicle.

After we had finished clearing the bushes off of the trail we walked back up to the truck and proceeded to drive slowly off the side of the road toward the logging trail. Once we were on the trail it was pretty slow going. While we drive along I kept seeing signs that someone had traveled this trail recently. There were low hanging tree limbs that had been broken off and a lot of disturbed and crushed bushes and plants. Finally I saw a clear set of tire tracks on the trail.

"It looks like someone's been through this way not too long ago," I said.

"Yeah," replied Landen. "Probably just some people out four wheeling. They love to drive old logging roads whenever they can find them. It's a lot easier than making their own roads."

"You think they're the ones that piled all of those bushes up at the top of the road?" I asked.

"Most likely," he answered. "But now that I think about it, it does seem a little odd. Usually if they find an old trail someplace they like to make it known to all the rest of the people who like to go four wheeling. Not try to hide it."

Although the road was bumpy and uneven, it cut right through some of the most beautiful countryside I'd ever seen. Large trees lined the old logging trail, accompanied by ferns in the wetter areas and lots of other green vegetation that I could not identify. It was exactly opposite of the dry barren land that lay on the other side of Wild Cat Ridge.

After driving down the trail for close to a half hour, we came to a big chain hanging across the road that was anchored between two large trees. It had a sign fastened to it that read, FERDERAL LAND! NO TRESSPASSING! Then in small letters underneath it read TRESSPASSERS WILL BE VIOLATED! I looked at Ted and he looked back at me. Then we both looked at Landen. All three of us burst out laughing. The sign looked somewhat official but the spelling and wording were atrocious.

"I guess that if we proceed past this point," said Ted, "there's a good chance we'll get violated." We all burst out laughing once again.

"Whoever constructed this sign wasn't an English major in school," replied Landen. "I can certainly assure you of that."

Although the sign was a bit humorous, the chain that went across the road was not a laughing matter. It effectively blocked the van from traveling any further down the trail. We all got out of the van and went over to examine the chain. It was made out of three quarter inch metal links, making it virtually indestructible. It was secured to the trees with two huge padlocks, one on each end of the chain that was wrapped securely around each tree.

"Well, gentlemen," said Landen, "it appears that we're going to have to continue on foot from here."

CHAPTER TWENTY-TWO

Back at the medical clinic, it wasn't long after notifying the proper authorities that an F.B.I. field agent walked into the laboratory where both doctors were standing discussing the treatment they were going to follow for radiation poisoning.

Pulling out his wallet and flipping a badge and I.D. at the doctors he spouted out, "Captain Frank Mason, F.B.I. I've been assigned to this case. I've got a few more Agents coming to assist me. They should arrive within the hour."

Dr. Benstowe looked at Dr. Abernathy and rolled his eyes. "I knew this was going to happen," he said.

"Now, Doctors," the Captain continued, "I want you to give me every piece of information that you have on this case including the names, addresses, phone numbers and professions of each of your patients."

About that time, Sheriff Arby walked into the room saying, "I just got a report about some kind of radiation poisoning around here." As he walked over to the Doctors he looked around and noticed the Captain. Turning back to look at the Doctors he said, "What's going on, Fred?"

Before Dr. Benstowe could answer, the Captain interrupted, "Just who are you?"

"I'm Sheriff Arby Fillmore," he answered. "I'm the law in this town. Now I'll ask you the same question," he said, looking down on the five foot eight inch man with a slight build and short red hair. "Just who the heck are you?"

"I'm Captain Frank Mason, F.B.I.," he replied. "Now, Sheriff, you go back to doing whatever it is that you do around this little town and you and I will get along just fine. I'm in charge here and I won't need your help."

"Is that right?" said the Sheriff, with an angry look on his face and bringing his tall heavy set frame up to its full height. "Well, I just want you to remember one thing and that is that this is my town and then you and I will get along just fine. I'm in charge of it and if I catch you doing anything around here that doesn't meet with my approval I'll throw your red-haired skinny little butt in jail. You got that Francis?"

"The name's Frank," said the Captain meekly, turning somewhat red in the face.

"Whatever," said the Sheriff, looking back at Dr. Benstowe. "Now, as I was saying, what's going on around here, Fred?" he asked the Doctor.

Dr. Benstowe turned to Dr. Abernathy and asked, "Lewis, could you please assist me in explaining the condition of each patient and what we believe the diagnosis is?"

"Certainly, Doctor," he answered.

The Doctors went into detail about what was originally thought to be some type of a flu virus or bacterial infection and had now been found to be radiation poisoning. They also explained their findings of how the poisoning had progressed between the five patients. They said that the first two patients were two paramedics and therefore they had the most advanced cases followed by patient number three who was the city coroner. Patient number four was a funeral home director and the last patient, patient number five, was the furnace operator at the crematorium.

"In the order that you've just explained of the seriousness of your patients," said Captain Mason, "it sounds to me like they must have all contacted this poisoning from a person who was radioactive."

Everyone turned to look at him.

"Please let me explain. First the paramedics go out on a call," he continued. "They check a victim out and find that the person is dead. They call in the coroner who takes the body over. He examines the body and pronounces that the victim is deceased. He then covers the body and loads it into his vehicle and takes it to the morgue to have the body processed." Everyone was still listening intently as Captain Mason continued. "Next comes the funeral home director, followed by the crematorium furnace operator."

"Makes sense," said Sheriff Arby. "But don't most of these people wear rubber gloves to protect themselves from such things like contaminates? And what about the furnace operator?" he continued. "He wouldn't even touch the body. Wouldn't it be in a box when he burnt it?"

"I've thought about that," said Dr. Benstowe, "and I'm not quite sure. Many times in different professions, people forget to put on their protective gloves…"

"In this case," interrupted Dr. Abernathy, "mere gloves might not prove effective depending on the intensity of the radiation. The furnace operator is the only one of the patients that has me puzzled. We'll need to interview each of the patients separately and pick their minds for more details. We must not be too harsh on them, though. We do not want to upset them too much."

"Well," said the Sheriff, "the only death that we've had around here in the last few weeks was that guy they found up there on No Pay Grade a few days ago."

"No Pay Grade?" asked Captain Mason. "What is a No Pay Grade?"

"It's a steep grade out on Highway 88," answered Sheriff Arby.

"How did the person die?" inquired Captain Mason.

"The Coroner here listed it as acute shock," replied the Sheriff. "We figured the guy must have been walking along the side of the road was either struck by a vehicle or something happened that caused him to go into shock."

"Do you have any proof what so ever?" the Captain asked.

"Not really," the Sheriff answered. "We're just going by what the Coroner determined.

"But the Coroner is one of the patients," said the Captain. "Just how credible is this person?"

The Sheriff thought for a minute then a slight smile crossed his face as he thought back to when the Coroner had pronounced Clarence Osborn dead and had listed the cause of death as a heart attack. Then it had turned out that old Clarence hadn't died after all. The Sheriff looked back at the F.B.I. Captain and said, "He's been correct in determining the cause of death most of the time."

"Excuse me!?" the Captain said loudly. "I don't think I heard you correctly. Did you just say *most* of the time!?"

"That's what I just said," answered the Sheriff.

"I'm sorry," replied the Captain. "Most of the time is not acceptable. It leads to confusion and in atrocities like this a coroner has to be right one hundred percent of the time!"

"If I may interrupt here," said Doctor Abernathy. "Distinguishing between normal shock signs and radiation poisoning would be extremely hard to do. The signs tend to mirror each other in both instances. When the human body goes into shock, it can be caused by a number of things," he continued, "loss of blood, internal bleeding and yes, radiation poisoning. It would be almost impossible to detect radiation poisoning unless you suspected it, in which case you would take different precautions. In most cases of radiation poisoning, nuclear reactors and such things that are known to be highly radioactive usually cause it. I'm not at all sure that's what we're dealing with in these cases."

"Let me see if I have this right," said Captain Mason. "We've got five documented cases of radiation poisoning. We have only one possible lead as to where these patients might have come into contact with radiation. Yet in order to get radiation poisoning you would need to come into contact with something that is radioactive. Tell me this, is it possible that this body that was found at the side of the road could have been radioactive?"

"When you're dealing with radiation poisoning," answered Dr. Abernathy, "anything is possible."

"In that case," said the Captain, "I'm afraid I have only one recourse. I'm going to have to quarantine this whole town. Nobody will be allowed in and nobody will be allowed out until we find out what caused this radiation poisoning and mitigate it. Now, Sheriff," he continued as he turned to look directly at the Sheriff, "I'll need a detailed map of your town that shows every road that leads in and out of town."

"I'll get that for you right away," answered the Sheriff. "But let me tell you this, you're gonna have your hands full if you're gonna try and lock down this town."

"That might be the case," replied the Captain, "but it has to be done. Otherwise, something like this that starts off to be only a few small cases could spread into a national crisis in no time at all. With that said, the Captain took his iPhone/All Frequency communicator out of his phone pouch and quickly pushed a button. Then he spoke into the iPhone device, "Captain Frank Mason, Jefferson ninety nine twenty, requests ten additional Agents and four Office of Emergency Services response teams equipped with Geiger Counters and iodine capsule dispensers."

Sheriff Arby looked at both doctors and said, "Do you realize how many units this guy's calling in? Each O.E.S. response team has five fire trucks manned with four officers in each truck. That's twenty fire trucks, not to mention all the F.B.I. Agents he's calling in."

Dr. Benstowe closed his eyes and said, "My, God! I knew this would happen!"

Dr. Abernathy looked a bit bewildered as he looked at Dr. Benstowe and the Sheriff. Finally he said, "The sooner we find the radioactive material that caused these five cases, the sooner things will be back to normal in your small town."

While Captain Mason talked on his iPhone, a black car pulled up to the clinic and parked and out stepped three men. The three men walked right into the clinic and as they did they flipped their ID badges at the receptionist at the front desk.

"Jim Daley, F.B.I." said one of the men. "I'm looking for Captain Mason."

"Yes," said the receptionist. "He's in the laboratory with the doctors. It's straight down the hall, the first door on your right."

CHAPTER TWENTY-THREE

Back on the logging trail, Ted got back into the driver's seat and backed the vehicle over to a partial clearing at the side of the trail, then got out of the van. Landen said, "OK, gentlemen, we have no idea how far we'll be hiking this trail, so we'll need to bring some supplies with us."

It was now close to nine o'clock and the sun was starting to climb high in the sky. Although there were a lot of trees in the area to help shade us from the sun, the further we traveled on the road toward the ridge the scarcer they were becoming.

Ted grabbed the shotgun from the back of the van, then he opened up a new box of beef jerky. "Here, everybody needs to take a few of these with you for the trail," he said.

I took four and slipped them into my pants pocket. Landen grabbed some and then got the digital camera from the front of the van and strung the long carrying cord attached to the camera down over his head so the camera would hang down on his chest. I opened up the cooler and grabbed two bottles of water. Ted and Landen did the same. We had no idea how far we'd be walking and, with the hot sun overhead, we wanted to make sure we had enough water. I took my cell phone out of my pants pocket and checked it briefly for any messages I might have missed. I changed the ring tone to vibrate and stuck the phone down into my hiking boot. This way I'd be able feel the vibration on my lower leg if I were to get a call.

When we all had gotten the supplies we'd be bringing with us, Ted locked up the van and we were on our way. We climbed over the chain that was blocking the road and began walking down the trail. As we began our journey, Landen asked Ted if he'd brought some extra shotgun shells with him.

"Yeah, I sure did," he answered. "There's two loaded in the rifle and I've got six extra shells in my pocket. Why do you ask?"

Before Landen could answer I interrupted, "Because, if he is anything like me, he's probably got a bad feeling about this. All three of us know that Red Tail Hawks don't hang chains across roads."

Landen gave me a serious look and said, "You're quite right, Jason. We might be in for a bit of trouble. Therefore, I think it might be best if Ted stays in back of us, about a hundred yards or so back and follows behind as we proceed along this logging trail. That way if we run into any trouble Ted can back us up by calling the Sheriff or possibly use the shot gun to protect us."

"That sounds good," Ted said. "We can use our cell phones like walkie-talkies to keep in touch."

"Excellent idea," said Landen.

Ted hung back as Landen and I continued down the trail and he gave us about a two-minute lead, then he began to follow us. While we walked along, I told Landen all about the Bird Farm and Devon's ranch and how beautiful the house was.

"He must make quite a lot of money at this bird business," replied Landen.

"According to Devon, that's how he paid for his ranch and all his furnishings," I said.

"Just how does he train these birds to do what he wants them to do?" asked Landen.

"It's all done by rewarding them with food," I answered.

"What sort of stuff does he feed them?" asked Landen.

"He didn't really say," I answered, "but I do know that he lets them out occasionally to find their own wild food. He said it taught them to be aggressive. Suddenly we heard hooves galloping in the distance. We stopped and listened. "They're getting closer," I said.

"It sounds like they're coming right at us," replied Landen.

Out of nowhere, a herd of wild mustangs burst out of the bushes and galloped down the trail in front of us. Toward the middle of the herd ran a half grown colt with a horn sticking out of the top of its head.

"Landen!" I yelled over the noise of the galloping mustangs. "Take a picture! It's a unicorn!"

Landen grabbed the camera that was hanging from around his neck on his chest and began snapping shots of the animal. The herd galloped on down the trail and disappeared through the bushes on the opposite side of the road.

"Did you get a good shot of that?" I asked excitedly.

While Landen reviewed the pictures he had taken, he said, "Yes. I got some excellent shots." He then held the camera out for me to take a look.

While I viewed the pictures that Landen had taken I gasped. I just couldn't believe my eyes. Such a beautiful creature thought to be a fantasy, but here it was, captured on Landen's camera. "This is amazing," I said. "Connie told me just the other day that Jimmy and Billy claimed to have seen a unicorn when they were over by Wild Cat Ridge, but we thought that it was just one of their tall tales."

"I can see where you would have thought that," said Landen. "I wouldn't have believed it myself if I hadn't seen it with my own two eyes." About that time, Landen's cell phone rang. "Yeah?" Landen answered.

"What's going on up there?" asked Ted.

"Just some wild mustangs running across the road," replied Landen. "We're going to continue on now."

As Landen got off the cell phone I asked, "Aren't you going to tell him about the unicorn?"

"In due time," answered Landen. "You have to realize that if I were to tell him right now he'd just want to run up here and Lord knows we don't have time for that right now."

While we continued on I realized he was probably right. We needed to make it to the backside of Wild Cat Ridge before the hot afternoon sun appeared in the sky. "What's your take on unicorns?"

"Well, Jason," he said, "I think it must be some kind of freak of nature. Unicorns were fictional creatures created by the great author William B. Downing in one of his first novels written way back in the seventeen hundreds. For us to actually see one trotting along with this herd would make me think that something has affected this herd's reproductive system. What else could it be? We both know that there are no such things as unicorns. Don't we?" he said, looking straight at me.

"Of course," I said. "But it's going to be kind of hard, knowing that there are no such things as unicorns, when we've got pictures of one."

Then Landen did something I'd never seen him do before. He actually laughed. "Well," he said as he got control of himself, "I guess we'll just have to try a little harder."

After we had hiked a good mile and a half on down the logging trail we came to a fork in the road. "What now?" I asked Landen.

He gave me a perplexed look and said, "I'm really not quite sure."

I examined both trails and I could see that one appeared to be more established. It had a well-worn look to it. The other looked newer and wasn't quite as worn. I looked over the terrain and noticed that the established road going toward the right looked to be more laden with trees. The newer looking road seemed to have less vegetation. "What direction is town?" I asked Landen.

"From the highway it was southbound," he answered.

I thought to myself for a moment. Knowing Wild Cat Ridge was west of town, that would mean that we would want to be traveling in a southwest direction. I used to be pretty good at finding directions back when I was in the Boy Scouts. As a matter of fact, the scoutmaster used to say the T in Jason T. Harmony stood for Tracker because I was the best in the troop when it came to the compass games we used to play. "Too bad we don't have a compass," I said to Landen. Then I remembered something that my Scoutmaster had always pounded into our heads, *Moss always grows on the north side of a tree.* I gazed at the trees around us. The moss was growing on the side closest to the direction of the established trail to the right of us.

Finally I said to Landen, "I believe this road going off to the right is the old logging trail. If we want to get to the back side of Wild Cat Ridge we need to take this other road." Then I pointed to the road that took a gentle curve to the left.

"Are you sure of this?" asked Landen.

"I'll stake my reputation as a tracker on it," I replied.

Landen gave me an odd look then he asked, "Your reputation as a what?"

I smiled and said, "Landen. Weren't you ever in the Boy Scouts?"

"No! Certainly not!" he answered. "I never had time for such nonsense."

"Well, trust me," I said. "This is the road we want to take."

With that established, he took out his cell phone and pushed his speed dial to reach Ted. "Ted," he said into the phone, "when you come to the Y in the road, follow the road that goes off to the left. That's the road we'll be taking."

CHAPTER TWENTY-FOUR

Back in town, the O.E.S. units were starting to arrive. Two response teams were pulling into town and the other two estimated their arrival time to be twenty-five minutes out. Captain Mason assigned the three F.B.I. Agents that had just arrived the task of working with the O.E.S. units to set up the roadblocks on every road going in and out of town. They were also in charge of contacting every radio and T.V. station within a five hundred mile radius to have the stations make announcements every fifteen minutes informing the public that the town of Jefferson City, Nevada was locked down. No one would be allowed in and no one would be allowed out until further notice.

Captain Mason and Sheriff Arby, along with both Doctors, were interviewing the five patients. After interviewing the first four patients, all signs pointed to the man that was found dead up by No Pay Grade as the source that caused the radiation poisoning. But they still needed to link the fifth patient, the mortuary furnace operator named Nelson, to the same dead man to be absolutely sure. They knew that he had cremated the man's remains, but there was no way he could have gotten close enough to the dead man to have been exposed to his body. The man would have been in a standard wooden coffin used to dispose of unidentified bodies and it was Nelson's job to simply hoist the coffin into the furnace with a small over head crane, fire up the furnace and burn the remains. After that the ashes were sucked out of the furnace with a large suction hose and sorted into an urn of some type or simply disposed of in a small plastic container. Each plastic container would be labeled and stored in a larger container that's in a shed that was outside of the building. The container looked like a dumpster but was specially designed to hold the small containers of ashes until they were disposed of in a reserved section at the county graveyard.

The Captain, along with everyone else, fully covered in a protective smock, walked into the room where Nelson was quarantined and said, "Hi. I'm Captain Mason of the F.B.I. I understand that your name is Nelson."

"That's right," Nelson replied in a rather weak voice.

"I've got some questions I want to ask you," the Captain said.

"I haven't robbed any banks or taken any hostages," Nelson said as he gave a weak laugh then reached for the controls on his hospital bed and raised his bed up to the sitting position.

"No, it has nothing to do with anything like that," said the Captain.

Nelson looked over at Sheriff Arby and asked, "Sheriff, do I need some kind of lawyer or something before I talk to this F.B.I. guy?"

Sheriff Arby gave Nelson a wink and said, "Nelson, you're not in any trouble. Just trust me on this one. The Captain is only trying to find out what made you sick."

"I'd like to find that out myself," said Nelson.

Captain Mason looked apologetically at the Sheriff and said, "Thanks for your help, Sheriff. I guess I was wrong, it looks like I will need your help after all."

"No problem," said the Sheriff. "You'll find that if we work together on this case we'll get things done a lot faster."

"Yes, you're absolutely right," said the Captain. "I'm sorry I started us off on the wrong foot." Then they both turned their attention to Nelson.

"Nelson," the Captain said, "last week you cremated an unidentified man. A transient found up on the side of the road by what you town people call No Pay Grade.

"Yes, I did," said Nelson. "I burnt his remains in the furnace."

"Did you have any close contact with the corpse?" asked Captain Mason.

"No. I just loaded his box in the furnace and burnt it," he replied.

"How close did you get to the coffin?" asked the Captain.

"Oh, I don't know," said Nelson. "Maybe ten or fifteen feet."

"You didn't get any closer than that?" asked Dr. Abernathy.

"No, sir," answered Nelson.

"Are you sure about that?" said the Captain.

"Yes. The boss has a policy that no one shall open the coffins when they are in our possession," Nelson said. "If anyone does open one of the coffins for any reason at all its grounds for termination. That's why I always make sure that I don't even get close to them. Then I won't have any problems."

Dr. Abernathy looked at Dr. Benstowe and shrugged his shoulders. "Perhaps there's something else that ties these five patients together besides the body," he said.

"I hate to say it," said Dr. Benstowe, "But if the body isn't it then it looks like we'll be chasing a red herring because there's no telling what it could be."

The Sheriff turned to the Captain and said loud enough for everyone to hear, "Well I guess the one armed dead man that Nelson cremated has nothing to do with this whole thing after all." The Captain gave the Sheriff an odd look and started to say something but the Sheriff gave him a wink and it stopped him from saying anything.

Nelson gave the Sheriff a surprised look and said, "I didn't cremate no one armed man."

"Sure you did, Son," said the Sheriff. "The transient only had one arm."

Without thinking, Nelson quickly replied, "He had two arms."

"And how would you know that?" asked the Sheriff.

"Because..." Nelson said, "I..." then Nelson stopped himself in mid sentence and didn't say another word.

"Because you what?" asked the Sheriff.

Nelson sat quietly and didn't answer.

"Because you what?" asked the Sheriff again.

"Well," Nelson said in a small voice, "I had heard that he had two. That he had two arms. That's how I know."

"And just who did you hear this from?" asked the Sheriff looking back at the Captain who was beginning to smile just a bit.

Nelson thought for a moment and then said, "I heard it from the guy who brought the casket over from the Funeral Home."

The Sheriff said, "Let me see if I got this straight, Nelson. The guy brings the casket over from the Funeral Home and when he drops it off he says *Oh, by the way, Nelson, this guy has two arms*. Is that how it went, Nelson?"

"No. Not exactly," answered Nelson.

"Well, then," said the Sheriff, "why don't you tell me exactly how it went?"

Nelson got a blank stare on his face as he tried to think of some way to answer the Sheriff's question. Finally the Sheriff said, "Look, Nelson, all we're trying to do here is find out what made you five people sick. If you know something, and you're not telling us, you better speak up now. Otherwise a lot more people might get sick and it will all be your fault."

Nelson sat quietly thinking to himself as the Sheriff continued. "Now, if you did something you weren't supposed to do, for instance, let's say, you looked in that casket for one reason or another, well, let me tell you this, none of us here have any intentions of telling your boss. That thought hasn't crossed our minds. All we're trying to find out here is what connects you five people together.

Nelson was silent for a few more moments, then he finally said, "I had heard that the guy's hands were black. I'd never seen somebody die and have their hands turn black. I mean, most black people have black hands, but this was different. A Mexican guy dying with black hands, I thought that they were kidding me. You know what I mean?"

"Yeah, Nelson, it does sound pretty hard to believe," said the Sheriff.

"Anyway," Nelson continued, "the boss was gone for the day and he had left me orders to cremate this guy, so before I torched him up I figured I'd open up that casket and take a look for myself. After all, how many chances does someone get to see something like that?"

"Were his hands black?" asked Dr. Abernathy.

"They sure was," said Nelson. "It was kind of spooky looking."

Dr. Abernathy turned to Dr. Benstowe and said in a low voice, "The transient died of overexposure to a highly radioactive source."

"Thank you, Nelson," said Sheriff Arby. "You try and get you some rest now."

"You're not going to say anything to my boss, are you?" Nelson asked.

"I told you I wouldn't and I'm a man of my word," said the Sheriff, then he turned and started to walk out of the room so Nelson could get some rest.

The doctors and the officers followed the Sheriff out of the room and then they all began to remove their protective clothing and gloves and place them in the can for disposal of such items.

"Sheriff, you did an excellent job in there," said Captain Mason. "I'm really impressed."

"It goes with the territory," said the Sheriff. "In a small town like this you get to know the people first hand and you learn how to talk with them. And most importantly, you earn their respect and trust. Speaking about important matters," the Sheriff continued, with a big smile on his face, "I think that maybe we had better get on down to the crematorium and find that transient's remains. We don't want to lose them just because we are having so much fun standing around here patting each other on the back."

"I agree," said the Captain, who was all business now. "We need to do it right away." The Captain took out his phone and pushed a button, "Mason here. I'm going to need one O.E.S.

unit to meet me at the crematorium over on Dunbar Street ASAP and make sure they bring a Geiger counter with them." With that, he got off the phone and asked the Sheriff, "What's the quickest way to get to this crematorium?"

"The quickest way is to jump in my squad car," answered Sheriff Arby. "With my flashing lights and siren I can get us over there in about two minutes."

"That will work," said Captain Mason. "Where's your squad car?"

"Right out front," answered the Sheriff. They both hurried out and got in the car. The Sheriff turned on his flashing lights and siren and took off with a vengeance.

Both Doctors stood there looking at them rush out and then turned to go back into the office to work on the paperwork that they still had to do.

CHAPTER TWENTY-FIVE

As Landen and I began to walk down the trail to the left, we noticed that there were fresh tire tracks along the way.

"Looks like there's been someone here not too long ago," I said.

"It sure appears that way," said Landen. "Probably the guy who wrote that sign and put the chain up across the road."

"You think maybe we better turn back?" I asked.

"Not yet," answered Landen. "We've come this far. We need to find out for sure if this bird is indeed being used for security purposes. And if so, we need to get a rough idea of what it's guarding."

Through the trees I caught a glimpse of what appeared to be the backside of Wild Cat Ridge. "Well, it shouldn't take us too long now," I said, "because I believe that's Wild Cat Ridge right over there."

While I pointed toward the ridge, Landen took his camera, pushed the zoom lens button and snapped a few close up shots. "Take a look," Landen said, handing me the camera from around his neck.

As I reviewed the photos, I could see that it was the backside of the ridge. For some reason, this side had a lot of vegetation. Not at all like the other side, which was dry and rocky. It seemed almost impossible that one side could be so different from the other. "That's the place we're looking for," I said to Landen, handing him his camera back.

He took the camera back and put it around his neck again then he took out his cell phone and called Ted. "Ted. Did you take the left trail back at the 'Y'?"

"Yeah, I sure did," answered Ted. "I've seen some tire tracks that don't look that old."

"Yes," said Landen. "We know about those."

"You think maybe you ought to wait for me to catch up with you guys?" asked Ted.

"Negative," said Landen. "We need you in back of us in case something does happen to us. That way you can go for help. We've seen the backside of Wild Cat Ridge so we know we're going the right way. Now, there is one thing I want to make clear. If you do see a Red Tail Hawk attacking us, you are to shoot the damn bird, not scare it. Do you understand?

Ted answered, "Yeah, I understand. It's just that I hate to kill things."

"I know this, Ted," said Landen. "But would you rather have a dead brother or a dead bird?" There was dead silence on the phone. Finally Landen said in a loud voice, "Ted! Tell me that you're not actually thinking over the option I just gave you!"

"No, no, of course not," answered Ted. "It's just, it's the way you phrased it, I mean, of course I'd rather have a live brother and a live bird. But if I had to choose I'd rather have a live bird."

"What did you just say!?" yelled Landen.

"I was just kidding," laughed Ted. "You know I'd pick you every time."

"That's better," said Landen. "Just make sure you keep your shot gun and don't let it out of your sight."

"Will do," answered Ted.

Landen got off the phone and stood still, looking down the trail, and then he turned and said, "Jason, we're going to have to keep our eyes and ears open from here on in. Every chance we get we need to stay under cover. Use trees and bushes, anything that we can to hide us from view."

I nodded my head in agreement and then said, "If this Red Tail Hawk is equipped with Devon's technology then we're visible from the sky by whoever is controlling the bird."

"Exactly," replied Landen. "It would just be a matter of where their surveillance lens is located and if they're paying close attention."

We continued to walk down the small road. After a while a slight breeze blew our way. I caught a whiff of a nasty, nauseating smell. "Oh, my God! What is that smell?" I asked.

"It smells like something dead," answered Landen. "Maybe there is a dead decaying animal of some sort nearby." When the breeze passed, the smell went away.

We continued on and noticed that the further we went, the fewer trees there were, until finally they began to disappear altogether. There was still the green shrubbery and bushes, but trying to keep ourselves under cover was beginning to become very difficult. We tried our best to stay close to the bushes at the side of the road. It became quite evident before too long that we'd be clearly visible on certain parts of the road.

Suddenly I felt a vibration on my leg. It was my phone that I had stuck in my hiking boot. I motioned for Landen to stop for a minute while I reached down and took the phone out of my boot. "Hi. This is Jason," I answered.

"Jason! Where are you?" asked Connie in a frantic voice. "The F.B.I. has locked down our town. There are fire trucks everywhere!"

"What in the world's happened?" I asked.

"I'm not sure," said Connie. "I heard from Billy's mother that it's something to do with radiation poisoning but I'm not sure if that's what it's about or not. Where are you?" she asked again.

"I'm on a trail, well actually, it's a small road," I said. "It's somewhere to the backside of Wild Cat Ridge. Ted and I, along with Landen, are trying to get enough information on this Red Tail Hawk case so we can hand the whole thing over to Sheriff Arby."

"How much longer are you going to be?" asked Connie.

"Hopefully just a couple of hours," I answered.

"I sure hope they let you guys back in town," she said. "What are you going to do if they don't?"

"Well," I said, "I guess we'll have to get a room at a motel someplace."

"Please be careful," Connie said. "You know I care a lot about you and Ted."

"I will," I answered, "and I'll relay the message to Ted. Now, why don't you and Jimmy stay in your house and lock your door until this whole F.B.I. thing is over with."

"Alright, we'll stay in the house and lock the door. But I want you and Ted to come back to town right now. Don't keep chasing that stupid bird! Please don't chase that stupid bird!"

"I'll let Ted know that we need to come back now," I said.

"Good. So I'll see you real soon?" Connie asked.

"Yes, we'll be back shortly," I answered. I knew that probably wasn't going to happen but I figured that it would make her feel better, for now, anyway.

"Take care," Connie said as she hung up.

$\infty\diamondsuit\infty$

When I got off the phone and was putting it back in my hiking boot, Landen asked, "What's going on?"

"Apparently the F.B.I. has locked down Jefferson City. Nobody can go in or out of town," I answered.

"What's this to do with?" he asked.

I replied, "Connie said that she heard that it's something about radiation poisoning."

"Well, I guess we were just lucky to get out of town when we did," he said.

"I suppose so," I said. Then I thought to myself, *was it luck or misfortune? Here we are out in the middle of nowhere looking for a Red Tail Hawk that could possibly attack and kill us both. If the hawk is protecting something, it's probably something we'd be better off not knowing anything about. And we're lucky we got out of town? I'm beginning to wonder.* Just then a breeze blew our way and with it came the disgusting stench that we had smelled a short time earlier.

"Man! That is foul smelling!" I said.

"It does smell a bit nasty now, doesn't it," replied Landen. "Maybe I'd better give Ted a quick call," he continued, "and inform him about the town being in disarray. He pushed his speed dial and got Ted on the phone. After telling him about what was going on back in town, I told him to tell Ted that Connie said to be careful. He relayed my message to Ted, and then replied, "Ted says for us to be careful. He's got the rifle to take care of him."

As the time passed, the trees completely disappeared and the hot sun established itself high in the sky. I'd been cautiously taking small sips of water as we walked along, trying to save as much as I could. But now I was more than half way through my first bottle. I figured that if it took me one bottle of water to get where we were going, it would certainly take every bit of the second bottle of water to get me back from where we came, so I make myself a pact, that when I had completely finished my first bottle of water, it was time for this boy to head back to the van whether we found out any more information on the Red Tail Hawk or not. Unlike Ted and Landen, I was doing all of this for the adventure, not for money, and the adventure part was getting pretty thin at this point.

From where we were on the road we could now clearly see Wild Cat Ridge down the side of the hill. It had a large mound at the base of it surrounded by what otherwise was a flat valley floor covered with green leafy plants. Landen took a picture of the area with his zoom lens and brought it up on the screen of his digital camera and began to study it.

"That's odd," he said.

"What's odd?" I asked.

Holding out the camera screen so we could both view the picture together he said, "That fern plant to the right of the picture has a bird perched on its top branch."

"What's odd about that?" I asked.

"Well, judging from the difference in size between the bird and the plant, that fern plant has got to be about seven feet tall or more," he replied.

"Now that you mention it, that is odd," I said. "Fern plants usually only get to be about four feet tall."

Landen snapped a few more shots with his camera and then we continued our journey.

The road now curved slightly toward Wild Cat Ridge and had started descending downward to the valley below. We'd traveled a short ways when suddenly a Red Tail Hawk appeared in the sky above us.

Landen immediately called Ted on his cell phone. "Ted!" he screamed into the phone. "There's a Red Tail Hawk above us! Be prepared to shoot!"

Ted answered back, "I can see it. It might be out of my range of fire for this shotgun. I'll try and get a bit closer."

"Well, hurry up!" yelled Landen.

The hawk began a fierce dive straight for Landen. As the bird came closer and closer to Landen, a shot rang out from Ted's shotgun. It missed the hawk. The hawk continued its powerful dive. Landen saw that the bird was diving straight for him and he began to run, waving his hands above his head to try and scare the hawk away. Another shot rang out, but it didn't stop the bird from its dive. Ted was too far away for his shotgun to be effective. I quickly thought back to Devon's Bird Farm and when I had seen his hawk diving for José. Devon had spoken a word loudly into his control system to stop the bird from its attack. It was an odd word. Something I'd never heard before. What was it? I thought to myself. I remembered it ended with 'dash'. Was it hold dash? Bold dash? Bald dash? All of the sudden the word came back to me. It was 'balderdash'. That's what it was. Although Devon had said that he used different control words for each of his birds, I found that very difficult to believe. It would be way too complicated. If this indeed were one of Devon's Hawks, then possibly this word would halt its attack the way it had at the Bird Farm. It was the only chance we had.

"BALDERDASH!" I screamed at the top of my lungs. "BALDERDASH! BALDERDASH! BALDERDASH!"

Ironically, the bird stopped its dive about ten feet from Landen's head and flew back up into the air and began to circle overhead.

I then yelled over to Landen, who was on his knees with his arms draped around his head to protect himself from the hawk, "It's OK, Landen! The bird stopped its attack! It's back up in the sky!"

Landen slowly uncovered his head and got back up on his feet, then looked in the air to see the bird was circling overhead. "What was that word you were yelling?" he asked. "Why did the hawk stop its attack?"

I explained how I'd overheard Devon stop one of his hawks from attacking by saying 'balderdash'.

"Well, that proves two things," said Landen.

"And what two things are those?" I asked.

"First, this hawk is from Devon's Bird Farm," answered Landen, "and secondly, you just saved my life and I want to thank you for that."

"You're quite welcome," I said. "I'm just glad I had the ability to stop the hawk. But we do have a problem," I continued, "this hawk is equipped with a receiver in one of its ears and somebody is controlling the bird as we speak. Although the bird is probably somewhat confused about what control word it needs to follow at the moment, it will definitely continue its attack before too long."

I'd no sooner gotten those words out of my mouth than the hawk began to dive again. This time it was diving straight for me. At the same time as I began to yell, Landen joined in. "BALDERDASH! BALDERDASH!" we yelled. The hawk again stopped its dive and flew away into the sky. But this time it immediately started its dive again. It was clear to see that whoever was controlling the bird was paying closer attention and becoming frustrated with the bird's behavior. When the hawk got about twenty feet above me, suddenly Ted appeared on the road behind me and fired both barrels of his shot gun into the bird.

The bird stopped its dive abruptly and fell to the ground on a small rise at the side of the road a few hundred yards back up the road that we had just traveled.

"Good shooting!" said Landen. "It's nice to see that you can actually hit something with that rifle of yours."

"Yeah," I interrupted. "He just shot seventy five thousand dollars worth of bird!"

"Wow! That would have paid for a lot of shotgun shells," said Ted, laughing.

"Well, I guess we are done here," I said. "All we need to do now is grab the dead hawk and bring it back to the Sheriff and let him take the case from here on in."

"That's the best idea I've heard all day," said Ted.

From out of nowhere I heard someone say, "Well, if it isn't Jason *Trouble* and his foul dancing friend."

I thought to myself, *Where have I heard that voice before?* I turned around to look and there stood Big Gus with two of his buddies.

Gus grabbed the shotgun out of Ted's hands and said, "The boss ain't gonna be too happy when he finds out you killed one of his birds." And with that, he hit Ted upside the head with the butt of the rifle, knocking Ted unconscious to the ground.

CHAPTER TWENTY-SIX

Back in town, Sheriff Arby and the F.B.I. Captain pulled into the parking lot of the crematorium. As they got out of the squad car and walked toward the office, an O.E.S. unit pulled up and parked at the side of the squad car. When the Sheriff and the Captain walked into the office, the Sheriff asked the man in charge where they might find the remains of the transient that was cremated this last week.

The man answered, "They'd be in the lock box at the back of the building. Why do you want them?"

"We need to check them out for contamination," answered the Sheriff.

"What kind of contamination?" he asked.

"Never you mind, what kind of contamination," said Sheriff Arby. "You just show us where they're at right now."

The man grabbed a key from his desk drawer and said, "Follow me, Sheriff."

He led them out the side door of the building. Captain Mason motioned for the men in the O.E.S. unit to come along with them. The men got out of the fire truck and the Captain yelled back at them, "Bring the Geiger counter with you." One of the men in the unit went back and grabbed the Geiger counter and then hurried to catch up with the rest of the unit.

When they got to the lock up container at the back of the building, the man from the crematorium unlocked the lock and started to open the door.

"Don't open that door!" yelled the Captain.

"Why not?" asked the man. "I thought you wanted to see the remains of the transient?"

"We do," answered the Captain, "but we need to do it very carefully. Bring the Geiger counter over here," the Captain ordered.

One of the men from the O.E.S. team ran up with the instrument and turned it on. With the Geiger counter engaged, he checked for radioactivity around the outside of the lock box and entrance area of the building. Then the Captain slowly opened the container. All the while, the O.E.S. man was checking for radioactivity.

"Are you getting any readings?" asked the Captain.

"Nothing to speak of," answered the O.E.S. officer.

With the door wide open, he slowly walked inside of the huge container, watching the Geiger counter carefully for any sort of reading.

"Where are the remains of the transient we wanted to check?" the Captain asked as he was looking around and then turned to the crematorium man with a questioning look.

"That would be the box to the right on the rear shelf," he answered.

"How do you know that without checking any file numbers?" asked the Captain suspiciously.

"Trust me," said the man. "This is a small town and that's the only person we've cremated in the last week and a half. But now that all you F.B.I. guys are in town," he continued, with a twinkle in his eyes, "I'm hoping that business will pick up a bit."

The Captain turned and gave him an odd look, then he had the O.E.S. man check out the box with the Geiger counter. It made a faint noise and the needle moved slightly.

"What was that?" asked Captain.

"It was a very small reaction. Nothing to be concerned about," answered the officer. "But to get a better reading it would probably be best if we emptied out the contents of the box and checked them closely. Let's get some masks, gloves and our protective suits on before we go any further."

"Good idea," said the Captain.

"I'll get some from the O.E.S. truck," said Sheriff Arby. "I'll be right back."

When the Sheriff came back with the supplies, they all put on their protective equipment and then proceeded to empty out the ash and remains out of the box onto a large piece of thick plastic that the man at the crematorium had supplied to them. The officer ran the Geiger counter over the remains slowly and it immediately gave a slight reading and gave off a faint noise in three different sections of the ashes.

"We're getting some readings," said the officer. "But they're very faint. Something with a reading this low wouldn't actually be harmful."

The Captain took a writing pen out of his shirt pocket and began sifting through the ashes. He quickly found a strange spot of melted material in one of the sections of ashes that had triggered the meter. He brushed it off with his gloved finger and then picked it up with his other gloved hand to examine it closer. It was oblong and flat, about one and a half inches in length at its longest point.

"What do you make of this?" asked the Captain, holding out his hand so the Sheriff could take a look.

As the Sheriff examined it, a look of surprise came to his face. "That looks like a piece of melted gold!" he said.

The Captain had the O.E.S. officer run the Geiger counter over the melted material. The meter jumped slightly and made a faint clicking noise.

"That's what we've been picking up on the meter," said the officer.

After sifting through the remaining ashes, they found two more melted pieces of material. They were both about the same size as the first.

Captain Mason looked at the Sheriff and said, "How in the world would a person get this much gold in their body? It certainly couldn't be from the gold fillings in their teeth."

The Sheriff said, "How does anybody get anything in their body? They swallow it, that's how. This guy must have swallowed some gold nuggets. And, judging by the size of the melted material, they were pretty good-sized nuggets. He was probably hoping to pass them through his bowels at a later date," the Sheriff continued. "He most likely stole them from somewhere and smuggled them out in his body. But unfortunately for him, before these nuggets were melted in the high heat of the crematorium furnace, they must have been extremely radioactive. That's how this guy met his demise."

"The whole thing doesn't make much sense," said the Captain. "First of all, where would a transient find so many gold nuggets? And secondly, how would gold get to be radioactive?"

"Then, I guess that is exactly what we need to find out."

"I think the first thing we need to do," said the Captain, "is to find out if this material is really gold. Do you have a good jeweler in town? One that can do a quick test on this stuff?"

"That would be Woolworth's Jewelers," said Sheriff Arby. "It's down on Main Street."

"Let's go!" said Captain Mason.

"What about these ashes?" asked the Sheriff as he turned his head to look at the ashes scattered on the plastic sheet. "We need to put them back in the box."

Mason turned to the O.E.S. officer and said, "Secure these remains back in their box and tag them for evidence." Then the Captain looked at the proprietor of the crematorium and said, "Don't remove these ashes from this lock up container! Don't release them to anyone! And don't take them anywhere! Is that **understood**!?"

The man gave the Captain a cynical look and said, "And just who in the heck do you think you are ordering me around like this?"

Captain Mason said firmly, "I'm the F.B.I.!"

The proprietor answered, "Well, you don't sign my paycheck. I'm in charge at this here crematorium!"

Sheriff Arby interrupted and said, "Look, will you just do us a favor and take good care of these ashes?"

"Sure," said the man. "I'll do it for you, Sheriff. But only 'cause I happen to like you." Then he looked back at the Captain and said, "Him, I don't like!"

The Sheriff gave out a chuckle as the Captain stood with a frown on his face and then gave the man a nasty look.

"Come on Captain," said the Sheriff, "time's a wasting."

They both walked briskly out and got back into the Sheriff's squad car. As they drove off the Captain asked, "What is wrong with that man? Doesn't he know that I could shut him down and have him arrested and throw away the key?"

"I'm sure he does," said the Sheriff. "Chances are he just doesn't care. If you don't mind me saying so," continued the Sheriff, "I think you need a lot less bark and a little more beg. You've got to understand that these people around here aren't used to outside people coming into town and disrupting their lives. There hasn't been anything like this going on around this area since the movie that was made here back in the sixties. I find that I get more cooperation from folks if I treat them like I treat my friends. Don't talk at them, talk to them."

"Perhaps you're right," said the Captain. "I'll keep that in mind." He was silent for a few seconds and then, turning his head to look at the Sheriff, he said, "What's that you said about a movie?"

The Sheriff smiled broadly and said, "Oh, that. That was a real fiasco, really turned this town upside down."

"What kind of movie was it?" asked the Captain.

"You ever hear of a guy named Elvis Presley?" asked the Sheriff.

"What kind of a question is that?" said the Captain. "I think everybody in the world knows Elvis Presley."

"Well," continued the Sheriff, "it seems he was engaged to star in a movie. Something called, *Harum Scarum*. The movie company got the OK to film most of the scenes on the B.L.M.

land outside of town, up the road a ways. The movie crew set up trailers and big tents out there and most of the people working on the film came into town every afternoon when they were done for the day. They would eat their meals here and they graced the local bars and different establishments throughout the town. I was just a kid back then, about eleven or twelve years old, but I remember the whole thing like it was just yesterday. Everyone would wait around for these people to come into town for the evening. When they would come, the whole town would go bonkers. All the young girls and older ones, too, would hope for a chance to catch a glimpse of Elvis. He didn't always come into town. He spent a lot of time out there on that B.L.M. land with his boys."

"With his boys?" asked the Captain.

"Yeah. He had a group of guys. I guess you'd call them his bodyguards and good time buddies that always hung around with him. Right before they had planned to begin making this movie there was a big uranium strike in the desert out by Ely, Nevada. So when Elvis heard they were gonna film in Nevada, he bought each of his boys a Geiger counter and he bought them all brand new dune buggies. They spent a lot of time out there on that B.L.M. land racing around with those dune buggies searching for uranium. When Elvis did come into town, the women would go wild. They'd start that screaming stuff and some of them actually would faint out right. Then about two weeks after they was here, one of his boys, Joey I think was his name, found something out there they all thought was uranium. Elvis hired some roustabout guy that worked with uranium to take a sample of the rock and bring it in to be tested. Meanwhile, he had a rough map and a claim for drawn up and filed it with the county. They was all going to be rich, not as if Elvis needed any more money, but his boys sure could use the dough. Anyway, they took the sample and had it tested. Turned out it was some type of radioactive waste. They said it had probably landed there from the nuclear test site over in southern Nevada when they did all those atomic bomb tests in the late fifties. Elvis's boys sure were mighty disappointed, but Elvis, being the good hearted guy that he was, had the rock sample enclosed in an air tight display case with a plaque that read, '**Jefferson City, Nevada is a 'Rock' in Town Thanks For The Hospitality Elvis**' He had it presented to the Mayor at the time and it still sits on a shelf at the Court House to this day."

"Wow! What a story," said the Captain. "Did you ever actually meet Elvis?"

"Yes, I did," answered the Sheriff. "I was standing on the corner helping my little sister sell Camp Fire Mints. The filming of the movie had wrapped up and we thought everyone had picked up and left for good. All of a sudden, this big black limousine pulled up and the back window slides open. Elvis appeared through the open window and asked, "Whatcha kids selling?"

My sister just stood there with her mouth wide open. Finally I said, "Camp Fire Mints, Mister Presley."

He said, "What's yer name, son?"

I said, "Arby."

"And what's her name?" he asked, pointing to my sister who still had her mouth wide open.

"She's my sister, Kelly," I said.

"Well, Arby," Elvis said, "why don't cha give me a box of them mints?"

I reached over and handed him a box of mints. He took the mints and reached out and shook my hand. I could feel him putting something in my hand as we shook. When he pulled his hand away I looked and there was a hundred dollar bill in my hand. I said, "Gee, thanks, Mister Presley."

He smiled and said, "Just call me Elvis, kid. That's what my friends call me. And could you do me one favor before I leave?"

"Sure, whatever you want. What is it?" I asked.

"Well, kid, could ya'll reach over and gently close your sissy's mouth so a fly or something don't land in it?" then he smiled and slid his window closed and the limo drove off. To this day my sister draws a blank every time I talk about it. She was so dumbfounded. She must have been in shock or something."

"I heard he had that effect on a lot of people," said the Captain. "He was truly a dynamic person."

As they drove through town, there was an O.E.S. truck parked at the side of Main Street with a crowd of people standing in a long line on the sidewalk.

"What's going on here?" asked the Sheriff.

"They're distributing iodine tablets to protect against radiation poisoning," answered the Captain. "It's standard protocol when dealing with radioactive materials."

"Maybe we better pull over and get some," said the Sheriff. "I don't think you've taken one and I know I haven't had any."

"You're probably right," said Mason. "But we don't have to stand in line. I'll call an agent and have him send them to us at the jewelry shop." The Captain got on his communicator and the Sheriff was quite surprised to hear the change in his attitude. Instead of shouting out orders, he was using the *please and thank you* words.

When they pulled up to Woolworth's Jewelry, one of the O.E.S. men met them and gave them each an iodine tablet enclosed in plastic wrap. As they tore open the packages and put the tablets in their mouths, the man gave them each a bottle of water to chase the pills down with. After taking the tablets, they walked into the jewelry store and found the owner, Mr. Woolworth, himself.

"Hi, Jeff," the Sheriff said to the owner.

"How are you doing today, Sheriff?" said Mr. Woolworth.

"Well, we're doing pretty good," said the Sheriff. "This is Captain Mason with the F.B.I.," the Sheriff said, turning toward Mason and gesturing with his hand. "We've got some material that we believe is gold that we'd like to have you verify for us."

The Captain reached into his shirt pocket and pulled out a baggie with the three pieces in question and handed it to the jeweler.

"Certainly," said the jeweler. "I'd be more than happy to help you in any way possible." He took them out of the bag. "Now, let me have a closer look at them." He turned them over in his hands, testing the weight and the color. He said, "It sure looks like gold. Let's do an electrode test on it to start off. That will give us a good idea to begin with. If it passes that, then we'll go from there." He took out a small testing meter with two wires that had alligator clips at the end of each wire. He plugged the wires into the side of the tester and turned it on to make sure that the tester was working. Then he took one alligator clip and clamped it on the material and took the other clip and clamped it on a terminal at the side of the meter itself. The needle on the meter went all the way over to one side.

"What's that mean?" asked the Sheriff.

The jeweler looked up at the men and said, "That indicated that it's gold. But to be one hundred percent sure, I need to take a scraping of the material and perform what we call an acid test." He then took a small minute part of the material and placed it on a glass-testing strip and disappeared into a back room. A few minutes later he walked back out into the show room. He had a very odd look on his face as he said, "This, Gentlemen, is the purest gold I've ever seen in my life. It's every bit of twenty-four carat gold and if I could give it a special rating, I'd say its twenty-four carat plus. Where in the world did you and the Captain find this gold?"

The Sheriff turned to the Captain and then looked back at Mr. Woolworth and said, "I really don't think you want to know the answer to that question."

The jeweler put the gold back into the baggy and handed it back to the Captain without saying another word. The Sheriff thanked him for his help. Captain Mason put the baggy back in his shirt pocket and they walked out of the store.

CHAPTER TWENTY-SEVEN

While Ted lay unconscious on the ground, Gus's men quickly grabbed Landen and I, then tied our hands behind our backs with long strips of leather. With our hands secured, they frisked us and took everything from our pockets. They tore Landen's camera from the strap around his neck and threw it on the ground. Then one of them smashed it with the heel of his boot. When Landen tried to protest, Big Gus slapped him across the face with the back of his hand and told him to shut the hell up. With the bottle of water that they took from my pocket, Gus cut the top off with a large buck knife and then poured the entire bottle over Ted's head. At the same time he yelled, "Get up you lazy bastard!"

As Ted slowly came to, Gus grabbed him by the back of his shirt collar and pulled him to his feet. The men immediately emptied his pockets and found the remaining shot gun shells and his cell phone. Looking at the guy who was holding Ted's cell phone in his hand, I saw that he was missing a good portion of his little finger on his right hand. I thought to myself *this must be the guy Slick Willy was talking about, the guy that kept buying all the bags of ice and the rock salt*. I didn't have a clue what this guy would want with the rock salt and ice way out here, but I had a bad feeling that I was going to find out. The man walked over and gave the cell phone to Gus, who had Landen's phone in his other hand.

Big Gus took the phone, then looked over at me and said, "Where's your cell phone, Trouble?"

"I don't have one," I said.

"You don't have a cell phone?" Gus said in a suspicious voice. He turned to his men and said, "Strip this guy down to his birthday suit and we'll just see if he's got a cell phone or not."

When the men came toward me I knew they'd find the phone that I had stuck in my boot, so I said, "Well, heck, yeah, I got a cell phone, Big Gus. Everybody's got a cell phone. I meant that I don't have one with me. I forgot it at home. But if you don't trust me, Ted's phone there has my cell phone number in it. Just push my number and see if you hear a ring. I guarantee you won't." I knew I was putting my neck on the line but it was a chance I had to take. Without any means of communication to the outside world we would most certainly die a slow death out here with the likes of these thugs.

The men began to grab me when Gus suddenly said, "Hold on, boys. Mr. Trouble's got a good point here. Why should we go through all the trouble of stripping him down when all I have to do is push this little button." As the men backed off, Gus looked at them and said, "You gotta use your heads, boys. It takes less energy." Then he pushed the button and put the phone to his ear. He listened while it started to ring, then he took it away from his ear and said, "Anybody hear a cell phone ringing?"

The men stood by me silently as they listened for a ring or a song, anything that would indicate that I had a cell phone on me. Although I felt the vibration against my lower leg, the men didn't hear a thing.

After letting it ring for a short time, Gus finally said, "Well it looks like Mr. Trouble was telling the truth after all." With that he turned off the cell phone and stuck both phones in his pocket. "Let's get these guys back to camp," said Gus. "We need to get back to business.

Big Gus and one of the men led us, while the other two men walked in back of us as they marched us down the road toward the bottom of Wild Cat Ridge. Near the bottom of the road we began to smell that horrible smell that we had noticed before, earlier in the day.

Gus shouted to one of his men that the pits were beginning to smell a little ripe. "You need to put some rock salt on it."

"I would," answered the man walking with Gus, "but we're all out of rock salt again."

Big Gus said, "I guess we need to send Pinky back down to buy some more."

The man with half his little finger missing said, "First you need to give me some more money."

"What do you do with all the money I give you?" said Gus.

"All the money you give me?" repeated Pinky. "Hell, with the prices that old coot charges down there at that Willy's Place, it takes every last penny I have on me just to get out of the place."

"Oh, I'm sure he can't be that bad," said Gus.

At that moment I saw my chance to try and get on talking terms with the men, so I spoke up and said, "Old Slick Willy would charge you a dollar for a penny piece of candy if he could get away with it."

Pinky looked at me and said, "Is that what they call him, Slick Willy? Huh. The name certainly fits."

"Yeah," I continued. "He's the kind of guy that would take a ten dollar bill from a blind man and give him change for a dollar."

Gus and the boys all began to laugh. Then Gus said to Pinky, "Maybe I'd better start sending you someplace else besides there."

"There's no other place close enough," said Pinky. "If we go too far away the ice will melt too much. Then we won't be able to pack the shipment."

Now it was becoming clear to me. The ice was being used to keep something cold and it wasn't beer or soft drinks. What were they doing out here? Were they poaching? Maybe they were using the ice to keep the meat cold while they shipped it somewhere for processing? That didn't make any sense. Why use expensive hawks for something as petty as that? It couldn't be a drug lab or marijuana operation. They wouldn't need ice to ship any of that.

Then I heard a cell phone ring. It was Gus's that he carried on a pouch attached to his belt. He took it out and said, "Big Gus here. Yeah. They got one of the hawks. No, the one on the West side is still good. We got all three of them right here with us. We're gonna take 'em down to camp." Then he paused and listened for a moment. He said, "Really, the whole town, huh? What are they doing in Jefferson City?" Then paused again and listened intently. He finally said, "The boys ain't gonna like that. Yeah, I know," he said. "While I got you on the phone, what do you want me to do with those last two wetbacks?" A pause and then, "Yeah, but they're not ready for the pit yet. OK, you're the boss."

When he got off his phone, the boys all looked at him. Finally one of them asked, "What ain't we gonna like?"

Gus looked at him and said, "We're not gonna be able to go into town tonight."

"Oh, come on!" said the man. "Saturday night's the only time we get a chance to get out of this place."

"Yeah," said the rest of the men. "What's with that?"

Gus turned to the rest of the men and said, "Now, don't you boys give me no trouble. I'm just as mad about this as you are. Let's get these guys down to camp. We got a lot of things we need to discuss."

As we got close to camp, I could see the pit that they were talking about off to the right side of the road, slightly off in the distance. It was surrounded by mounds of dirt and a tractor with a loader bucket on it was sitting off to the side. Judging from Gus's phone conversation with the boss, whoever that was, there were two 'wetbacks' that the boss told Gus to put into the pit. Were they talking about two illegal Mexicans? The odor coming from the pit reeked of death. Were they going to put these two souls to their death? Where had these two come from? What would draw them way out here to the wilderness of Nevada? Instantly my mind flashed back to the newspaper that Uncle Lester's elephant had been wrapped in. There was that ad for

Mexicanos to make many pesos in Nevada. Could that perhaps be connected in some way with what was going on here?

In the distance I could see a large canvas tarp propped up with tree branches to form a lean-to type structure. There were two large pickup trucks parked in a surrounding area. Off to the side sat a flat bed trailer with a ball hitch. That explained how the tractor that was sitting by the pit had gotten here. Toward the center of the area was a circle of rocks with some smoldering ashes inside, probably used for cooking meals. Standing over by the lean-to was another man. Counting Gus and the three men with us that made five of them. This must be the camp they were talking about. But why have it out in such a dry barren area? Why not put it closer to the base of Wild Cat Ridge by the mound with all the green shady plants?

When we were marched into camp by Gus and the boys I could see that the one man was holding an iPhone. He looked at us, then looked at Gus and said, "I take it that these three here are the reason the bird wouldn't follow its commands."

"These three here," said Gus, "are the reason the bird is dead!"

"Dead!" said the man. "No wonder I haven't been able to get any response from this iPhone. Does the boss know they killed one of the birds?"

Gus said, "Yeah. And the boss ain't too happy about it either."

"What's the boss want to do with them?" asked the man.

"The boss gave me orders," said Gus. "You'll find out pretty quick."

"Who are these guys, anyway?" asked the man. "And what are they doing poking around out here?"

Big Gus gestured his hand toward Landen and Ted and answered, "Evidently these two here are the Meade Brothers. A couple of small time gumshoes from Jefferson City. And this one over here," he said pointing toward me, "is just plain trouble. I guess they're working for the Sheriff investigating the mysterious Red Tail Hawk attacks."

All the men started laughing. Then one said, "They ain't mysterious to us." Then they all started laughing again.

"What do you want us to do with them?" asked Pinky.

"Take 'em out of the way over there by the trailer for now and sit them down out in the hot sun," Gus ordered.

I could tell that this wasn't going to be a pleasant experience. I hadn't had a sip of water for quite some time and I knew that it had to be extremely uncomfortable for Ted who had a big knot on the side of his head where he'd been hit with the shotgun butt. Landen also had to be pretty miserable. He had dried blood in his handlebar moustache from a nosebleed after Gus had backhanded him across the face.

After we were sat down by the trailer in the hot sun, I asked both Landen and Ted if they were doing OK.

"I guess I'll live," said Ted, "But I've got one heck of a headache."

Landen said, "I sure could use a drink of water about now."

"Try not to think about it," I said. "Thinking about water will only make it worse."

From where we were by the trailer, we could see two men off in the far distance using pick axes by the large mound. "Do you suppose those are the two Mexican fellows they were talking about?" asked Landen.

"It must be," I answered. "I wonder what they're doing with those pick axes?"

"It looks like they're digging into that mound," said Ted. "Maybe they're digging footings for a foundation or something."

Landen shook his head in disgust. "I think that knock upside your head must have affected your brain," he said, "because you're certainly not thinking properly."

"What do you mean?" asked Ted, with a cross look on his face.

"First of all, dear Brother," said Landen, "footings require cement and second of all, even if you were able to get a cement truck out here, which is highly unlikely, why would anybody in their right mind want to build a structure on the side of a circular mound?"

Ted thought for a minute and then responded, "Well, dear brother, has it ever crossed your mind to ask yourself, what would a circular mound be doing out here in the first place?"

Landen looked at the mound off in the distance and said, "Now that you mention it, that is rather odd. It looks a bit out of place, doesn't it?"

"It sure does," I said. "It's strange how everything around it is so green and over growing, yet here not even a mile away it's all dry and dead looking. You know, I read a Jules Verne novel when I was a kid," I continued, "called, *When It Fell To Earth*. It was about a large meteor that was falling toward earth undetected for years. The closer it got to earth the more havoc it created with the earth's gravity pull and weather conditions. It turned lush green fertile regions into dried up deserts and turned deserts into tropical paradises. When it finally fell to earth it hit with such magnitude that it caused earthquakes and mass destruction throughout the area. I realize that Jules Verne wrote science fiction novels but a lot of his fiction became a reality as time passed."

"Yes," said Landen, "Jules Verne wrote great science fiction novels, but let me just play devil's advocate. Let's say that large mound over there was a meteor that had fallen to earth. Something that big would certainly have had to cause a catastrophic disturbance when it struck the earth, yet nothing was ever noted or recorded in any journals or books of history."

"What about the 1906 earthquake in San Francisco?" Ted said smugly. "Wasn't that a catastrophic disturbance?"

Landen was taken aback. He couldn't believe his brother Ted had just trumped his theory. "That's a brilliant piece of philosophy," he said. "I hadn't thought of that."

Ted replied, "Well, I guess that knock upside the head didn't scramble my brains after all."

"Not as far as you could tell," mumbled Landen under his breath.

"What was that?" asked Ted.

"I said there's a far off smell," answered Landen.

"Probably that pit," I said, laughing.

"Jason!" snapped Landen. "This is not a laughing matter!"

"I know. I know," I said apologetically.

"If this mound is an actual meteor," said Landen, "then there's a good chance that it's radioactive."

"Maybe that would explain that unicorn we took a picture of," I said. "Wouldn't something radioactive affect those horse's reproductive systems?"

"Yes, it definitely would," said Landen. "But if it is radioactive then those two men with the pickaxes over there would have a bad case of radiation poisoning."

"How long could someone be exposed to something like that without having any ill effects?" I asked.

"Not long. Maybe a minute or two, tops," Landen answered.

"How long would somebody last under radioactive conditions such as that?" Ted asked.

"Well," Landen said, "if that large mound is indeed a meteor and it is radioactive, then it would certainly be one of the highest forms of radioactive materials existing on Earth. I'd say a person would last maybe four or five days at the most. Then their body would stop functioning altogether. All of their organs would shut down one by one in rapid succession."

"Sounds pretty gruesome," I said.

Landen replied, "Yes. It would be a very painful death."

We could hear Gus say in a loud voice, "OK, Boys, now that you're all here, we've got a lot of stuff to do and a short amount of time to do it in. First of all, the boss wants us out of here ASAP. Everything needs to be gone, lock, stock and barrel."

"Why? What's going on?" asked one of the men.

"For one thing," said Gus, "that damn Mexican," he paused for a second and then continued. "You remember the one who was so cocky?"

"You mean the one named Felipe?" asked Pinky.

"Yeah, that's the guy. Anyway, it seems that when he snuck outta here he didn't die in the brush like we thought. He made it to the main road."

"You mean he got away?" asked another man.

"Well, not exactly," answered Gus. "They found him dead up on the road."

"Not good," said Pinky.

Gus said, "Not good at all. But they didn't just find him dead, they found that he was radioactive, too."

After hearing that, Landen's eyes opened up wider than usual and he continued to listen closely.

"Now they've got the whole town locked down and the boss said there's F.B.I. Agents crawling all over the place, along with O.E.S. engines and crews. This whole thing's turned into a big mess. The boss is starting to get a little nervous and wants us to shut the operation down until things cool off."

"What about the rest of the gold?" Pinky asked.

Gus turned toward Pinky and said, "We need to pack up what we've got and drop it off at Turner's place so we can make some more fishing weights."

"Do we have enough silver spray paint?" asked Pinky.

"We should," answered Gus. "The boss bought two cases of the stuff. Right now," Gus continued, as he looked straight at Pinky, "I need you to make a quick trip to that Willy guy's place and pick up one last load of ice and rock salt."

"I'm on my way," said Pinky, hurrying toward one of the pickup trucks.

While we sat in silence listening to Gus bark out orders to the remaining men, the hot sun was becoming very uncomfortable. I hadn't gotten over my sunburn from two days ago and now here I was sitting in the hot sun again, begging for more. It was not yet clear what Gus had planned for us three but the chances of us getting out of here alive were beginning to look pretty slim.

Ted leaned toward me and whispered, "Did you hear him mention the word gold?"

"Yeah," I answered. "I also heard him say something about Turner's."

"You don't suppose he's talking about that old Turner's Foundry, do you?" asked Ted.

"Probably one in the same," I answered.

"But that place hasn't been used since the end of the Depression," said Ted.

I looked over at Landen and asked, "Wouldn't this gold they're talking about be extremely radioactive if they're digging it out of that meteor?"

"That's debatable," answered Landen. "The outer crust of the meteor would be highly radioactive but the closer you got to the center, the less radioactive it becomes. It's more likely than not," continued Landen, "that if there is any gold at all in that meteor it would have to be in the inner layers."

CHAPTER TWENTY-EIGHT

Sheriff Arby and Captain Mason got back into the squad car and proceeded down the street. The Captain looked at the Sheriff and asked, "Got any ideas?"

"I think we need to examine our clues," answered the Sheriff. "We've got five people with radiation poisoning. We've got a transient that apparently died from radiation poisoning. We've got that same transient that swallowed the gold nuggets. And last of all, we've got the three pieces of gold that were radioactive before they were melted down."

"It seems like everything points toward radiation and the gold," said Mason thoughtfully. "And without any idea where this gold came from, it appears like we're at a dead end." After a few seconds of silently thinking, Mason continued, "It seems that the only other thing that you got in this town that is possibly radioactive is that show rock you were talking about at your Courthouse."

The Sheriff looked at Mason then said, "Do you think that rock might be connected to this in some way?"

"I'm not sure," said the Captain. "But right now it's the only lead we've got."

"I guess you're right," said Sheriff Arby. "Let's go take a look. Besides, I haven't seen that rock for quite a while. Maybe it will bring back some pleasant memories."

"I don't know about memories," said Mason, "but I'd kind of like to see the thing just for the sheer history and legend that goes along with it."

They drove into the Courthouse parking area and got out of the squad car. They walked up the stairs and went to the front door, then the Sheriff took a ring of keys off of a clip fastened to his belt and found the key that unlocked the door. They walked in and the Sheriff turned on the light fixtures.

"There," he said. "I know it's daytime but it's a lot easier to see in here with the lights on. When they built this place they were worried that convicts on trial might try to escape by jumping through a window."

"Yeah, I see what you mean. The lights really help you to see. It's rather warm in here, don't you think so?" said the Captain.

"Give it a minute," said the Sheriff. "I turned the A/C on when I turned on the lights but it takes a while to cool this place down. Come on over here," the Sheriff said as he walked over to the opposite wall, pointing at a mounted display box with a shelf underneath it. "The rock is right over here in this box if you want to take a good look."

"Yes," said the Captain. "I'd like that." When they came up to the shelf the Captain's eyes widened just a bit. "Wow! That is some rock! It's so odd looking." He continued to stare at the rock and then said, "I've never seen anything like it in my life."

"That's what everybody says when they see it for the first time," said the Sheriff. "They act like it's something from out of this world."

The Captain got closer and looked at the plaque that went with the rock and read it out loud. " '*Jefferson City Is A 'Rock-In' Town Thanks For The Hospitality Elvis'* Incredible!" he said. "This thing's probably worth thousands of dollars."

"That's what we figure," said the Sheriff. "That's why we keep it here in the Courthouse. So it doesn't grow legs and walk away."

"Where did you say they found this?" the Captain asked.

"Out there on that B.L.M. land north of town," answered the Sheriff.

"Well," said the Captain slowly, "you are aware of what the B.L.M. stands for, aren't you? It stands for Bureau of Land Management. Which means that it is land owned by the Federal Government?"

"Yes. I'm aware of that," said Sheriff Arby. "Why? What are you getting at?"

Captain Mason, still looking at the rock in the display case said, "Then, actually, this rock is Federal property."

The Sheriff gave him a stern look and said, "Well, the way I look at it is this, Captain, the rock might be Federal property. Legally it makes no difference to anyone. But I'll tell you this, the airtight box and the plaque were a present to this town from Elvis and that's not Federal property. So anytime you want to take that radioactive rock out of that there airtight box you go right ahead. The bottom line here is, that box stays mounted to this wall in this Courthouse here in Jefferson City. And that is all I'm going to say about it."

The Captain gave Arby a rather apologetic look and said, "No, no. I didn't mean I wanted to take the rock. I was just merely pointing out the fact that B.L.M. land is Federal property. That's all." After a few seconds of silence, the Captain said, "I remember you saying something about a map."

The Sheriff gave him a suspicious look and then said, "We already know the rock came from Federal land."

The Captain said, "No, I'm not going there. The rock belongs to the town and it will be kept here. I just thought we might take a look at the map. Maybe we could find some type of clue to the radiation poisoning. Something that would tie in the transient and the five patients over there at your clinic."

"Good idea," said the Sheriff. "I believe there's a copy of it over at the City Hall. Let's see if I can get one of these dedicated City employees to come down here on their Saturday off and give us a hand." The Sheriff made a quick phone call then he said, "Phyllis, the head clerk, will be down there directly. She said to meet her there. Let's go ahead and lock this place up and get on over there. We don't want to keep her waiting."

The Captain took one last look at the rock in the case and then said, "Yep, that thing is quite unusual."

The Sheriff locked up the Courthouse and they both got back into the squad car and drove off toward City Hall.

When they arrived at the City Offices, Phyllis was just pulling up in her car. As she got out, Sheriff Arby walked over and introduced Captain Mason. "He's with the F.B.I.," the Sheriff said.

"My goodness," said Phyllis. "What's all the excitement about around here? The roads are all blocked off and the F.B.I. is all over town. What happened? Did someone rob a bank?"

"No, nothing like that," answered the Captain. "We're just investigating a radiation scare."

"Well, I sure hope everything is going to be OK," she said.

"Don't worry," said the Captain. "Everything will be fine."

Phyllis turned to look at both the Sheriff and the Captain and then said, "Well, I guess you boys are here to look at some documents, so let's go on inside and see what you need."

When they got in the Records Room, Phyllis asked, "What year records are you looking for, Sheriff?"

"They'd be back in the sixties," answered the Sheriff.

"All that stuff in on micro film index cards," she said. "You'll need to step over here to one of these computers in our work area and type in a name." The Captain followed as she led the Sheriff to a computer desk. She turned on the machine and said, "What exactly are you looking for? Some kind of Grant Deed or something like that?"

The Sheriff replied, "Well, actually we're looking for a claim form that has a map attached."

The woman looked at the Sheriff and raised one eyebrow. After looking at the two of them for a second or two she said, "You're kidding me, right, Sheriff? Is this just some kind of a joke?"

"No, I'm afraid he's quite serious," interrupted the Captain.

"Yes," said the Sheriff. "We're looking for the claim form that was filed years ago when Elvis and his boys found that rock that's over at the Courthouse."

Phyllis stood there staring at them both as though she was in a trance, not speaking, not moving a face muscle. Finally she said, in a very sharp voice as she walked toward them, "You mean to tell me that you called me all the way down here on my day off for this shenanigan that you're trying to pull on me?"

The Captain and the Sheriff both backed away from her as she continued walking toward them, her voice erupting with a tirade of words aimed at them, "You told me over the phone that this was an emergency! You said this was important!" she said, pointing her finger at each of them. She kept walking toward the two men as they continued to back up. "Do you realize that I was at home enjoying a first run movie with my husband and kids? And now, here I am in the middle of your game, while the two of you play your little joke on me. And by now I have probably missed the best part of the movie. All because of this!" she said, while she threw her hands up in the air.

Finally the Sheriff shouted out, "Phyllis! Get a hold of yourself!"

She stopped short and looked at the Sheriff. "Now look," continued the Sheriff, "I know this sounds kind of kooky, like it must be a joke or something, but we're dead serious here. We'd like to take a look at that old claim form to see if we can find any pertinent information."

Phyllis looked at both men and then said, "I'm sorry. I shouldn't have talked to you boys like that. But to be quite honest with you, I wouldn't have any idea where to find something like that. We deal mostly with Grant Deeds, Birth and Death Certificates, you know, that sort of thing. If, and that's a big if, if it was filed, it would have been filed as a land usage permit request with the Federal Government because, as I've heard tell, they found that rock out there on the B.L.M. land." After thinking for a moment, she continued, "But they would have had to file it in triplicate because the land is located in the County of Jefferson."

"So, what would we look under?" asked Sheriff Arby.

"Well, it would certainly help if we knew who filed for the permit," answered Phyllis.

"Why don't you just type in the name 'Elvis' and see what comes up?" said the Captain.

"I'd be great if it was that easy," said the Sheriff, "but the request for the claim wasn't made by him. It was done by that roustabout guy that was handling the whole operation out there."

"You don't have any idea what his name was?" asked Phyllis.

"Not a clue," answered the Sheriff.

"Let me think a bit," said Phyllis. Then she said, "I suppose we can go by the year and check that way. But let me warn you, it will be like looking for a needle in a haystack because there are tens of thousands of items recorded. What year would you like to start with?" she asked.

The Sheriff thought for a minute, back to when he and his sister had actually met Elvis, when they were selling the mints. "That would have to be nineteen sixty-one," answered the Sheriff.

"Nineteen sixty-one it is, then," she said, typing in the year. Instantly, a page of names and dates came on the screen. "Now, gentlemen, this could take all day, so I'm going to show you the process and let you carry on by yourselves. If you look closely at the screen you'll see each item recorded has a reference number to a book. These books have been put on microfilm and index cards that show each page. Those cards are over here in this file," she continued as she led them both over to the file card index on the other side of the room. "Each has a book and series of page numbers. When you find the book and page you're looking for, you take out the file card and install it in one of these projectors over here," she said, pointing to a row of projectors sitting on a long table. "After you view the file card, if it's the document you're looking for, then you simply walk in this room over here," she said, as they followed her into the next room, "and stick the card in this special copier. Center it on the document that you want printed by looking in the viewer to locate it and print out a paper copy of the document. Do you have any questions?"

The Sheriff looked at the Captain, then they both looked back at Phyllis. Sheriff Arby said, "It kinda sounds like you're getting ready to go someplace."

"You're very perceptive, Sheriff," Phyllis said. "I am going someplace. I'm going home to finish watching what's left of the movie with my family."

"But you can't leave us by ourselves," said the Captain. "We don't know how to work this stuff."

"You're both big boys. I'm sure you'll figure it out," she said as she grabbed her purse and headed out the front door.

The Captain looked at the Sheriff and said, "I guess we're on our own."

The Sheriff said, "It sure looks that way." He looked at the computers sitting on the computer stands and said, "Well, I guess we'd better get busy here."

"I've got an idea," said the Captain.

"What's that?" asked the Sheriff.

"It looks like there are five computers here. I'll get a few of my agents over here and we can use all five computers at the same time and narrow the time line down."

"Good idea, Captain," said the Sheriff.

In no time at all the five computers were in use searching for the fabled document. After working for several hours, one of the Agents shouted, "I think I've found something, Captain!"

The Captain and the Sheriff both got up from their computers and hurried to see what the Agent had found. It was a claim form requesting the mineral rights to a certain section of property located twenty-two degrees west of Township twenty-five and a section of Township twenty-six. Just north of a monument named Tranquility Ridge.

"Have you ever heard of something called Tranquility Ridge?" the Captain asked Arby.

Laughing, the Sheriff said, "Yes. But I haven't heard it called that in years."

"Where's it located?" asked Mason.

"It's outside of town," answered the Sheriff. "On the B.L.M. land. But these days everybody calls it Wild Cat Ridge."

"Evidently there another page here, Cappy," said the F.B.I. Agent. "It looks like some sort of a map."

"This must be what we're looking for!" said the Sheriff.

They took the microfilm card out of the projector and walked over to the copier and after a short time of trial and error, they printed out copies of the two documents.

Looking at the claim form, the Captain said, "This claim was requested by a guy named Bert Barkley."

"That must have been the name of the roustabout that they hired to test the rock sample," said the Sheriff.

"I wonder where this guy is today? You know, whatever became of him? Just for the heck of it," said Captain Mason, "Let's run this guy's name through our F.B.I. computer data base filing system and see what we come up with." The Captain walked over to a computer sitting in the office and turned it on to access the Federal Files. After a moment or so he typed in numerous code words and entered into the F.B.I. Network. After several minutes and the process of elimination, he said, "Here we are, Sheriff. His full name was Bert Robert Barkley. He was born on May 12th 1935. Unfortunately, he passed away about six months ago. He was married to a Martha Frances Barkley who is deceased also. They had one child, a girl named Frances Constance Barkley."

Sheriff Arby replied, "End of story, I guess."

"Kind of looks that way," said Captain Mason.

Just then, the F.B.I. Agent who had found the claim called out to them from the other room. "Hey, Cappy! Come look at this!"

The Captain and the Sheriff hurried in to take a look at whatever the agent had found.

"I typed this Barkley guy's name into the document computer and look what I found," the Agent said. "He refiled for the same mineral rights claim in his own name in 1967 but the Federal Government denied it. Then he resubmitted it in 1982. The B.L.M. denied that request also. After that he waited fifteen years and resubmitted the claim once again in 1997. That claim was denied and that's the last entry that is listed in the file."

"Hum," said the Captain, turning toward the Sheriff. "I thought you said that the rock material they found out there was some type of nuclear waste from those atomic bomb tests."

"That's what everyone was told," said Sheriff Arby.

"Well, something just doesn't add up here," said Captain Mason. "If it were just some type of worthless material, why would this Barkley guy keep trying to obtain the mineral rights to this B.L.M. land?"

"It does make you wonder, doesn't it?" the Sheriff answered. "Another thing that's rather odd is that it was this Barkley guy who ran the test on the material."

CHAPTER TWENTY-NINE

It had been quite a while since I had heard from Connie. I figured that it must be about four o'clock by now and I knew that Connie must be quite worried about Ted and me. I wished that I could get my hands on my cell phone or at least feel the vibration on my leg. I just wanted to have some sense of something normal around me. We all sat as still as possible so as not to attract attention from any one.

As Pinky drove off in the pickup truck for Willy's place, Gus barked out orders to the other men. "Two of you boys start taking down that lean-to and fold that tarp up nice and neat." Two men ran over and began taking the poles down that supported the large tarp and then folded the tarp up. They placed everything into the back of the big truck.

Gus looked around to make sure everyone was working as fast as they could to get everything cleaned up and cleared out. He noticed that two men were just standing there, so he pointed at them and shouted out, "You two hook that flat bed trailer up to the big truck."

"You got it, Big Gus!" one of the men shouted as the two of them hurried over toward the trailer to get the job done. "What do ya want us to do with these three bums over here?" one of them asked as they got close to the trailer that we were sitting against.

"Push them out of your way!" yelled Gus back at them.

The men grabbed us one by one and hurled us off to the side.

Gus said to the last one of his boys, "Get your hands out of your pockets and get busy!"

"What do you want me to do, Big Gus?" he asked.

"Put on that radiation garb over there," said Gus, "and walk over and tell them two Mexicans to put the clean gold in the carrying box and pile the rest of the outer crap back into the hole, then cover it up. I want it to look natural. Understand?"

"Yes sir, Big Gus," he said. "Consider it done."

While the two men were preparing to hook the trailer up, one of them screwed the cap on a bottle of water he'd been sipping from and set it on the flat bed trailer. When they raised up the trailer and hooked it up to the pickup truck, the bottle rolled off unnoticed by them into the dry bushes.

Ted looked at me and said quietly, "I sure could use a sip of that water right about now."

"Try not to think about it," I said. "They'll give us some water before too long."

"Do you really think they will?" asked Ted.

"Sure they will," I said, trying to smile. "I haven't lied to you yet, have I?"

Ted thought for a moment and said, "I don't know. Have you?"

"Of course not," I said, still trying to keep a slight smile on my face. "Now try to think about something else for awhile."

Ted closed his eyes and drifted off. I knew I'd just lied to him. There was no way these people were going to give us water. But I had to keep his hope alive and keep his spirits up. Without hope we wouldn't stand a chance.

With the trailer hooked up and the lean-to taken down and put into the truck bed, Gus waited for Pinky to get back from Slick Willy's place. The men were kept busy tidying up the area by scattering the rocks that had served as their cooking pit and covering up the ashes so that there was no visible sign that they had been there at all.

The man walked back from where the two Mexicans were busy working. As he began to take off his radiation protection suit he told Gus, "The gold's in the lead lined box and I got them Mexicans covering up the outside of the mound. You know," he continued, "them Mexicans ain't doing too good. One's having trouble standing up and the other one is all bloated up."

"Well," said Gus, "I'm kind of glad to hear that."

"What do you mean?" he asked in a rather shocked tone.

Gus gave him a mean look and said, "Because we're going to do the humane thing and put them out of their misery just as soon as Pinky gets back."

Hearing that news, Ted's eyes opened up wide. "Did he just say he's going to put us out of our misery?" he asked me.

"No, Ted," I answered. "He's talking about those Hispanics over there. Evidently they've got advanced stages of radiation poisoning."

When Pinky drove up after going to Willy's, one of the men drove the tractor over and loaded up the rock salt from the back of the pickup truck into the bucket of the tractor. He then drove it up to the pit and off loaded it to the side. While he was busy unloading the rock salt, the rest of the men rearranged the ice in the back of Pinky's truck to accommodate the shipment they were about to load up. One man slipped on the radiation protective garb as Pinky got in the truck and backed up part of the way toward the meteor. Then Pinky stopped and waited while the two Mexicans stumbled over with the small lead lined box and placed it on the bags of ice in the back of the truck. The two workers then covered the box in bags of ice while the man in the radiation garb supervised the operation.

When they were nearing the completion of their task at the truck, the man who was driving the tractor back from the pit area came up to where the two Hispanics were leaning against the side of the truck bed. He lowered the front loader bucket and shouted out, "Get in!"

The two Hispanic men looked at him not quite understanding what he wanted them to do.

"Get in!" he shouted again pointing to the bucket. "Ándale! Ándale!"

The two men were too weak to fight. They slowly drug their spent bodies into the bucket and lay against the back of it. The man lifted the bucket up and drove off toward the pit.

With the gold in the lead lined box, it was not quite as dangerous but when it was covered and kept at low temperatures with the ice, it stabilized the alpha particles and made them virtually harmless. When the gold was taken to the foundry and processed at close to two thousand degrees, the heat melted the gold and neutralized the neutrons and protons and made it suitable for marketing with very low levels of radioactive particles, if any at all.

When the man with the tractor got to the pit area, he raised the bucket high over the open pit and tilted the front. The two men went sliding out of the bucket and into the pit, screaming weak screams of fear with whatever life they had left in them.

Landen looked at Ted and I and said, "This is out and out murder. We need to do something."

"There's nothing we can do," I said. "Our hands are tied behind our backs and if we make too much of a fuss they'll put us in that pit with those poor souls."

While the man on the tractor spread bucket after bucket of dirt on top of the two Mexicans, another man scattered the bags of rock salt in-between the layers of dirt. The weak screams faded until, soon, there were no screams at all. There was just the sound of the tractor engine running. Tears came to Landen's eyes as he heard the last faint scream fade away.

Ted looked over at me and in a matter of fact tone asked, "Do you think that's what they've got planned for us?"

"I sure hope not," I said, not even wanting to think about it and feeling very shaky. "It seems to me that if they were going to bury us in that pit they would have already done it by now."

Just then, when the man got back there with the tractor, he yelled at Gus, "Got anything else you want me to put into the pit before I cover it up for good?" After that was said the man glanced over at the three of us sitting in the hot sun. Chills ran down my back just thinking about what was about to happen to us.

Then Big Gus pointed to several big bags sitting on the ground close to where the lean-to had been. "Yeah," he said, "take them bags of garbage and stick them in there and then cover it up nice and neat. I don't want anyone to be able to tell what we've been doing out here."

The man threw the garbage into the bucket and drove back to dump it into the pit and then finished covering it up. A sigh of relief fell over me when I heard him yell out that they were all done covering up the pit. Still, I knew Big Gus had something planned for us three and I was sure it wasn't going to be nice. After covering up the pit and grading the area with the tractor, the pit looked like it had never been there at all. The man then drove the tractor over to the trailer and, with a little help from some of the boys, got it loaded and strapped down on the trailer.

With the camp all cleaned up and the gold ready to transport, Gus called all the men together one last time. "OK, boys. Listen up!" Gus shouted out. "Here's the plan. We're going to take the gold over to the old Turner place and process it. On the way out of here we're gonna pick up the vehicle the three low-lives came here in and drive it up past the Dell Ridge Exit and abandon it at the side of the road so they can't trace these guys back to here. And when we're all done with that, I got a little surprise for you boys."

"What's that Big Gus? Yeah, what's that Big Gus?" the men all began to shout out at the same time as if in unison.

"Well, boys," Gus said, "we ain't gonna go to town tonight."

"What cha mean we ain't gonna go to town tonight!" said one of the boys. "That ain't no surprise!"

"SHUT UP STUPID AND LET ME FINISH!" yelled Gus. "Anyway, we're not going to town tonight but we're going up to that motel in Dell Ridge and we get to spend a few weeks up there."

The boys all let out with a cheer. "That place is like a country club!" shouted one of the boys.

"Yeah!" said another. "They got a real nice bar up there!"

"And it's all compliments of the boss!" said Gus. "Now let's get going."

When the boys were all getting ready to leave, Big Gus walked over to us with a rope in his hand and looked down at us sitting in the sun with absolutely nothing around to shade us. He had a smile on his face as he said, "Well, Trouble, this is where we part ways." He tied our feet together so that there was no way we could stand up to try and get out of the sun when they all left. "You know, I could of thrown you and your two shit head friends here in that pit with them wetbacks and you'd be meeting your creator right about now. But instead I figured I'd give you a fighting chance. You boys can either shrivel up in the hot blistering sun and die out here or you can figure yourselves a way out of this mess. Either way it's outta my hands now." Gus gave another yank at the ropes binding us all together to make sure they held and then turned and walked off toward the truck to get a ride with the boys.

One of Gus's men yelled out, "They sure look like buzzard bait to me!" and the rest of the boys started laughing like a bunch of wild hyenas.

"What about the other hawk?" one of the men asked Gus.

"The boss said to leave it and the cameras out here. That way when we come back we'll be ready to pick up right where we left off," Gus replied.

With that said, they all got into the two trucks and drove out of the camp area and proceeded to the trail going out toward the highway.

We listened as their trucks drove off in the distance until the noise finally faded away.

"What are we going to do?" asked Landen.

"Whatever we do, let's think it out first," I answered. "There's no sense wasting a bunch of energy trying things that might fail because we don't have much energy left in us."

With the sun bearing down on us it was almost impossible to think. It was probably five-thirty, maybe six o'clock at the latest. We still had another two and a half hours at least to tough it out in this hot sun. And with no water, the odds of us making it were next to none.

Finally, Ted turned to me and said, "Jason? I don't think we're going to make it out of this alive, so I need to tell you something."

"What's that, Ted?" I asked.

"You won't be mad at me, will you?" he asked.

"No. No. Of course not," I said.

"Well," Ted continued, "do you remember the other night when you were in Arizona and no one could get hold of you?"

"Yeah. What about it?" I said with my curiosity starting to get the best of me.

"Well, Connie and I…"

"Connie and you what?" snapped Landen. "Spit it out, man!"

"Well, Connie and I got a little intimate," Ted said.

"You got a little intimate?" I asked.

"Well, actually," said Ted, "we got a lot intimate."

"You dirty bastard!" I said, struggling to get my hands and feet loose so I could get up and punch him on the other side of his head and give him matching bumps.

"Calm down!" said Ted as I struggled with all my might to get loose. "You said you wouldn't get mad!"

"That was before I knew what you were going to say!" I shouted. Suddenly, from all my struggling and from sheer determination, I felt my right hand slipping out from the leather strap it was tied with. I turned to Ted and said, "Make me mad! Make me real mad!"

"OK," said Ted. "Do you remember that time when we were kids and your Dad found out that you were smoking cigarettes and he spanked you till you couldn't sit down for a week?"

"Yeah, I remember that," I said. "How is that going to make me mad?"

"Well," said Ted with a bit of a smile on his face, "I'm the one who told him."

"That's it, you lousy pig!" I shouted. "You're dead meat now!" As I struggled again with all my might to get loose so I could give him what he deserved, my sweaty hand slid completely out of the leather strap. "I'M FREE!" I shouted pulling both hands out from in back of me.

Ted immediately cowered over toward his brother trying to hold his head down saying meekly, "Don't hit me. Don't hit me. I'm all tied up."

"There's no time for squabbling now," I said. "We need to untie these straps and this rope so we can get out of this blistering sun."

I untied the rope from around our feet and stood up. It felt good to get back on my feet. I immediately helped Ted and Landen untie the leather straps that were holding their hands. We were free men at last. Now the first thing we needed to do was to get out of the sun, so we ran over to some giant ferns and bushes, then collapsed in the shade.

"We need to keep our distance from that meteor," said Landen. "We certainly don't want to get contamination from the radiation."

When my body cooled off just a bit and I was able to think clearer, I remembered the bottle of water that I'd watched roll off the flat bed trailer and into the bushes earlier in the day. That was our only hope of survival. I gathered my strength and made a wild dash back into the hot sun for the bottle. Hopefully it wouldn't be too hard to find. I was lucky. It hadn't rolled far. I grabbed it and ran back for the shade.

Landen tried to grab the bottle out of my hand as soon as I returned but I pulled it away from him and held it up in the air. "Listen!" I yelled. "We've got a long way to walk to get out of here and this is the only water we have, so we need to ration it. Each of us will take one small sip. It won't be thirst quenching but it will help keep us alive. Understand?"

"Yeah, I understand," said Landen ashamedly.

"Yeah," said Ted. "Makes good sense."

We each passed around the bottle and took a small sip. My face felt like it was on fire from the over-exposure I had received sitting in the sun. I looked around at some of the green plants that were closer to the meteor. I spied, what appeared to be an aloe vera plant. But if it was then it was the biggest one I'd ever seen. It stood well over fifteen feet tall and was about six feet in diameter. I thought back to the nature class I had taken one weekend with my Boy Scout Troop. I was told that '*aloe vera*' were the Indian words for '*cool fire*'. Evidently they used the sap from the leaves to treat burns. I walked over to the plant and picked a few of its hard succulent leaves, snapped one in the middle and squeezed out the sap. Then I rubbed the sap from the inside of the leaf against my burning face. In a few seconds my blistering face started to cool. I rubbed some more on my neck and arms.

"Ted, Landen!" I yelled. "Come here!" When they came over to where I was I said, "Use some of this plant. It will treat your sunburn and cool your skin."

After we all had treated our skin with the aloe vera sap, and with our skin starting to feel somewhat better, we walked far away from the meteor area and regrouped in the shade.

"My phone!" I shouted. "I forgot all about my phone!"

I reached into my boot and pulled it out. I began to wonder why I hadn't felt it vibrate since Gus had called my number. Certainly Connie would have tried to call. She was not aware that I'd found out what had gone on with her and Ted, so I would think she would be getting worried about us and wonder how we were. When I opened up my cell phone I was horrified. It had shut itself off. I immediately turned it on only to see *Low Battery* flash across the screen.

"I'm an idiot!" I shouted.

"What's the matter?" asked Ted.

"Oh, I forgot to charge my phone last night before I went to bed," I said in disgust.

"Don't be so hard on yourself," said Landen. "I've done that once or twice myself."

"I know," I said. "But this is so important to us. It might have been our only way out of here." Just then I thought of an idea. I remembered back to when I was a kid and I had a transistor radio with a nine-volt battery. When the battery would get weak I used to heat it up in a pan on the stove for a minute or so and the heat would put a temporary charge on the battery. It would never last too long but it worked for a short time. I wondered if something like that would work on my cell phone battery. I quickly took the battery out of my phone and found a rock sitting in the hot sun. I ran to the rock and lay the battery on it then ran back into the shade. I had no idea if it would actually work but I knew that at this point it certainly wasn't going to hurt.

While I waited to see if the battery would charge, I noticed that Landen had picked up two small tree branches and was securing them together with one of the leather straps that our hands had been tied with.

I looked at Ted and asked, "What's he making?"

Ted said, "I'm not sure."

Landen looked over and saw the both of us staring at him. "I don't want either of you to laugh at me but I'm making a holy cross as a grave marker for those poor souls buried in that pit."

"We wouldn't laugh at you," said Ted.

"Of course not," I said. "As a matter of fact I think it's very righteous of you. We'll stop by and put it by the pit on our way to the road."

While Landen worked on the cross I broke off some large fronds from a nearby fern plant.

"What are you going to do with those?" asked Ted.

"I figured we can tie them together at the stems and put them over our heads to keep the sun off our necks and faces," I replied.

"Good idea!" said Ted. "I'll unravel some of the rope our feet were tied with and we can use it to tie the leaves together with."

In a short while I had one of the hats complete. It was shaped something like an Indian teepee. When I put it over my head, Ted and Landen started to laugh. Although the situation we were in at the moment wasn't very funny, a little humor didn't hurt. It helped relieve the tension.

I looked at them through the small openings in the leaves and said laughingly, "I'm thinking of marketing it. I'm going to call it 'Tropical Teepee Topper' or 'T T T' for short. It'll be the new sensation. Everybody will want one."

As Ted busied himself constructing two more toppers, I walked over and picked up my cell phone battery off of the rock. I walked back over to the shade and took the fern leaf hat off my head. When I stuck the battery back in the phone I could see that it was still weak but somewhat stronger than before. I immediately pushed Connie's number on my speed dial.

"It's ringing!" I shouted out in joy. It continued to ring...two...three...four... *Why isn't she answering?* I asked myself. On the seventh ring her answering machine came on, *"Hi. You've reached the Fowler Residence. We're not in at the moment so please leave a message at the sound of the beep."* I quickly turned off my phone to save the weak battery. There was no sense in leaving an urgent message if Connie wasn't home. Besides, it would just worry her when she returned. The best thing for me to do right now is to call 911 for help. I turned my phone back on and dialed 911.

In a few rings a woman answered, "This is 911. What's your emergency?"

"Hi. I'm Jason T. Harmony..."

"Could you please speak up sir? I'm having trouble hearing you," the woman said.

"I'm Jason Harmony!" I repeated loudly. "We need help!"

"What seems to be the problem?" she asked.

"We've been left to die!"

"Just a minute," she said. "You keep saying 'we'. How many people are with you?"

"Two!" I shouted. "Two people! We have no water! We're out on the B.L.M. land by Wild Cat Ridge! Could you please send help!" As I listened for her reply, all I could hear was silence.

"**HELLO? HELLO?**" I took my phone away from my ear and looked at the screen. It was blank.

"What did they say?" asked Landen.

"Nothing," I answered. "My phone just went dead."

"But you were talking to the 911 operator," said Ted.

"Yes," I said. "But I'm not sure how much she heard before my phone stopped working."

"Well, let's just hope that she heard enough," said Landen.

"I sure hope so," I said. "Either way, we need to start our long walk out of this place while we still have some water left."

We all put on our 'toppers' and got ready to leave. Landen grabbed his cross and we started on our way. When we came to the pit area, Landen triumphantly stuck his cross into the dirt. We knelt down and blessed all of the poor men who were buried in that horrible pit. When we were finished we headed back toward the narrow dirt road on our walk to the Highway.

CHAPTER THIRTY

The Captain looked at the Sheriff and asked, "Where exactly was this transient found? Was it close to this B.L.M. land?"

"Not far from it," the Sheriff answered. "It was on the highway by the old logging claim." The Sheriff turned to the F.B.I. agent and said, "Let me see a copy of that map Barkley filed." As the Captain and the Sheriff studied the roughly drawn map, the Sheriff pointed toward the edge of the map and said, "The highway would be located over here. I'll tell you what, let's drive up there and I'll show you exactly where we found the guy."

"Great!" said the Captain. "Let's go."

While the Sheriff and the Captain prepared to go, the Captain turned to the three F.B.I. Agents and said, "I want you men to follow the Sheriff and myself. We might need a little assistance."

"Yes sir, Cappy!" said one of the men. All three men followed the Captain to their cars as Sheriff Arby locked up the County Building.

When Sheriff Arby got into the squad car where the Captain was waiting for him, they took off for the highway and were followed closely by the three F.B.I. Agents.

After driving for a minute or so, they came to one of the roadblocks that Captain Mason had set up blocking the roads in and out of town. As they rolled up to the O.E.S. officers who were controlling the roadblock, Captain Mason rolled down his window and flipped his badge I.D. and asked one of the Officers, "Had any trouble?"

"No sir, Captain!" he replied standing straight as if he were at attention.

"You haven't let anybody in or out, right?" continued the Captain.

"Just the one lady," answered the Officer. "Nobody else."

The Captain looked at the Sheriff and then turned back to the Officer. "The one lady?" he asked. "What one lady?"

"The one your office called about and said to let through," replied the Officer. "The undercover C.I.A. woman, sir."

"First of all," said the Captain, getting quite red in the face, "my office doesn't give any orders! I give the orders! And secondly, we're not associated with the C.I.A. We're independent organizations, so we'd have no way of knowing if there were a C.I.A. agent in town! What did this woman look like?" the Captain asked, getting very upset.

The Officer replied, "Good looking woman. She had blonde hair and was quite shapely."

"What was the license plate number of her vehicle?" asked the Captain sharply.

"You know," said the Officer, "I didn't really notice."

"What kind of car was she driving?" barked the Captain.

"That I did notice," said the Officer. "It was a blue one."

The Captain turned to the Sheriff and said impatiently, "Does it sound like anybody you know?"

"Not right off hand," replied the Sheriff.

The Captain turned back to the Officer and said, "Did you I.D. her?"

"Yes, sir!" answered the Officer. "I wrote her name down on our clipboard. Let me go get that for you sir."

The Captain looked up and closed his eyes and said out loud, "God, what did I do to deserve this?" Then he opened his eyes and said to the Sheriff, "Thank God for small favors."

The Officer hurried back over to the squad car with the clip board in his hand and said to the Captain, "Sir. It was a Miss

Frances Barkley, sir. But her real name was Margaret Thatcher. She said she's working undercover, sir."

Sheriff Arby started laughing and said, "This is getting better as we go along. Ask him some more questions, Captain."

Just then, Captain Mason's eyes opened wide and he exclaimed, "BARKLEY! That's the name of the guy that filed for the claim."

"Wasn't his wife's name Frances?" asked the Sheriff.

"It was," replied the Captain. "It was also his daughter's name. The Captain turned back to the O.E.S. Officer and asked, "How long ago did you let this woman through here?"

"It was about an hour ago, sir. Let me check the clipboard for the exact time. Yes, one hour ago," the Officer replied.

The Sheriff looked at the Captain and said, "We need to get an A.P.B. out on this woman right away."

"Yes," Mason said. "We definitely need to find her so we can get the answers to a few questions."

Arby radioed his dispatch and said, "Put out an All Points Bulletin on a blue late model car with an attractive woman driver with long blonde hair. Left the town of Jefferson City approximately sixty minutes ago. Direction of travel unknown at this time."

After the Sheriff was finished, the dispatcher said, "Sheriff, we just got a call in from 911 a few moments ago. They said the caller's transmission was somewhat garbled and broken but the operator was able to obtain that it was a Jason Harmony and something about two people who have no water. She thinks it might be some kind of prank call. But she did hear the word 'help,' so she thought she'd better report it."

The Sheriff replied, "Yes, Jason T. Harmony. He's been working with the Meade Brothers. He's not the type of person to make a prank call. Did the operator get a location on where he was calling from?" asked the Sheriff.

"Yes," answered the dispatcher. "The operator picked up a G.P.S. signal from his cell phone. It appeared he was located west of Highway 88 somewhere north of town."

"Humm," said the Sheriff. "That would put him somewhere over on that B.L.M. land. I'm heading up toward Highway 88 right now. I'll take a look around and see what I can find." After that, the Sheriff and Mason took off from the roadblock and headed for the Highway.

When the Sheriff turned onto the Highway, the three F.B.I. Agents were right on his tail. The Captain looked out the back window of the squad car at his three agents in hot pursuit and then turned to the Sheriff and asked, "Have you ever tried to lose an F.B.I. Agent that was on your tail?" Before the Sheriff could answer, the Captain continued, "It's impossible," he said. "We train our Agents on a tedious obstacle course. Each Agent must complete five hundred hours of training and pass two hundred different scenarios and tests."

As the Captain continued to talk about the driving abilities of his Agents, Sheriff Arby was nearing No Pay Grade. When he started climbing the Grade he stepped down on the accelerator pedal and increased his speed to seventy-five miles per hour.

The Captain continued to brag about his agents. "They have to take a one hundred hour re-certification course every year.."

The Sheriff interrupted the Captain and turned his eyes briefly toward him and said, "Are you trying to insinuate that there's no way I could lose your boys, even if I felt like it?"

"That's exactly what I'm saying," replied the Captain, with a smug smile on his face. "These boys are good!"

"Well, let's just see how good they are," said Sheriff Arby. By now he was almost to the top of the Grade traveling seventy-five miles an hour in the fast lane. As he neared the last cutout in the center lane divider, and with the F.B.I. Agents right on his tail, he slammed on his brakes and locked them up to the horror of the F.B.I. Agents in the car directly in back of him. With their faces pale white and their eyes almost popping out of their heads, the driver quickly switched into the right hand lane passing the squad car at a high rate of speed as the Sheriff skidded into the road divider cutout and then turned onto to the other side of the Highway, heading in the opposite direction, and sped away, leaving the F.B.I. Agents heading to the top of No Pay Grade with absolutely no place to turn around except for the Dell Ridge Exit, which was quite a ways up the road.

With that accomplished, the Sheriff turned to the Captain, who still had his hands glued to the dash from the quick maneuvering, and said, "Your boys might be good but they ain't nothing to write home about." Then he let out a great big belly laugh. When they were close to where the transient had been found, the Sheriff pulled over to the side of the road and parked.

"This is the place, right?" asked the Captain still trying to get his composure back.

"Yep!" said Sheriff Arby, pointing to a place on the shoulder of the road. "It was right over in that area." When the Sheriff stepped out of the squad car, he noticed the Meade Mobile traveling up No Pay Grade on the other side of the road. He quickly turned to the Captain and said, "Get a hold of your boys and tell them to stop where they're at and wait for a funny looking van to pass them, then follow it. If it pulls over for one reason or another, have them detain the occupants until we get there."

The Captain got on his radiophone and relayed the Sheriff's message to his Agents. He turned to the Sheriff and asked, "They want to know how they'll be able to tell what kind of van is a funny looking one?"

"Trust me," said the Sheriff. "They'll know! But if it helps them any, tell them it has Meade Investigations written on the sides."

When the Captain finished relaying the message to his Agents he turned to the Sheriff and asked, "What does the van have to do with anything?"

"Well," replied the Sheriff, "you remember the 911 call that I was talking to my dispatcher about?"

"Yeah," said the Captain. "What about it?"

"The guy that made the call," said the Sheriff, "works with the two brothers that own that truck. They were doing a little bit of detective work for me. It seems rather strange that they'd be heading in that direction. I need to have a little chat with them."

Then the Sheriff started walking toward the area where the transient was found and said, "Let's go over here and take a look around."

"OK," said Captain Mason. "I'm right behind you."

While they both walked over and were looking around, the Captain stopped and stared down the side of the road a ways. "What do you see?" asked the Sheriff.

"Looks like some tire tracks down there coming up from out of the bushes," answered the Captain.

"I believe you're right," said Sheriff Arby, starting to head down toward the tracks. When he got to the tracks he knelt down to take a closer look. He looked up at the Captain and said, "Mason, that's exactly what they are. Dirty tire tracks coming from right down there." The Sheriff pointed down to the heavily vegetated area off the side of the road.

"Let's go have a look see," said the Captain.

"Watch your step," cautioned the Sheriff as they both started to climb down the bank.

Once they got down the bank it wasn't long before they discovered the shrubbery covering up the entrance to the old logging trail.

"Gee, I forgot all about this old road," said the Sheriff. "It's been years since they used this for logging."

"Looks like somebody's been using it quite a lot lately," replied the Captain.

"You know," said the Sheriff, "just looking at this old road makes me think it has something to do with that 911 call they got from Jason T."

"You're probably right," said the Captain. "Do you want to try and drive the squad car down here and follow it for a ways?"

"I'm thinking we'd probably get stuck," said the Sheriff. "Can you call for one of the O.E.S. units? They got them long wheel base fire trucks. Probably wouldn't have any trouble at all driving this old road."

"You're right," said the Captain. "I'll get one out here right away." After calling for the O.E.S. truck, they both climbed back up the bank and waited for the truck to arrive. It wasn't long before they saw the truck coming up No Pay Grade with its lights flashing and its siren blaring. It drove through the cutout in the center divider and came to a halt at the rear of the squad car.

The men jumped out of the truck and the Sheriff and Captain both pointed out the old logging trail. "We want you to drive that old logging road and keep your eyes open," said the Sheriff. "We got a 911 call and it's just possible somebody might be in trouble out there."

While the men got back into the truck, the Sheriff walked over to the driver and said, "Make sure you men keep in radio contact with us."

"Will do, Sheriff," said the driver as he drove down the bank toward the old logging trail.

The Captain and the Sheriff watched as the fire truck disappeared down the trail, then walked over and got back into the squad car. "I guess we'd better go on up and see what your boys are doing," the Sheriff said, looking at the Captain.

CHAPTER THIRTY-ONE

The farther we walked up the narrow road, the heavier our topper hats became. After walking for less than a mile, Landen turned to me and said, "Jason, I need a sip of water. My throat is so dry it hurts."

"OK," I said, "but just one small sip. This water has got to last us all the way out of here. And just remember, if we run out of water we won't get out of here alive." I handed him the bottle and he lifted up the bottom of his teepee topper and took a small sip and then handed it back to me. "What about you?" I asked Ted.

"No," answered Ted. "My throat's not completely dry yet. I can go a while longer."

When I stuck the warm bottle of water back into my pocket I thought to myself, *This water is so hot that if I was back home I would have never bothered to swallow it. I would have spit it out once it touched my mouth.* It's kind of funny how you don't appreciate something so slight and unnoticed until you don't have it anymore.

While we walked along in our teepee hats, the animals that scampered by looked at us oddly, not knowing if we were some kind of a new walking variety of tree or just weird looking humans. Down the road we could see the trees off in the far distance. It would easily take us an hour to get to their shade. Although our heads were shaded with our hats, the rest of our clothes were scorching from the rays of the hot sun. Suddenly, Ted tripped and fell to the ground. His head was still swollen from the blow he'd received from the butt of the shotgun.

"Are you alright!?" I yelled as I knelt down by him.

"My knee," he said, in a very painful voice. "My knee hurts pretty bad."

I rolled up his pant leg and examined his knee. There was a small cut, probably from a sharp rock when he fell.

"Here, try to stand up," I said holding my hand out for him to grab onto.

As I stood up, he tried to stand up with me and immediately started to fall. I quickly reached over and grabbed his shirt and pulled him back up. He got his balance but when he tried to put his weight on his right leg he started to fall again. "It's not going to work," he said. "I can't walk. Just leave me here and when you get out and get some help you can come back for me."

"Oh, no. That's not going to happen," I said. "I'll get you out of here if I have to carry you out."

"After what I did to you?" Ted said in a small voice.

"What did you do to me?" I asked.

"You know, going behind your back with Connie when she's supposed to be your girlfriend and all," Ted replied.

'You know, Ted," I said, "I've been thinking about that and it takes two people to 'tango', as they say. If Connie really cared for me as much as she put on then she would have never gotten intimate with you. Especially when she was supposedly so worried about me because she hadn't heard from me when I didn't arrive at the airport on my scheduled flight."

"Well," said Ted, "I know it wasn't right what I did, but if it's any conciliation to you, Connie came on to me. I didn't force myself on her. I should have thought before I acted. But it all happened so quickly and it felt so right at the time."

I looked at Ted and said, "Don't beat yourself up. I would have done the same thing if the shoe were on the other foot. Now we need to get you out of here." I took out the bottle of water and handed it to him. "Here, take a sip," I said.

While Ted took a small sip of water, Landen looked at me and said, "How are we going to work this?"

"I guess the best way is one of us on each side of him," I responded. "That way he can limp along with us."

When Ted was done sipping the water, I took a quick sip then handed the bottle to Landen, who took a small sip. When he handed the bottle of water back to me, I held it up to gauge its contents. There was now less than half a bottle left. I knew that unless a miracle happened, there was no way we were going to have enough water to make it to the Highway.

Landen and I stood up and pulled Ted to his feet. We placed ourselves on each side of him and he put his arms over our shoulders. We started walking down the narrow road again, this time the three of us were arm in arm. The pace that we were walking this time was much slower and time consuming. For every two steps we had taken before, now we were getting one. On and on we plodded in the blistering sun. There was no relief in sight, just the endless step, step, step down the narrow track and the relentless sun beating down on us.

After traveling some distance, Landen said, "I need to take a break for a moment. My back and legs are about ready to give out."

We stopped briefly and all of us rested by a large bush that partially shaded the area. After resting for a few minutes we each took another sip of water and started our walking ordeal once again. I knew now that our only hope of getting out of this alive lay in whether the short call I had made to the 911 operator had made any sense to her and whether she had heard our location.

We continued walking again for what seemed to be over an hour but in reality was probably only twenty minutes. We again stopped to rest and as we rested I took out the water bottle and handed it to Ted. He took a small sip and passed it back to me. I, in turn, gave the bottle to Landen who took a small sip and then handed the bottle back to me. I raised the bottle to my lips and I felt the last few drops of water trickle from the bottle. I held the bottle up and shook it up and down over my open mouth. A few small drops slid out and then the bottle was completely empty. It was quite clear now that we were not going to make it much further. The shady tree area was still over a mile away. If we could at least make it to there then we wouldn't die shriveling up in the hot sun.

Although we all knew that we had no more water, we had to get walking again and try to make it to the trees. When we started walking again we had only gotten about the equivalent of a city block when we started to hear the sound of an engine off in the distance.

"Oh my God! They're coming back!" Landen shouted. "We've got to hide!"

I thought to myself for a moment. Certainly the surveillance camera that the boss was using was still intact someplace high on the ridge. Although one of Gus's boys had been controlling the hawks with the iPhone, I'm sure that the boss had the capacity to control the hawks as well. So if the boss was watching us and knew we were trying to get out of this place alive, why wouldn't the boss simply use the other Red Tail Hawk to finish us off rather than having Gus and his boys come all the way back? Maybe, just maybe, it might be help coming. Perhaps that 911 operator had gathered more information than I had thought. Either way we were out of water and there was no place to hide. The few bushes that were around were not big enough to hide us. Our only hope was to make it to the trees.

I quickly turned to Landen and said, "Calm down. You're only wasting your energy getting upset like this. We need to keep going. It's our only chance."

He turned and looked at me and I could see the tears in his eyes. Then he said in a matter of fact tone, "You're right. We must continue. Whatever happens is completely in God's hands."

Now our progress was slow, but steady. We were determined to make it to the shade. The further we got, the louder the engine noise became until suddenly, from out of the trees on the narrow road ahead of us, we could see the shiny red glare of an O.E.S. Fire Truck. We immediately started waving our hands and shouting. The truck stopped and the men inside stared at us as if we were something alien in nature, something that they could not recognize.

"What's wrong?" asked Ted. "Why are they staring at us?"

Glancing over at Ted and Landen standing there in their teepee toppers, I began to laugh. "They probably think we're some kind of tree men from outer space," I said through my laughter. With that I took off my topper and waved it in the air over my head.

After a few moments, the fire truck started toward us. When it reached us, the men got out of the truck. As they trotted over to assist us, an officer asked, "Are one of you men Jason Harmony?"

"Yes, that's me," I said. "I'm Jason T. Harmony."

"What's the 'T' stand for?" asked the officer.

"Teepee topper," I said, with a big smile on my face.

"Boy," he replied, "that's one heck of a middle name. Were you born in a teepee or something?"

I realized I'd probably never see this guy again so I figured I'd give him something to talk about. "Yeah," I answered. "My parents are full blooded Cherokee."

"Wow!" he said. "You sure couldn't tell it by looking at you." Then he said, "Evidently you called 911 about an emergency," he continued. "The Sheriff sent us out here to look for you."

While one man brought us over some bottled water, two more men were busy putting a make shift splint on Ted's leg so he would be able to walk. They cleaned the dried blood off of Landen's face with a saline solution and cooled some bottled water with ice packs and poured it on some gauze dressing to place on the blistered areas of my face.

While we sat at the back of the fire truck in the shade we told the Officer about our ordeal with Big Gus and his boys. "You need to radio the Sheriff right away," I said. "They're heading up to the Old Turner Foundry. They've also taken the Meade Mobile and they're supposed to abandon it somewhere up the Highway."

"I'll give him a call right away," said the Officer, hurrying to the radio in the front of the truck.

I then turned to Ted and said, "If we can borrow one of these men's cell phones, maybe we should give Connie a call. She's probably worried sick by now."

"You give her a call," said Ted. "She's supposed to be your girlfriend."

"Wait a minute," I said. "You're the one that got intimate with her. You give her a call."

"No!" said Ted forcefully. "I think you should be the one to call her."

"I disagree with you," I said. "I think you should have the honors."

Landen finally interrupted us and said, "Will you two please stop your bickering? You're making my head throb. Give me a darn phone and I'll give her a call." One of the men standing by us handed Landen a phone to use then walked away from us. Landen looked back at the two of us and said, "Now, what's her number?" We both rambled off her number almost in unison. Landen stood there with the phone to his ear listening to the ringing. He then turned to us and said, "It's going to her answering machine. What do you want me to say?"

Ted looked at me and I looked back at him. "She's still not home?" I said. "What's with that?"

"It sounds to me like she's not worried about either of us," replied Ted.

After thinking about it for a second or two, I said to Landen, "Just tell her Ted and I picked up a couple of topless dancers and we're on our way to Vegas."

"Do you really want me to tell her that?" asked Landen.

"Yeah," said Ted. "Unless you can think of something spicier?"

Landen relayed our message into the phone and then called out to the man that we were done with the phone and handed it back to him when he walked back over to us. Meanwhile, the Officer finished his radio transmission to the Sheriff and came back to inform us of the outcome.

"The Sheriff told me to let you know that he's got some F.B.I. Agents following your van right now," said the Officer. "He's on his way to assist them as we speak. In the meantime, he wants you boys to come on back to town with us."

We squeezed in the fire truck with the rest of the men. Although it was a tight squeeze, I was just thankful that we were alive and on our way out of this place that almost became our final resting place.

CHAPTER THIRTY-TWO

Back up the Highway, the three F.B.I. men watched as the Meade van pulled over to the side of the road and stopped. The F.B.I. men quickly pulled over about a block down the road to keep surveillance on the van. In a few moments they saw a pickup truck pull over and the men who were in the van jumped into the pickup and then it sped away. The agents called Captain Mason to report on what had just happened.

When the Captain answered, the Agent in the driver's seat relayed to Mason, "Cappy. The van has been dumped at the side of the road just past the Dell Ridge Exit. We are now following the vehicle that picked up the driver and the passenger of the van."

"Good job," said the Captain. "For your information, we just got a report from O.E.S. that there are two vehicles involved in this incident. Both are pickup trucks and one is towing a flatbed trailer with a small tractor on it. According to the same source, five men are involved. They are known to be armed and are considered to be extremely dangerous."

"I copy that, Cappy," said the Agent. "We observed the truck towing the trailer go by shortly after the van pulled over. We have both vehicles in sight and are proceeding with caution. What's your location?"

"We're just passing Dell Ridge right now," responded the Captain. "We're about a minute behind you. I've got additional agents responding. I've also called for our chopper out of Reno," continued the Captain. "It's got an E.T.A. of ten minutes."

"Sounds like we're loaded for bear," replied the Agent.

"We're here to take care of business," said the Captain, in a matter of fact tone.

After driving for a short time, the two pick-up trucks pulled off the Highway at Ten Mile Road and proceeded to the old foundry with the F.B.I. and Sheriff close behind. Once Gus and the boys were at the foundry, they backed the pick-up truck with the shipment of gold through the large open door. They all got out of the vehicles and prepared to fire the old furnace up. They quickly started the fire with seasoned wood and old coal left there from years past.

While they were distracted by the work in the foundry, the F.B.I. Agents and the Sheriff pulled up not too far down the road and began to watch from a distance. It wasn't long before the air was full of the thumping sounds of helicopter blades slicing through the sky. When Captain Mason made radio contract with the copter, it began to make a wide circle around the old building. Soon two more F.B.I. units pulled up alongside the Sheriff's squad car.

The Captain spoke into his hand held communicator, "You men in Chopper Twelve ready your weapons and prepare for action. The ground units are going in."

"Copy, Captain," responded the chopper. "We're ready when you are."

With that Captain Mason ordered the ground units in to surround the old foundry.

Sheriff Arby reached into the car and grabbed the bullhorn hanging under the dash and spoke those famous words every law enforcement officer dreams of saying one day, "We've got you surrounded! Come out with your hands up!"

Big Gus quickly grabbed the shotgun out of the pick-up truck and took aim at where the loud noise appeared to be coming from. He got his sights on a vehicle and with a pull of the trigger he blasted the front windshield out of the Sheriff's squad car.

The Sheriff and Captain Mason took cover behind the open front doors of the squad car. Big Gus immediately hid by the side of the old foundry door.

The Captain looked over at the Sheriff and said, "I'll have my men open fire."

"No, wait," replied the Sheriff. "Let's give these boys one more chance to surrender." The Sheriff got back on the bullhorn and said, "If you value your lives, I would suggest you throw out your weapons and come out with your hands high in the air. These F.B.I. boys here have got a brand new automatic nuclear thermo blaster that they're anxious to try out. I hear tell it can fry a guy from the inside out. The amazing thing about it is that it zeros in on a person's body heat. It goes right through solid structures. All these boys have to do is set it at ninety-eight point six degrees and aim it in the general direction of the person or persons they want to zap. When they pull the trigger it's just like one of them there guided missiles. You can run and hide but it don't make no difference. It'll find you. When it does you don't even know you've been zapped. It takes a full sixty seconds before you begin to feel a little tingle inside. Then it spreads quickly. Before long it's all over but the crying. The only way you can stop the effects is by taking a large dose of sodium phosphate. I'll tell ya, it's the damndest thing I've ever seen."

The whole time the Sheriff was talking, the F.B.I. Agents were trying to hold their laughter back. When the Sheriff was done, it didn't take Gus and his boys long to weigh the odds. Here they were in a dilapidated old foundry building. The only weapons they did have were a shotgun with a few shells that they had taken from Ted and a handgun that Pinky carried.

"I think they're bluffing us," said Pinky. "I never heard of any such weapon."

"Well, the thing is," said Gus, "even if they don't have that weapon, we ain't in no position to have a shoot out with these boys."

"Hey, Big Gus!" hollered one of his boys, "What is that sodium phosphate stuff? Do we got any of it?"

"Of course not you big dummy!" answered Gus. "You got to have a prescription to get that kind stuff. Now, boys," continued Gus as he looked around at the open door of the foundry, "let's get the heck outta here before they decide to zap us!"

With that, they threw out their weapons and walked out with their hands high in the air. The agents quickly surrounded them and placed them securely in handcuffs.

The Sheriff and Captain Mason walked over to Gus and his boys and then Captain Mason began to interrogate them. "You know what you men have been involved in is a federal offense," said the Captain. "If I don't get some answers, I might just lock you all up and throw away the key! Now," continued the Captain, "how did you men find out about that place on the B.L.M. land?"

The boys all looked at Big Gus. Then Big Gus looked at the Captain and said, "No comment!"

"Are you men working for somebody or are you working alone?" asked the Captain.

"No comment!" answered Big Gus.

The Captain turned to Sheriff Arby and said, "Let's take these men back to town where we can separate them and probably get better results interrogating them on an individual basis. Meanwhile, we can run a rap sheet on them and see if these guys have been in any trouble before."

"That sounds like a good idea," said Sheriff Arby. "What are we going to do about the radioactive material in their truck?"

The Captain replied, "I'll call in the F.B.I. special units to handle that. I'll also have one of my men stop by and drive that abandoned van back to town."

The F.B.I. Agents loaded up Gus and his boys in the back of their units and headed for town.

CHAPTER THIRTY-THREE

A Nevada State Patrol unit sitting at the side of the Highway spotted a blue car speeding down the road that matched the description in the all points bulletin that had been released a few hours ago. He immediately flipped on his lights and siren and sped off in hot pursuit after the speeding vehicle.

"Boulder Dispatch. This is Trooper Nineteen in pursuit of a blue vehicle that matches the description of the A.P.B."

"We copy that T-19. Do you have a plate number?"

"That's negative," answered the Trooper.

"What's your location?" asked Dispatch.

"I'm about thirty miles from the Arizona State Line," replied the Trooper.

"Copy that," said Dispatch. "We'll alert all officers in that vicinity as backup. We're also contacting the Arizona State Patrol and advising them of the situation. Do you need additional Patrol units?"

"That's negative on the Patrol. The officers are fine," said the Trooper. "I'll keep you advised."

"Copy," said Dispatch.

After the Arizona Dispatch was contacted by Trooper 19, the State Patrol set up a roadblock at the State Line.

Trooper 19 continued on his high-speed chase down the highway when another trooper contacted him. "T-19, this is T-21. Do you copy?"

"That's affirmative. I read you loud and clear. What's your twenty?"

T-21 answered, "Look in your rearview. I've got your back."

"Copy," said Trooper 19. "Kick back and enjoy the ride cause it doesn't look like this lady has any intention of stopping anytime soon."

"Will do," replied Trooper 21. "Let's play follow the leader."

Around dangerous curves and near head on collisions and passing slower traffic, the Troopers stayed close behind the lady in the blue car.

After a few minutes Boulder Dispatch came back on the radio. "T-19, this is Dispatch."

"Copy, Dispatch. This is T-19. Go ahead."

"I just want to give you a caution," said Dispatch. "The Hoover Dam by-pass is not yet completed so they're stopping traffic and inspecting vehicles going over the dam as per the 9-1-1 Terrorist Act. So be advised, traffic on Route 93 is backed up several miles before the dam."

"I copy that, Dispatch," said Trooper 19. "Could you dispatch a few units from the Boulder City Police Department to head this way to try and intercept this mad hatter before we have one heck of a pile up?"

"I copy you, T-19," said Dispatch. "Let me check availability."

In a few moments, dispatch replied, "I have two units starting that way. They're equipped with spike strips. They'll be trying to lay them down when the vehicle approaches."

"Copy," said T-19.

"We'll call this incident Blue Chase. T-19 will be the incident commander. I want all units involved to go to tack channel Amy 43." With that, Dispatch called for all units to check back.

"Copy 19 as I.C.?"

"I.C. 19 copies."

"Does T-21 copy Amy 43?"

"21 copies"

"Does Boulder City Car 3 copy?"

"3 copies."

"Does Boulder City Car 5 copy?"

"5 copies."

"Good luck, gentlemen," said Dispatch. "I'll keep my fingers crossed."

The two Boulder City units quickly proceeded up the Highway away from the dam and stopped about five miles out and prepared to throw the spike strips out on the opposite side of the road.

"Boulder City units, this is T-19."

"Yes, T-19. Go ahead," said one of the Officers.

"My GPS puts me seven miles out from the Hoover Dam," said the Trooper, "so keep your eyes peeled."

In no time at all the Officers saw the vehicles approaching. With spike strips in hand, they waited for the split second needed to perform such a dangerous and challenging maneuver. With the blue car several hundred yards away, the strips were tossed out. Bingo! BOOM! BOOM! BOOM! Three tires instantly blew out. The Officers immediately pulled in the strips from the road ensuring that the units following the blue car would not be in jeopardy.

Slamming on her brakes, the car slid sideways down the road while the officers watched from a safe distance. Within a matter of a few seconds, the car came to rest against a small bank at the side of the road. Troopers and Officers instantly surrounded the car, all with guns drawn. The blonde woman was ordered out of the car. She was placed in handcuffs and read her rights and then put into the back of Trooper 19's squad car. As per mutual agreement with the Federal Government, Trooper 19 was assigned the duties of transporting the woman back to Jefferson City for the F.B.I. to question.

CHAPTER THIRTY-FOUR

The O.E.S. truck dropped all three of us off at the Wal-Mart parking lot so I could pick up my car and take Ted and Landen back to the Detective Agency Office. Once there, Landen got out to go to the office. He said he had paperwork to do.

Ted turned to me and said, "Are you going over to check on Connie?"

"I was thinking about it," I said. "Why? Do you want to come, Hop-a-long?"

"Just because my knee is twisted is no reason to call me Hop-a-long," said Ted, with a cross look on his face.

"I'm sorry," I said. "Let me rephrase that. Would you like to come along, Gimpy?"

Ted started to smile just a bit and answered, "Yeah. Let's make sure she's OK."

We drove over to Connie's place in my car. When we got there I got out of the car and went around and opened the passenger door to help Ted get out. Ted gave me a thankful look and then said, "You know you should have just left me back there on that B.L.M. land to die, as much trouble as I've been to you."

"If the tables were turned, would you have left me out there?" I asked.

"Well, no. Certainly not," Ted answered. "But that's different. You didn't get intimate with my girlfriend."

I said, "Let's figure this thing out. You liked Connie as a girlfriend, right?"

"Yeah. I did," answered Ted.

"Well, it just so happens that I liked Connie as a girlfriend also," I continued. "Connie's the one who's been playing us both. We don't need to be angry at one another. In fact I think we need to have a long talk with that lady.

"You're right," said Ted.

As I helped him out of the car I saw a small branch lying on the ground that had broken off the old elm tree in Connie's front yard.

"Just a minute," I told Ted as he leaned up against the car.

"What are you doing?" he asked me when I walked over and picked up the branch.

"This looks like it's just your size," I said walking back over to the car. I held it out to him and said, "Give it a try."

"What do you want me to do with it?" asked Ted.

"Use it as a cane," I said. "It will help you walk so you don't have to lean against me all the time."

"Yeah, but I like leaning against you," Ted said smiling.

"Yeah, I know," I replied. "But people are starting to talk."

Ted leaned his body weight on the small branch and began to walk, all by himself but with a pronounced limp, down the walkway to Connie's front door. "Hey! This works pretty good," he said, with a smile on his face and a slight bounce in his walk.

"Just watch your step," I replied. "I'd hate to see you fall and twist your other knee."

When we got onto the front porch I reached over and knocked loudly on the door and waited for it to open. After waiting a minute or so Ted said, "Why don't we try the door bell?"

"Good idea," I said while I pushed the button.

Still no answer, I said to myself. Ted leaned over and looked in the front window, "I don't see anybody inside," he said. "Do you think everything is OK?"

"I'm not sure," I answered. "I told her to stay in the house with little Jimmy and to lock the door until all of this F.B.I. stuff was over."

"Maybe something's wrong," Ted said with a bit of panic in his voice. "Somebody might have broken in and tied them up."

I reached over and tried the front door knob. It was unlocked and the door opened up. "Maybe we better go in and check to make sure nothing has happened to them," I said getting quite concerned myself.

"Yeah, maybe we'd better do that," Ted said.

As we walked in the front door, we both started yelling for Connie and Jimmy but there was no answer. "You check the kitchen area and front bedrooms and I'll check the bathroom and the two rear bedrooms," I said.

While Ted limped around the front of Connie's house checking the rooms there I walked to the rear of the house and checked the bathroom and master bedroom. When I stepped into the large bedroom I immediately noticed that all the drawers were open in the dresser and the closet door was wide open. Everything was in disarray, as though somebody had gone through and picked out what they wanted and left the rest. Wow! I thought to myself. What in the world happened here? Was Connie in some kind of trouble? I walked out of the room and went into the spare bedroom. When I opened the door I got the surprise of my life.

"Ted! Come here fast!" I called out. I walked further into the room and saw a very sophisticated computer system. There on the screen was an image I won't forget for the rest of my life. When Ted came limping in the door I said, "Take a look at this." What we saw on the screen was the B.L.M. land we had barely escaped from alive, just hours before. The view was from the top of Wild Cat Ridge.

While Ted stared at the computer screen he shook his head from side to side. "I can't believe this!" he said. "It looks like Connie's been involved in this thing all along."

"Not only involved," I said, "but it appears as if she's the boss. I think it's time we go down to the Sheriff's office and have a talk with Arby."

"I hate to say it," replied Ted, "but I believe that's what we need to do."

We began to walk out of the front door and, as we were closing it, we could see Jimmy waving at us from the front of Billy's house where he was standing with his friend and Billy's mother.

"Uncle Jason! Uncle Ted!" he yelled.

We went over and Billy's mother said, "Connie was called out of town because her mother was dying in the hospital. She left Jimmy here with me for a few days until she returns." Then she got a concerned look on her face. "You two look worried," she continued. "Is there something wrong?"

Before I could answer Jimmy said, "Yeah. You two look like you've been in a knock down drag out fight. What happened to your leg, Uncle Ted?"

"Oh, it's just a scratch, kid. Nothing to worry about," Ted said quietly.

"Yeah, we're fine," I said, as lightheartedly as I could muster. "We're just a little worse for wear. By the way, did Connie give you a number where you could get hold of her in case of an emergency?" I asked Billy's mother.

"No," she said. "Connie told me that she'd call when she got there," replied Billy's mother.

"Well, we'd better get going," said Ted. "We've got a lot to do."

After that we said our goodbyes to Jimmy, Billy and his mother and, together, Ted and I went back to my car and got inside. When I started the engine and put the car in drive, I remembered about the newspaper that I had thrown in my wastebasket back at my apartment. I told Ted that I wanted to make a quick stop at my place.

I drove over to my apartment and ran inside quickly while Ted waited in the car. After I had retrieved the paper, I grabbed the extra battery for my cell phone that I keep charged for emergencies. After placing it in my phone and putting the other one on the charger, I ran back out to the car and got in the driver's seat. I handed Ted the paper as I started to drive. "Here," I said. "Take a look at this."

While Ted looked over the ad, I could see he had a disgusted look on his face. "Whoever placed this ad is an out and out murderer!" he said. "They lured these poor people over here on the pretense of becoming rich. Then the only reward they do get is to be buried alive in a pit."

"We need to give this ad to the Sheriff," I replied. "Maybe he can trace the 1-800 number to the person who placed the ad." I continued to drive, heading straight to Sheriff Arby's office.

CHAPTER THIRTY-FIVE

On the other side of town, Sheriff Arby and Captain Mason pulled up to the Sheriff's Office accompanied by the other F.B.I. Agents. They unloaded Big Gus and his boys and took them inside for booking. The Sheriff and the Captain gathered the I.D.'s of the boys and processed their names through the computer bank for a current print out of their arrest records. After receiving the printouts they looked them over carefully.

The Sheriff finally turned to the Captain and said, "You thinking about making a deal with one of these guys?"

"Yes. It appears we're not going to get any of them to talk," said the Captain. "Maybe if I offer the cleanest one a light sentence for turning State's evidence we can get him to play ball."

"It looks like this here Theodore Rupin guy has about the cleanest record," said the Sheriff.

"Which one is he?" asked the Captain.

"He's the one they call Pinky," answered the Sheriff. "It looks like he's only been arrested two times in his life. Once for vehicle theft when he was nineteen and once for assault a few years ago."

"The rest of these boys should still be in prison, what with all of the crimes they've committed," said the Captain shaking his head as he continued to read over the reports.

The Sheriff walked into the holding area and took Pinky out of his cell. "What's going on?" asked Pinky a bit fearfully.

"You'll see in a minute," said the Sheriff.

He led Pinky into a conference room where the Captain was sitting at a table. "You look like a pretty smart guy to me," said the Captain, looking at Pinky.

"One of the smartest," said Pinky in a slightly bolder tone.

"Well, here's the deal," said the Captain, "you're looking at twenty to life in prison. But if you turn State's evidence and cooperate with me I can cut that down considerably."

"How much time are you talking about?" asked Pinky.

"I can get you three to five in a country club prison," replied Captain Mason.

"I'm listening," said Pinky. "What do I have to do?"

"You have to tell me everything you know," Mason said. "You'll have to testify against your friends and anyone else involved in this incident."

"Yeah, if I do that," sneered Pinky, "they'll kill me for sure."

"No! No! That won't happen," answered the Captain quickly. "We'll arrange to have you put into the Witness Protection Program. They'll give you a new identity and a different state to live in."

"Let me get this straight," said Pinky, as he looked the Captain straight in the eyes. "If I rat on these guys I get a new identity?"

"That's right," said the Captain.

"What about my share of the money I've made with these guys? Do I get to keep that too?" asked Pinky.

"I'm afraid we can't do that," answered Captain Mason. "But we will start you off with a bank roll."

"How much would that be?" asked Pinky.

"In most cases," said the Captain, "it's equal to a year's salary at a good paying job. Probably around fifty thousand dollars."

"Hey, that don't sound too bad," said Pinky.

"And before you're released from prison," continued the Captain, "they'll set you up in a good paying job. You'll be a respectable citizen. But you'll have to walk the straight and narrow. If you're found to be involved in any illegal activities at any time for the rest of your life you'll forfeit the agreement and be put back in prison to serve out the original twenty to life sentence."

"You mean they'll put me in with everybody I ratted out?" asked Pinky with his eyes wide in horror.

"That's right," said the Captain. "So if you want this deal you've got to go completely straight."

Pinky thought for a few moments and then replied, "If I make this deal with you how do I know you'll keep your end of the deal?"

"Because, first of all, it will all be in writing," the Captain said. "And secondly, I give you my word."

"OK," said Pinky after thinking for a minute. "We got ourselves a deal."

As they shook hands the Captain motioned for one of his agents to bring in a contract. After filling out the necessary details, Pinky and the Captain both signed the contract. The Captain had the video recorder, which was supplied to him by one of the Agents, turned on and Pinky began to talk.

"It all began about six months ago. I was working in a Las Vegas Casino as part of a security team. That's where I met Big Gus and the rest of the boys."

"What Casino was it?" asked the Captain.

"The MGM Grand," answered Pinky. "Anyway," he continued, "everything was going pretty good. We all became friends and started hanging out together on our time off. I got to know just about everybody that worked at the place. They had this break room there that all the employees hung out in on their break time and lunch times. One day when I went in to the room I saw Gus there and he was talking with this dealer named Fran. She was a real good-looking lady and she had started telling him about some secret her father told her on his deathbed. She said it was her inheritance of sorts because he didn't have any material items to leave for her. Her father told her that there was enough gold to choke a horse but that it was hidden inside a radioactive force. It was there for the taking, she said that he told her. All you have to do is figure out how to retrieve it, her father had said to her. He gave her an old map that he'd had for years and explained to her just where it was located. But you have to be careful, her father cautioned her, because the land doesn't belong to me, she said he told her. He said that it was U.S. Government Land. She said he told her that getting the gold out shouldn't be any problem though, because it's close to roads and it's also far enough out that people rarely go around the area. It was in a pretty secluded area. She said that he told her that the dangerous part is the radiation. He told her that it could kill you in no time at all. She said that he told her that radiation suits will protect you for a short time but they wouldn't be effective in this type of operation. They would be too cumbersome to work in and they are too easily compromised. You would need some type of robot system to get through the radioactive crust; she said her father told her. Then Gus kind of laughed and said, *"Where are you gonna find a robot?"* Fran just smiled her seductive smile and said she had somebody working on it."

"Who did she have doing that?" asked the Captain.

"Some high stakes card player she met at the tables," said Pinky.

"Did he actually supply robots?" questioned the Captain.

"No," replied Pinky. "He supplied a substitute."

"What was that?" the Captain asked.

"Illegal Mexicans," said Pinky.

"That's disgusting," said the Captain sharply. "To treat humans like they were disposable."

"It wasn't my idea," Pinky said. "I just did what I was told to do."

"What was the card player's name?" asked the Captain.

"None of us boys could ever find out his real name. We just referred to him as The Card Man."

"So what kind of deal did this Fran lady offer Gus?" questioned the Captain.

"She wanted him to put together a crew of men to run the operation," answered Pinky. "It would be their responsibility to install a series of surveillance cameras and to set up all the security devices. The men would have to keep a constant watch on the area and divert any intruders to the area. She was prepared to pay him ten thousand dollars up front for operational expenses and once the operation got underway each member of the crew would get twenty thousand dollars in each of their individual bank accounts for every twenty-five pound shipment. It worked out in the ballpark of about thirty percent of the take."

"Not a bad ballpark," said the Captain.

"Nope. It sure worked for me," said Pinky. "She set up bank accounts for all five of us guys and sure enough, after we finally got everything set up and working out there and when we were done with the first shipment, twenty thousand dollars was deposited in my account. Gus said that we'd all be rich men before the summer was out."

"What about these illegal Mexicans?" asked the Captain. "Where did they come from?"

"I'm not really sure where they came from," replied Pinky. "All I know is they came in on the Greyhound Bus. I picked them up at the bus depot every time we needed to re-order."

"Re-order?" asked the Captain.

"Yeah. They didn't last for more than five or six days because of the high level of radiation exposure."

"What did you do with them after that?" inquired the Captain.

"Gus had us dig a deep pit out there and when they were too sick to work we dropped them off into the pit and buried them," answered Pinky.

"How many did you murder?" asked the Captain.

"I guess it was twelve or so," said Pinky, "and we didn't actually murder them, we just put them out of their misery."

The Captain turned and looked at Sheriff Arby who was sitting in a chair off to the side just listening to the conversation. They both shook their heads. Then the Captain continued his questioning. "I know you melted down the raw material to get the pure gold," said the Captain, "but what did you transform the gold into?"

"We poured it into fishing weight molds and made one ounce fishing weights out of it," Pinky answered. "Once we had around twenty-five pounds, we painted the weights silver so they looked like lead and then shipped them."

"Where did you ship it to?" asked the Captain.

"Some place in Arizona called Blue Bird Incorporated. I sent each shipment through the UPS station here in town," answered Pinky. "From there the gold was fenced through some Mexican drug lord for around eighty cents on the dollar."

As Pinky continued to tell the Captain what he knew, an F.B.I. Agent knocked at the door of the meeting room. Looking through the glass pane on the door, Captain Mason motioned for him to come in. "Yes, what is it?" asked the Captain.

"We've just received word from the Doctors at the clinic," said the Agent. "They report that all five patients are showing signs of marked improvement. They're expected to make a full recovery."

"Good news," said the Captain. "I'm glad to hear that."

"Now that we know the cause of the radiation poisoning," continued the Agent, "is there any further need to lock down the community? The people are starting to get a little restless."

"I can see no reason to continue the lock down," answered the Captain. "Let's go ahead and open up the road blocks. Release all O.E.S. units. Tell them they did an outstanding job and thank them for their help."

CHAPTER THIRTY-SIX

When Ted and I got to the Sheriff's Office we were surprised to see so many cars of the same make and model parked in front of the office.

"Must be those F.B.I. Agents that are in town," Ted said looking at the cars.

"Yeah. They must have something going on in the Sheriff's Office," I said. "Let's go in and see what it is."

When we walked in the door, two well-dressed men wearing dark glasses immediately met us.

"Can we help you?" asked one of the men.

"Who are you?" I asked.

"F.B.I." he answered. "And just who are you?"

"I'm Jason T. Harmony and this is my side kick, Ted Meade," I said.

"Does your side kick always walk around on a tree limb?" the Agent asked, looking at Ted's makeshift cane.

"Not usually," I said smiling somewhat shyly. "He hurt his knee earlier today while we were making our way out of the B.L.M. land in back of town."

"Oh, you must be the guys that were trapped out there," replied the Agent.

"Yep. That's us," I said.

"Well, that would explain those awful sunburns you have," he said.

"Yes. We were left out in the sun to die," Ted replied.

"Oh, by the way," said the Agent, "we brought that fancy van back for you guys. It's parked in back of the station house."

"Thanks," said Ted. "We were wondering what happened to it."

Looking at the newspaper in my hand the Agent asked, "Is there something we can do for you?"

"Yeah. We need to speak with the Sheriff right away," I said. "I've got some information I think he might be interested in."

"Well, he's in the interrogation room with our Captain right now," answered the Agent. "But let me go see if I can get him for you."

With that said he walked down the short hallway. A minute or so later he returned followed by the Sheriff and a short skinny man with red hair.

The Sheriff smiled broadly and said, "Well it looks like you guys have been out basking in the sun. It must be nice to be able to come and go as you please." Then he said, "All kidding aside, I'm really glad to see you guys made it out of that place alive. I don't know what I would have done without my two favorite detectives." He turned and gestured toward the slim man standing by his side and said, "This is Captain Mason with the F.B.I. and Captain, these are two of those detectives I was telling you about." Turning toward Ted he announced, "This is Ted Meade." The Captain shook hands with Ted. Then turning toward me the Sheriff said, "And this is Jason T. Harmony."

The Captain reached over and shook my hand and then asked, "What's the 'T' stand for, Jason?"

"Tired," I said.

"Tired?" he replied.

"Yeah. It's been a long day," I answered.

I handed the newspaper ad to the Sheriff and as the Sheriff and Captain Mason started to read it I explained how I'd gotten the paper when I was in Arizona. I then said, "If you can trace the 1-800 number maybe you can find out who took the ad out. We should be able to find the person that supplied the illegal aliens for this mining operation."

"That would probably be The Card Man," said the Captain looking at the Sheriff. The Captain handed the paper to one of his Agents and told him to have the 1-800 number checked out through headquarters immediately.

"We've also got some more information I think you'll want to know about," I said.

"What's that?" asked Sheriff Arby.

"We think Connie Fowler is the boss of the whole operation."

"Yeah, we found a sophisticated computer system in one of the bedrooms in her house," said Ted. "She's one of the people who have been controlling the Red Tail Hawks."

"Controlling the Red Tail Hawks?" asked Sheriff Arby. "The last report I got from you guys said nothing about anybody controlling any Red Tail Hawks. You said the hawk incident should be treated in a secondary manner. That it posed no threat."

Ted looked at me and I looked back at him. Then we both looked back at Sheriff Arby.

"Well?" said the Sheriff. "Isn't that what you said in your report?"

"Well, we did say the case was pending," said Ted rather softly.

"Yeah, we've been working on the pending part of the case," I said with a big smile on my sun burnt face.

"Landen is over at the office right now writing you out a full report," said Ted.

Captain Mason interrupted, "What's this about someone being able to control Red Tail Hawks?" he asked.

"It's a long story," I said. "The Sheriff can brief you on it when he gets Landen's report."

"That's fine," said the Captain.

"Just a minute," said the Sheriff. "Wasn't Connie's son, Jimmy, the boy that was originally attacked by the Red Tail Hawk?"

"Yes," answered Ted. "We can't figure that one out yet."

"Connie Fowler," said the Captain talking to himself out loud. "We need to run her name through our system and see what we come up with." Then he said out loud, "How do you spell that?"

"Here, I'll write it down for you," I said as I grabbed a pen and a blank piece of paper off the Sheriff's desk.

When I handed the paper to the Captain, he walked over and gave the paper to one of his Agents who promptly went over to the computer in the Sheriff's Office and started typing in an access code.

"Are we done with Theodore Rupin?" one of the F.B.I. Agents asked the Captain.

"Yes. I think we've got all the information we need from him for now," answered the Captain. "Why don't you two men escort Mr. Rupin to a motel for tonight and keep him under wraps. We will process him tomorrow."

"Will do, Cappy," said the Agent as he walked back into the interrogation room.

∞◇◇◇∞

When the Agents brought Pinky out of the interrogation room in handcuffs, a surprised look came over his face when he saw Ted and I standing in the hallway.

"Well, look who the Sheriff picked up," I said to Ted in a loud voice.

"Thanks to your tip," said Sheriff Arby, "we caught the whole gang at the old foundry on Ten Mile Road."

Pinky gave me a sour look and said, "Well, if it isn't Mr. Trouble. I thought you would be dead by now."

"Nope. We made it out of there alive," I said. "But no thanks to you and the boys."

"Whoever named you Trouble sure knew what they was doing," said Pinky, "cause you been nothing but trouble to Big Gus and us boys."

As they led Pinky on out of the building, Sheriff Arby asked, "What's this about your name being trouble?"

"That's just a private joke between me and Big Gus," I answered.

"Well, that's odd," said Sheriff Arby.

"What's that?" I asked.

The Sheriff smiled and said, "I always thought the T stood for Tenderfoot." Then he gave out a hearty laugh.

In no time at all the F.B.I. Agent who had been working on the Sheriff's computer came back into the front office with a printout in his hand.

"Captain. I've got the information you requested," he said. "The 1-800 number was traced to a guy named Clark."

My ears perked up when I heard the name Clark. "That wouldn't happen to be a Devon Clark, would it?" I asked.

"Why, yes it is," replied the Agent. "How did you know that?"

"Just a lucky guess," I said.

"Also," the Agent continued, "this Connie Fowler woman is none other than Francis Constance Barkley. She is the daughter of Bert Barkley. He is the man who filed the claims on the B.L.M. land."

"Now it's all starting to add up," said the Captain. "This Clark guy must be the person they call The Card Man. Do me a quick favor and see if, by any chance, he's also the owner of a place in Arizona called Blue Bird Inc.?"

"Right away, Sir," said the Agent.

As the Agent went back to the computer to do as the Captain had requested, suddenly a voice came over the Sheriff's radio in the office.

"This is Trooper 19 on frequency 46.23. How do you read me?"

"You're coming in loud and clear," said the Sheriff. "What can we do for you?"

"Is this the one and only Sheriff Arby I've heard so much about?" said the Trooper.

"This is Sheriff Arby. Go ahead."

"Sheriff, I'm about five out with a looker in my back seat that belongs to an A.P.B. I'm supposed to deliver her to an F.B.I. Captain named Mason. Do you have his frequency?" asked the Trooper.

"That's affirmative," said the Sheriff. "But he's standing right here. Just a minute," said the Sheriff. The Sheriff motioned to Captain Mason to come over to the radio, then handed him the microphone.

"This is Captain Mason."

"Captain, this is Trooper 19. I've got a bag of goodies for you. What's your location?"

"I'm at the Sheriff's Office," answered the Captain.

"Copy that," said Trooper 19. "I'll be there in a few."

"I copy you," replied the Captain, then he put the microphone back on the Sheriff's desk.

I turned to Ted and said softly, "I think they might be talking about Connie."

"It kind of sounds like it," said Ted.

The Sheriff came over and confirmed the news for us. "They're bringing in your friend Connie or whatever her name is," said the Sheriff. "She should be here shortly."

Ted and I waited for the Trooper to bring Connie to the Sheriff's Office. The F.B.I. Agent walked back over to the Captain and handed him another computer readout.

As the Captain looked it over, the Agent began to talk. "This Clark guy does own Blue Bird Inc. He also owns a place called Clark's Bird Farm."

"Very interesting," said the Captain. "Call headquarters and have them send some Agents out to pick this guy up immediately."

"Will do, Captain," said the Agent.

As the Agent went off to contact headquarters, a squad car pulled up by the Sheriff's Office. A Trooper got out and opened the back door and ushered an attractive blonde lady out of the back seat and in toward the front door of the Sheriff's Office. While Ted and I watched through the window, at first glance we thought that there must be some kind of mistake.

"That's not Connie," said Ted. "Connie's got black hair."

After looking closer I said, "That's Connie, alright. She's wearing a blonde wig."

When the Trooper led her into the office she took one look at Ted and I and burst out into tears and crying. "I didn't mean for things to turn out this way," she said through her tears. "It was all going to be so perfect. Then Jimmy and Billy had to go hiking out there on the B.L.M. land." She paused for a few moments and then blurted out loudly, "I told them to stay away from there! I told them not to go out there! But did they listen?"

The Sheriff interrupted and said, "You probably would have been better off telling them to be sure and go out there. Kids that age do just the opposite of what you tell them to do."

Connie gave the Sheriff a dirty look as if to say, *I didn't ask for your input.* Then she turned back to Ted and I and continued to rant, "And you two! You just couldn't let this Red Tail Hawk thing drop! You just had to keep pushing things! I was starting to get so annoyed with you!"

"Is that why you had Big Gus and his boys leave us out there to die?" I said in an unconcerned tone.

"I didn't want that to happen!" Connie replied loudly. "This was my inheritance! You two were screwing around with it! When I first met you guys," Connie continued, "all I wanted to do was to distract you away from that stupid bird! But dimwitted Fran who wears her heart on her sleeve, well, I had to fall for both of you!"

"That's enough talk," said the Sheriff, leading Connie away. "The Captain wants you in the interrogation room."

As Connie was being led away she stopped and turned back and looked at Ted and I and said, "I know you two are hurt and don't want anything to do with me, but could you please get a hold of Jimmy's father and let him know what has happened and have him come and take Jimmy?"

"Sure," I said. "Just give us his name and number. Ted and I will contact him."

"Don't worry about little Jimmy," said Ted. "We'll make sure he's taken care of."

After getting the information about Jimmy's father, I stepped outside the door of the Sheriff's Office so I could call and make the arrangements for him to meet us and pick up Little Jimmy at the Meade Detective Agency office and to give him the directions on the easiest way to get there. I also made a call to Billy's house to let his mother know what was going on and to ask her to please have Jimmy ready to go when we got over there to pick him up.

When Ted and I were getting ready to leave the Sheriff's Office we overheard one of the F.B.I. Agents telling the Captain that Devon Clark had been arrested by the F.B.I. in Arizona and that the Federal Government had seized his property.

Looking at Ted, I said, "Boy, these F.B.I. guys don't mess around. They get right down to business."

"Yeah," said Ted. "Maybe we'd better get on out of here before they find something to detain us for."

"That sounds like a good idea," I replied. "Besides, we've got to go by and pick up Little Jimmy."

When we left the Sheriff's Office, Ted walked around to the back parking area and got into the Meade Mobile and drove off for the Detective Agency while I followed him in my car.

After dropping off the van and telling Landen a little of what had happened and that we were going to pick up Jimmy, we both drove over to Billy's house in my car. We didn't say much on the short drive over there.

When we got close to Billy's house, Ted asked, "Where, exactly is Jimmy's father coming from?"

"He's coming from Colfax, California," I replied. "He said that the drive should take him about two hours."

"Does he know how to get to the Detective Agency?" asked Ted.

"He said that with the directions I gave him he should be able to find it pretty easily," I answered. "But just in case he gets lost I gave him my cell phone number."

"Colfax, California," Ted said out loud. "Is that a' pretty nice place?"

"Yeah," I answered. "It's a pretty nice town. Jimmy's father said he owns a small ranch just outside of town," I continued, "so Jimmy should really enjoy it there."

"That makes me feel a lot better," said Ted.

"Yeah, it makes me feel better, too," I replied.

"Did the Sheriff call Mrs. Barnes and let her know that we're supposed to come by and pick Jimmy up?" Ted asked.

"Yes, he did." I answered. "And I called her to let her know the situation and to have Jimmy all ready to go. She said she'd have him all packed up and waiting."

∞⟨⟩∞

When we got to the Barnes' house, Jimmy was waiting for us on the front porch with Billy. Mrs. Barnes came out, when she heard us drive up, with a suitcase and set it down by Jimmy.

"We went over to Jimmy's house and got a lot of his clothes. What are they going to do with the rest of the things in the house?" Mrs. Barnes asked.

"Mr. Fowler said that he and Jimmy would come back next weekend and try to square everything away," I answered.

Jimmy thanked Mrs. Barnes for her help and then he turned to say good-bye to Billy. He held out his hand to shake Billy's. He had a serious look on his face as if he was trying to hold back tears.

I said, "Why don't you two boys give each other a big bear hug?"

With that the boys grabbed each other and began to hug as they tried to hold back their tears.

Jimmy said to Billy, "You can come and visit me and my Dad."

"Yeah. That would be cool," said Billy.

"And I'll be back next weekend," said Jimmy.

"That's right," said Billy. "We'll see each other next weekend."

"And, Jimmy," said Mrs. Barnes, "you're always welcome to come and visit us any time you want to."

"Thanks, Mrs. Barnes," said Jimmy, walking over and giving her a big hug. Then Jimmy grabbed his suitcase and walked over to my car. We all got in and waved goodbye as we drove away and headed toward the detective agency.

"Let's stop by and pick up a pizza," I said. "I'm getting kind of hungry."

"That sounds good to me," said Ted.

"Yeah! That's a great idea!" shouted Jimmy from the back seat. We stopped by the Straw Hat Pizza Parlor and picked up an extra large pizza with the works and brought it back to the agency.

When we walked in the front door, Landen was sitting at the computer desk working on the report for Sheriff Arby.

"Hey! Something smells good," he said looking up from the computer screen.

"We brought you some pizza," I replied with a big smile on my face.

"Who's your friend?" Landen asked, looking at Jimmy.

"Oh, that's right, you two haven't met yet," I said. "Landen, this is Jimmy Fowler. Jimmy, this is Landen Meade."

Landen stuck out his hand to shake Jimmy's small hand and said, "Glad to meet you, Jimmy."

"Jimmy's father is going to stop by in a little while and pick him up," Ted said.

"Yeah! I'm going with my Dad to his ranch in Colfax," replied Jimmy.

I placed the pizza on the meeting table and said, "Everybody dig in."

After eating three pieces of pizza and drinking a large Coke I was full. I was so full, in fact, that I felt like taking a nice long nap. All of a sudden we heard a car pull up out front.

"I bet that's your father," I said to Jimmy.

In no time at all there was a knocking sound at the door. Ted walked over and opened the door. The man standing there said, "Hi. I'm Bill Fowler," sticking out his hand to shake Ted's hand. "You must be Jason."

"No, no. I'm Ted," he said, shaking hands. "That's Jason over there." He motioned toward me standing by the table.

I walked over and held out my hand. As we shook hands, Jimmy came over and his dad gave him a big hug.

"I missed you, Son," he said.

"I missed you too, Dad," said Jimmy.

After Bill finished giving Jimmy a big hug, he turned toward me and said, "Can I talk with you outside for a moment?"

"Sure," I said. Then looking at Jimmy I said, "We'll be right back, Jimmy."

"OK, Uncle Jason," Jimmy said, hurrying back over to the pizza.

When we went outside, Bill asked, "How much does Jimmy know about what's going on with his mother?"

"Well, he knows she's been arrested and that she's in some kind of trouble," I answered. "But he doesn't know exactly what kind of trouble she's in."

"What kind of charges is she facing?" Bill asked.

"Accessory to murder, for one," I said, "and I'm sure there will be a lot more filed against her. I'm just not sure what they'll be."

"How is Jimmy taking it?" he asked.

"He seems to be fine," I replied. "He was especially excited when he heard you were coming to take him home with you."

Bill smiled broadly and said, "You know, I've been trying to get custody of him for the last five years but his mother never stays in one place long enough for me to file papers."

"Well, I think it's safe to say that won't be a problem from here on out," I said.

"I'm glad I'll finally get custody of Jimmy," Bill replied, "but I didn't really want it to happen like this."

We talked a while longer, then we went back inside to get Little Jimmy ready for his drive to Colfax.

After putting Jimmy's suitcase in the trunk of the car we all said our good-byes to Jimmy, shook hands with Bill and stood out front and waved as they both drove off for Colfax.

I turned toward Ted and Landen and said, "I think I'm going to call it a day and go home and put some Carnation's Evaporated Milk on my sunburn."

"Evaporated milk?" asked Landen.

"Yeah. It's an old family remedy that Sheriff Arby told me about earlier today."

"It sounds kind of messy," said Ted.

"Yeah, it does sound like it's a bit of a sticky wicket," I said laughing. "But if it gets rid of the pain it's worth it."

"Let me know if it works," said Landen as I walked out to my car.

"You'll be the first person I call," I said as I got into my car and shut the door. I waved to them as I drove off.

On the drive home I thought about how lucky the three of us were to be alive and about all the things that had happened in the last week or so. It seemed almost unbelievable that all this could have happened in such a short amount of time. We've gone months around our town of Jefferson City without even a hint of this much activity.

When I got to my apartment I gently cleaned my sunburned skin and carefully applied the evaporated milk to the areas that were affected. Once the milk started to dry I put on some loose nightclothes and crawled into bed and immediately fell asleep.

CHAPTER THIRTY-SEVEN

I was awakened from a sound sleep early the next morning by the sound of the phone ringing. I slowly reached over to the nightstand and picked up the receiver.

"Hello?"

"Hey, Jason. This is Ted."

"Hi, Ted. What's going on?" I said.

"Jason! You need to look at the Sunday paper ASAP!" Ted said loudly.

"Why? What's going on?" I asked.

"All I can say is, one of those O.E.S. Officers that rescued us must have had a camera on them," Ted answered. "Just take a look at the paper. You'll see what I'm talking about."

I got off the phone and put on my robe to walk out onto the front porch and get the paper. When I unfolded it and looked at the front page I couldn't believe my eyes. There was Ted, Landen and myself standing on the trail on the B.L.M. land with our 'teepee toppers' draped over our heads. There was a big headline above the picture that read, *HOME GROWN HEROS*. The two page article that went with the picture told all about the radioactive gold and the murdering that had taken place on out at the B.L.M. land by Big Gus and his boys. I hadn't even finished the article yet when my home phone started ringing off the hook. People I hadn't heard from for months were calling and telling me how good of a job I'd done catching those criminals.

∞✕✕∞

Later in the day I met with Ted and Landen at the detective agency because Ted had called to tell me that there was some urgent business that Landen needed to talk with me about.

When I walked in the front door of the agency I saw a bottle of champagne sitting on the conference table. Landen and Ted came over and shook my hand and then Ted walked over and popped the cork on the champagne bottle. As the champagne leaked over the side of the bottle, Ted poured it into three glasses sitting on the table.

Landen picked up a glass and held it in the air and said, "I wish to make a toast." Ted and I each picked up a glass and held them up and Landen continued. "Here's to the three best detectives in the State of Nevada!"

"Salute!" I said as I drank a sip of champagne from my glass.

"And here's to the Meade Detective Agency!" Landen toasted.

"Salute!" I said as I took another sip of my champagne.

"And here's to our new partner, Jason T. Harmony!" said Ted as we all touched glasses.

I went to take a sip of my champagne and then I realized what Ted had just said. "Partner?" I questioned.

"Yes, partner!" Landen answered. "We want you to be a partner and a full time detective with the Meade Detective Agency."

"Wow!" I replied. "I don't quite know what to say."

"You don't have to say anything right now," said Ted,

"Yes. Think about it for a week or so," replied Landen, "and let us know by the end of this month. I think it's a given fact that Ted and I wouldn't have made it out of that B.L.M. land alive if it wasn't for you," Landen continued. "You've shown skills, knowledge and just plain common sense, all of which are qualities that make for a world class detective. In fact, I would say, a World's Finest Detective! With you on our team there's no limit to the success we can achieve!"

While Landen continued praising me a tear came to my eyes. I'd never felt so appreciated in my life. After we finished our small celebration, I bid Ted and Landen good-bye and went back home to do some serious thinking about their proposal.

I didn't sleep much that night. The next morning I went in early to work so I could have a talk with Mr. Henderson. When he did arrive at the shop I followed him in as he opened up the door.

"I saw your picture in the paper yesterday," he said as we walked into the shop. "That was sure an impressive looking hat you were wearing."

"You liked that, huh," I said with a smile on my face.

"No! I didn't say that," answered Mr. Henderson, chuckling just a bit. "I said it was impressive."

As I walked over to start a pot of coffee I said, "I need to talk with you when you get a minute."

"Yeah. I kind of thought you might," he replied as he walked into his office and turned on the light. "Bring me a cup of coffee when it's done and let's sit down and have a chat."

As I waited for the coffee to finish brewing I wondered exactly what I would say to him. He'd been my boss for close to five years now. I liked him as a boss and also as a friend. He'd been very good to me and always treated me with the utmost respect. It kind of felt like I would be betraying him if I were to just pick up and leave with such short notice.

When the coffee was done, I poured us each a cup and carried them both into Mr. Henderson's office.

"Have a seat, Jason," he said as he took a sip of his morning coffee. Then he began to talk. "You know, I didn't always want to be the owner of an Auto Repair Shop. No sir. When I was much younger I wanted to be a Country and Western singer. I was pretty good too," he continued. "People thought I had what it took to get to the top. I loved singing and playing my guitar as the audience watched and cheered."

"What happened?" I asked. "Why didn't you continue?"

"Well," he confided, "I met a pretty young lady and, before too long, we got married. The next thing you know, we started having kids. I never could figure out what caused that," he said, giving me a wink. "Anyway, I knew it wasn't fair to my wife and kids for me to be gone all the time playing in some joint and leaving them home all alone, so I quit the music business after a few years and did the second best thing I liked to do."

"What was that?" I asked.

"Why, wrenching, of course," he answered. "I wrenched for a few years, then I got my big chance to open my own Auto Shop and the rest is history," he said, taking another sip of coffee.

Before I could say anything, he continued to talk. "Now Jason, you're an excellent mechanic and I know you like what you do. But you don't love it. There's something that's tearing at your heart and it won't leave you alone until you give it a try. Detective work," he said, "that's what you love to do. So I'm going to give you your chance while you're still young enough to follow your dream. Now, you haven't had a real vacation in the five years you've been working for me, so here's what I'm going to do. I'm going to give you two weeks off with pay, starting today," he said. "I want you to take a trip some place where you won't be bothered with the hustle and bustle of your everyday life. I want you to get away from your friends and family and coworkers and go out and do some soul searching. Decide what you want to do with your life. At the end of two weeks," he continued, "I want you to come back and tell me your decision. If you want to try your hand at being a detective, I'll consider these two weeks as your two-week notice. If you want to continue your mechanic job, just remember you're always welcome here."

I thanked him and shook his hand and then walked back out of the shop to my car. As I got into my car, I realized that Mr. Henderson was a whole lot smarter than I'd ever given him credit for. Heck, I hadn't even told him what I wanted to talk to him about. Maybe he'd sensed it from reading the newspaper article. Whatever it was, I knew I'd always be grateful to him for giving me this chance. The only thing I needed to do now was to figure out where I wanted to spend these next two weeks.

CHAPTER THIRTY-EIGHT

With the thought of gold still fresh in my mind from the case we'd just wrapped up, I decided to try my hand at a little gold panning. I'd heard of this place in Colorado outside of Cripple Creek where a guy could do a little backpacking and panning in small streams. He could get to be at one with nature. So here I was, looking at this beautiful woman sitting helplessly in this creek waiting for my assistance. As I walked thru the stream, stepping from stone to stone, I finally reached her and held out my hand for her to grab a hold of.

As she took my hand and got to her feet, she said, "My name is Bonnie. What did you say your name was?"

"Jason," I said. "Jason T. Harmony."

"What's the T stand for?" she asked.

"Thoughtful," I said, as she gazed deep into my eyes.

ABOUT THE BOOK

I woke up one morning with an idea and some words that had come to me in my sleep, the start of the novel, so to speak. "Hey, Stud! Not you, Stupid! I'm talking to my horse." As you might imagine, one-liners don't make a book. After the first page and a half, the idea was done. What now? Where does the story line go from here? I asked myself these questions and more. A few days later, in the early morning hours, 4:30 a.m. to be precise, I looked up at the sky and said, "God, my father, if you want me to write this book, give me a sign. Give me some kind of story line to continue my work." Suddenly, in the early morning darkness, a Red Tail Hawk flew overhead about ten feet above me. That's it, I said to myself. That's the sign. But it's going to be kind of hard writing a book about a Red Tail Hawk. Needless to say, I put my mind to work creating a mystery novel around a Red Tail Hawk. After a few months and over a hundred pages under my belt, I sat on the same porch at around the same time of morning, drinking another cup of coffee, when suddenly the same Red Tail Hawk flew over. This time, after looking a little closer, I said out loud, "Wait a minute. That's not a Red Tail Hawk. That's an owl." *"Gee, you think so?"* I seemed to hear a voice say from the heavens. *"I give you one simple assignment and you blow it!"* Sorry about the mix-up, God. Next time I'll try to do better.

Made in the USA
Lexington, KY
17 July 2011